BLACK RUN

ANTONIO MANZINI

Translated from the Italian by Antony Shugaar

FOURTH ESTATE • *London*

BLACK RUN

A Novel

Fourth Estate
HarperCollins*Publishers*
1 London Bridge Street
London SE1 9GF
4thestate.co.uk

First published in Great Britain by Fourth Estate in 2015
First published in the United States by Harper in 2015
Originally published in Italian as *Pista nera* in Italy by Sellerio Editore in 2013

1 3 5 7 9 8 6 4 2

Copyright © Antonio Manzini 2015
Translation copyright © HarperCollins*Publishers* Ltd 2015

Antonio Manzini asserts the right to be identified
as the author of this work in accordance with
the Copyright, Design and Patents Act 1988.

A catalogue record for this book is
available from the British Library.

Hardback ISBN 978-0-00-811900-3
Trade paperback ISBN 978-0-00-811901-0

Page design by Fritz Metsch

Printed and bound in Great Britain by
Clays Ltd, St Ives plc

MIX
Paper from
responsible sources
FSC
www.fsc.org   **FSC C007454**

To my sister, Laura

The mountain cannot frighten one who was born on it.
—FRIEDRICH SCHILLER

In this life
it's not hard to die.
But to make life
is trickier by far.
—VLADIMIR MAYAKOVSKY

CONTENTS

BLACK RUN

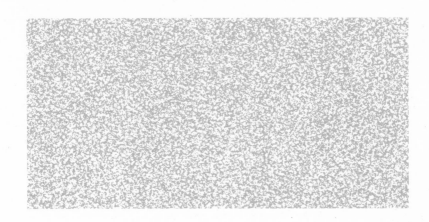

THURSDAY

The skiers had all gone home, and the sun, which had just winked out behind the craggy blue-gray peaks that were shredding a few scudding clouds, was still tinting the snow pink. The moon was waiting for darkness so it could light the whole valley until the next morning dawned.

The ski lifts were no longer running, and the lights were out in the chalets at higher elevations. The only sound was the low muttering engines of the snowcats running up and downhill, grooming the pistes that twisted around boulders and stands of trees down the mountain slopes.

The next day marked the beginning of the long weekend, when the ski resort of Champoluc would rapidly fill with out-of-towners eager to dig their skis into the snow. The runs had to be in perfect condition.

Amedeo Gunelli had been assigned the longest run. The Ostafa. Stretching almost a mile in length, and about sixty yards wide, this was Champoluc's main piste, and it was used by ski instructors with their beginner students as well as expert skiers to experience freeriding. This was the slope that took the most work, and it had often lost its snow cover by lunchtime. In fact, there were plenty of bare patches, unsightly stretches of rocks and dirt, especially at center piste.

Amedeo had started from the top. He'd only been doing this job for three months now. It wasn't hard. All you had to do was remember how to work the controls on this treaded monster and keep calm. That was the most important thing. Keep calm and take your time.

He had his earbuds in, with Ligabue's greatest hits blasting on his iPod, and he'd fired up the joint that Luigi Bionaz, the head snowcat operator and his best friend, had given him. It was thanks to Luigi that he had this job and a thousand-euro paycheck every month. Perched next to him on the passenger seat were a flask of grappa and his walkie-talkie. Everything he needed for the hours of hard work ahead.

Amedeo pushed snow in from the sides, spreading it and smoothing it over the barest spots, chopping it with the tiller while the rakes flattened it till the surface was smooth as a pool table. Amedeo was good at his job, but he didn't much like working alone like that. Folks seem to think that mountain people prefer the solitary life of a hermit. Nothing could be further from the truth. Or nothing could be further from the truth as Amedeo conceived it. He liked bright lights, loud noises, and lots of people talking all night long.

"Una vita da medianoooo," he sang at the top of his lungs, to keep himself company. His voice reverberated off the

Plexiglas windows as he focused on the snow, which was turning a pale blue in the moonlight. If he'd stopped to look up, he'd have glimpsed a breathtaking spectacle. High above, the sky was dark blue, like the ocean depths. By contrast, all along the mountain ridges it was orange. The last slanting rays of sunlight tinged the perennial glaciers purple and the underbellies of the clouds a metallic gray. Towering over everything were the dark flanks of the Alps. Amedeo took a slurp of grappa and glanced downhill. A nativity scene made up of roads, houses, and twinkling lights. A dreamlike vision for those who hadn't been born and raised in those valleys. For him, a squalid and heartbreaking diorama.

"Certe notti la radio che passa Nil Jàng sembra avere capito chi seiiiii …" He sang along to the words of the song by Ligabue: "Certain nights when the radio plays Neil Young as if it knew who you really we-e-ere …"

He'd finished the first run, a wall. He turned the cat to head downhill toward the second section and found himself facing a stretch of black piste—a black-diamond run. Like in karate, the black classification meant the most challenging kind of run. It was frightening. An expanse of ice and snow with no end in sight.

Only guys who'd been doing this work for years and who could spin the snowcat around like a tricycle would even dare to venture down that steep, twisting track, full of switch-back curves and sheer drops, that led down to the main run. Anyway, that was a stretch that didn't require grooming. It was supposed to be left the way it was. It was too tight, for starters. If you took it wrong, the treads would lose their grip, and before you knew it the snowcat would flip over, pinning you under tons of metal and hot grease. The skiers could groom it themselves, gradually smoothing the track as they descended. Someone had to go up just once a month, with a plow blade, and that was only when things had been pushed as far as they could go and the icy mounds that had built up absolutely had to be flattened out. Otherwise, on those blocks and slabs of ice, cartilage and ligaments, ankles and knees snapped and sprained regularly and unpredictably.

The light on the walkie-talkie on the seat next to him blinked. Someone was calling him. Amedeo yanked out his earbuds and grabbed the device. "Amedeo here."

The radio crackled, then the voice of his boss, Luigi, emerged through the static: "Amedeo, where are you?"

"I'm right in front of the wall at the top run."

"That's enough. Head downhill and do the section below, near town. I'll take care of the top section."

"Thanks, Luigi."

"Listen," Luigi added, "remember to take the shortcut down to town."

"You mean the lane?"

"That's right, the one that runs from Crest—that way you don't have to cross the piste that Berardo's cleaning. So take the shortcut, you got that?"

"Got it. Thanks!"

"Forget about 'Thanks.' Make sure you buy me a glass of white before dinner!"

Amedeo smiled. "That's a promise!"

He stuck the earbuds back in, shifted into the lowest gear, and rumbled off the slope.

"*Balliamo un fandango … ohhhh,*" he went on singing. "We dance a fandango." Again, Ligabue.

Overhead, heavy cloud cover suddenly filled the sky, blocking out the moon. That's how it always works in the mountains: before you know it, the weather veers around as fast as the winds at high altitude. Amedeo knew that. The weather forecast for the weekend was ugly.

The snowcat's powerful headlights lit up the slope and the dark mass of fir and larch trunks lining it. Through the black branches he could still see the lights of Champoluc below.

"*Balliamo sul mondoooo ohh,*" he sang. "We dance on the world."

He'd have to drive past the ski school and the snowcat garage, then head downhill toward town, and from there work the slope uphill.

He flicked the scorched filter of the joint out the window. Just then, the headlights of another snowcat blinded him. He lifted one hand to shield his eyes. The cat climbing the hill pulled up level with him. It was Berardo, another driver.

"Hey, are you high? You blinded me!"

"Heh-heh …" Berardo snickered idiotically.

"Listen, Luigi's taking care of the top. I'm heading down to do the bottom of the piste, near town."

"Got it," replied Berardo, whose nose was already bright red. "You want to get a glass of white at Mario and Michael's tonight?"

"I'm supposed to treat Luigi, so I'll be there anyway. I'm heading down to the end of the slope!" Amedeo shouted.

"Take the Crest lane—I've already finished the run up above!"

"Don't worry, I'll take the shortcut! Later!"

Berardo went on his way. Amedeo, on the other hand, turned toward Crest, as ordered. Crest was a small cluster of mountain houses above the slopes. Nearly all the houses were uninhabited except for a hut and a couple of villas owned by people from Genoa who loved skiing more than they did their own city. From there, he'd go through the woods to the short-cut, which would take him eight hundred yards downhill. He'd give the end of the run a quick groom and then finally came the glass of white wine and cheerful conversation and laughter with the Englishmen who no doubt were already drunk. He went past the few lights on in the village, then left it behind him. The lane that the snowcats used was clear and distinct.

"Ti brucerai, piccola stella senza cielo …" Hitting the high notes. "You'll burn up, little star without a sky."

He headed downhill, proceeding cautiously down the track, which was used only in the summer by off-road vehi-cles heading for the village of Crest. The headlights mounted on the snowcat's roof lit the shortcut brightly. There was roughly zero likelihood of driving over the edge.

"Ti brucerai …"

No problem. The treads were gripping perfectly. The cabin was tilted to one side like a thrill ride, was the only thing. But even that was fun.

"Ti bruceraiiii."

Then the tiller hit something hard and the snowcat bounced on its treads. Amedeo turned to see what the vehicle had hit. Must have been a rock or a patch of dirt. Out the rear windshield, the lights illuminated the churned-up snow on the lane.

But there was something wrong. He could see it immediately, right in the middle of the lane.

A dark stain stretching at least a couple of yards.

He braked hard.

He removed the earbuds, set the iPod aside, turned off the engine, and got out to check.

Silence.

His boots sank into the snow. In the middle of the lane was the dark patch.

"Christ, what the hell is that?"

He started walking. The closer he got, the more the stain in the middle of the shortcut changed color. At first it was black, but now it was purplish. The wind was whistling faintly through the needles of the fir trees, scattering down feathers in all directions.

Small, white, weightless feathers.

A chicken? Did I hit a chicken?! Amedeo muttered to himself.

He kept walking through the deep snow, sinking in five or six inches at every step. The down feathers covering the snow lifted into the air, spinning in tiny whirlwinds. By now the stain was brown.

What on earth did I hit? An animal?

How could he have missed it? With the cat's seven halogen lamps? And anyway, the noise would have chased it away.

He'd almost walked right over it when he finally saw it for what it was: a stain of red blood, churned into the white blanket of snow. It was enormous, and unless he'd run over a whole henhouse, that was way too much blood to have come out of a single piece of poultry.

He steered clear of the stain and carefully edged around it till he got to the point where the red was brightest, almost shiny. He crouched down and looked carefully.

Then he saw.

He turned and took off at a run, but he didn't make it to the woods. He vomited all over the Crest shortcut.

A cell phone going off at this time of night meant trouble, as sure as a certified letter from Equitalia, the Italian equivalent of the IRS. Deputy Police Chief Rocco Schiavone, born in 1966, was flat on his back in his bed, eyeing the big toenail on his right foot. The nail had turned black, on account of the filing cabinet drawer that D'Intino had carelessly dropped on Schiavone's foot while hysterically searching for a passport application. Dottor Schiavone hated Officer D'Intino. That very afternoon, after yet another idiotic move pulled by that cop, he'd sworn to himself and the entire citizenry of Aosta that he'd make sure he got that moron transferred to a godforsaken police station somewhere far from the sea, down at the opposite end of the Italian peninsula.

The deputy police chief reached out his hand and grabbed the Nokia that kept ringing and ringing. He took a look at the display. The caller number was police headquarters.

That rated an 8 on the scale of pains in the ass that ran from 1 to 10. Possibly a 9.

Rocco Schiavone had an entirely personal hierarchy up and down which he ranked the pains in the ass that life senselessly inflicted on him every day. The scale actually started at 6, which covered anything that had to do with keeping house: grocery shopping, plumbers, paying rent. The number 7 included malls, banks, medical clinics, and doctors in general, with a special bonus for dentists, and concluded with work dinners or family dinners, though all his living relatives, thank God, were down south in Rome. An 8 on the hierarchy began, first and foremost, with public speaking, followed by any and all bureaucratic procedures required for his job, going to the theater, and reporting to chiefs of police or investigating magistrates. At number 9 came tobacco shops that weren't open when he needed a pack of cigarettes, cafés that didn't carry Algida ice cream bars, running into anyone who wanted to talk and talk endlessly, and especially stakeouts with police officers who needed a bath.

Topping the hierarchy, the worst and the most dreaded, was a rating of 10. The top, the worst, the mother of all pains in the ass: the investigation he wasn't expecting.

He hoisted himself to a sitting position on both elbows and pushed ANSWER.

"Now who's busting my balls?" he barked.

"Dottore, this is Deruta."

Special Agent Deruta. Two hundred and twenty-five pounds of useless body mass vying valiantly with D'Intino for the title of stupidest member of police headquarters staff.

"What do you want, Michele?" roared the deputy police chief.

"We have a problem. On the slopes at Champoluc."

"And where do we have this problem?"

"At Champoluc."

"And where is that?"

Rocco Schiavone had been shipped north to Aosta from the Cristoforo Colombo police station, in Rome, the previous September. Four months later, all he knew about the geography of the city of Aosta and its surrounding province was the locations of his apartment, police headquarters, the courthouse, and the local trattoria.

"Champoluc is in Val d'Ayas!" Deruta replied, in an almost scandalized tone of voice.

"What's that supposed to mean? What's Val d'Ayas?"

"Val d'Ayas, Dottore, is the valley above Verrès. Champoluc is the most famous village in that valley. People go there to ski."

"Okay, fine, so what?"

"Well, a couple of hours ago someone found a corpse."

A corpse.

Schiavone let the hand holding the cell phone flop onto the mattress and shut his eyes, cursing through his teeth. "A corpse ..."

That was a 10 on the scale of pains in the ass. Definitely a 10. Possibly 10 with a bullet.

"Can you hear me, Dottore?" the telephone crackled.

Rocco raised the device back to his ear. He sighed. "Who's coming with me?"

"Your choice. Me or Pierron."

"Italo Pierron, every day for the rest of my life!" the deputy police chief responded promptly.

Deruta acknowledged the insult with a prolonged silence.

"Deruta? What, did you fall asleep?"

"No, I'm at your orders, Dottore."

"Tell Pierron to come, and to bring the BMW."

"Do you think the jeep might be better for high-mountain driving?"

"No. I like the BMW. It's more comfortable, and it has better heating and a radio that works. The only people who take the jeep are those losers the forest rangers."

"So should I tell Pierron to come get you at your apartment?"

"Yes. And tell him not to ring the bell."

He dropped his phone on the bed and closed his eyes, laying his hand over them, palm down.

He heard the rustling whisper of Nora's negligee. Then her weight on the mattress. Then her lips and warm breath in his ear. And finally her teeth, nibbling at his earlobe. At any other time, these were all things that would have aroused him, but right now Nora's foreplay left him completely indifferent.

"What's going on?" asked Nora in a faint voice.

"That was the office."

"And?"

Rocco pulled himself up into a sitting position on the bed without even glancing at her. He slowly pulled on his socks.

"Can't you talk?"

"I don't feel like it. I'm working. Leave me alone."

Nora nodded. She brushed aside a lock of hair that had fallen in front of her eyes. "So you have to go out?"

Rocco finally turned and looked at her. "Well, what do you think I'm doing?"

There Nora lay, stretched out on the bed. Her arm, thrown over her head, revealed her perfectly hairless armpit. Her crimson satin negligee caressed her body, emphasizing with an interplay of light and shadow her generous curves. Her long, smooth dark hair framed her face, white as cream. Her black eyes looked like a pair of Apulian olives freshly plucked from the tree. Her lips were thin, but she knew just how to apply the right amount of lipstick to fill them out. Nora, a magnificent specimen of womanhood, just a year over forty.

"You could be a little nicer about it, couldn't you?"

"No," Rocco replied. "I couldn't. It's late, I have to drive up into the mountains, I have to kiss the whole evening with you good-bye, and in a little while it's probably going to start snowing, too!"

He stood up brusquely from the bed, went over to sit in an armchair, and put on his shoes: a pair of Clarks desert boots, the only type of footwear that Rocco Schiavone knew. Nora lay on the bed. She felt a little dumb, made up and dressed in satin. A table set for dinner, and no guests attending. She sat up. "What a shame. I made you raclette for dinner."

"What's that?" the deputy police chief asked glumly.

"Haven't you ever had it? It's a bowl of melted fontina cheese with artichokes, olives, and little chunks of salami."

Rocco stood up and pulled on a crewneck sweater. "Nice and digestible, I gather."

"Am I going to see you tomorrow?"

"How the hell would I know, Nora! I don't even know where I'm going to be tomorrow."

He left the bedroom. Nora sighed and stood up. She caught up with him at the front door. She whispered: "I'll be waiting for you."

"What am I, a bus?" Rocco shot back. Then he smiled. "Nora, forgive me, this is just a bad night. You're an incredibly beautiful woman. You're unquestionably the top tourist attraction in the city of Aosta."

"After the Roman arch."

"I'm sick and tired of Roman rubble. But not of you."

He kissed her hastily on the lips and pulled the door shut behind him.

Nora felt like laughing. That's just how Rocco Schiavone was. Take him or leave him. She looked at the pendulum clock that hung by the front door. She still had plenty of time to call Sofia and go see a movie. Then maybe they could get a pizza together.

Rocco stepped out of the downstairs door, and an icy hand seized his throat.

"Fucking cold out here!"

He'd left the car a hundred yards from the front entrance. His feet, in the pair of Clarks desert boots he was wearing, had frozen immediately upon contact with the sidewalk, frosted with a white covering of goddamned snow. A cutting wind was blowing, and there was no one out on the streets. The first thing he did when he got into his Volvo was turn on the heat. He blew on his hands. A hundred yards was all the distance it took to freeze them solid. "Fucking cold out here!" he said again, obsessively, like a mantra, and the words, along with the condensation from his breath, flew up against the windshield, fogging it white. He started the diesel engine, punched the defrost button, and sat there staring at a metal streetlamp tossing in the wind. Grains of snow fell through the cone of light, sifting through the darkness like stardust.

"It's snowing! I knew it!"

He put the car in reverse and drove out of Duvet.

When he parked outside his apartment building on Rue Piave, the BMW with Pierron behind the wheel was already there with the engine running. Rocco leaped into the car, which the officer had already heated to a toasty seventy-three degrees. An agreeable feeling of well-being enveloped him like a woolen blanket.

"Italo, I'm hoping you didn't ring the buzzer to my apartment."

Pierron put the car in gear. "I'm not an idiot, Commissario."

"Good. But you have to lose this habit. The rank of *commissario* has been abolished."

The windshield wipers were clearing snowflakes off the glass.

"If it's snowing here, I can just imagine up at Champoluc," said Pierron.

"Is it up high?"

"Five thousand feet."

"That's insane!" The greatest elevation Rocco Schiavone had ever attained in his life was 450 feet above sea level at Rome's Monte Mario. That is, of course, if you left out the past four months in Aosta, at 1,895 feet above sea level. He couldn't even imagine someone living at 5,000 feet above sea level. It made his head spin just to think about it.

"What do people do at five thousand feet above sea level?"

"They ski. They climb ice. In summer, they go hiking."

"Just think." The deputy police chief pulled a Chesterfield out of the policeman's pack. "I prefer Camels."

Italo smiled.

"Chesterfields taste of iron. Buy Camels, Italo." He lit it and took a drag. "Not even stars in the sky," he said, looking out the car window.

Pierron was focused on driving. He knew that he was about to be treated to a serenade of nostalgia for Rome. And sure enough.

"In Rome this time of year, it's cold, but often there's a north wind that clears away the clouds. And then the sun comes out. It's sunny and cold. The city's all red and orange, the sky is blue, and it's great to stroll down those cobblestone streets. All the colors are brighter when the north wind blows. It's like a rag taking the dust off an antique painting."

Pierron looked up at the sky. He'd been to Rome once in his life, five years ago, and it smelled so bad that he'd thrown up for three days running.

"And the pussy. You have no idea of the sheer quantity of pussy in Rome. I'm telling you, maybe only in Milan will you find anything comparable. You ever been to Milan?"

"No."

"You don't know what you're missing. Go there. It's a wonderful city. You just have to understand how it works."

Pierron was a good listener. He was a mountain man, and he knew how to stay silent when silence was called for and how to speak when the time came to open his mouth. He was twenty-seven, but you'd guess he was ten years older. He'd never left Val d'Aosta, aside from the three days in Rome and a week in Djerba, the island off Tunisia, with his ex-girlfriend Veronica.

Italo liked Rocco Schiavone. He liked him because he wasn't one to stand on ceremony, and because you could always learn something from a guy like him. Sooner or later he'd have to ask the deputy police chief—though he insisted on using the old rank of *commissario*—just what had happened in Rome. But their acquaintance was still too new, Italo sensed, and it was too early to delve into details. For the moment, he'd satisfied his curiosity by poking into documents and reports. Rocco Schiavone had solved a substantial number of cases—murders, thefts, and frauds—and had seemed to be well on his way to a brilliant and successful career. And then suddenly the shooting star that was Rocco Schiavone veered and fell, slamming to earth with a rapid and silent transfer to Val d'Aosta for disciplinary reasons. But just what the stain on Rocco Schiavone's CV had been, that was something he never managed to find out. The police officers working at headquarters had talked it over among themselves. Caterina Rispoli argued that Schiavone had risen above his station. "I'll bet you he stepped on somebody's toes and that somebody had the power to have him shipped north; that kind of stuff happens all the time in Rome." Deruta disagreed; he felt sure that someone as capable as Rocco Schiavone was an annoyance, especially if he lacked a political patron. D'Intino suspected sex was at the bottom of it. "I'll bet he took somebody's wife or girlfriend to bed and got caught." Italo had a suspicion all his own, and he kept it to himself. His guess had been guided by Rocco Schiavone's home address. Via Alessandro Poerio. High on the Janiculum Hill. Apartments up there ran to more than eight thousand euros a square meter, or a thousand dollars a square foot, as his cousin, who sold real estate in Gressoney, had told him. No one on a deputy police chief's salary could afford an apartment in that part of town.

Rocco crushed out his cigarette in the ashtray. "What are you thinking about, Pierron?"

"Nothing, Dottore. About the road."

And Rocco looked out in silence at the highway, pelleted by falling flakes of snow.

*   *   *

Looking up from the main street of Champoluc, he could see a patch of light in the middle of the woods. That was where the body had been found, and now it was lit by halogen floodlights. If he squinted, he could just make out the shadows of policemen and cat drivers working the scene. The news had spread with the speed of a high-mountain wind. Everyone stood around at the base of the cableway, their noses tipped up toward the forest, midway up the slope, each asking the same question, which was unlikely to be answered anytime soon. The English tourists, drunk; the Italians with worried faces. The locals were snickering in their patois at the thought of the hordes of Milanese, Genovese, and Piedmontese who would find out tomorrow morning that the slopes were closed.

The BMW with Italo at the wheel pulled to a halt at the foot of the cableway. It had taken an hour and a half from Aosta.

Driving up that road, navigating the hairpin curves, Rocco Schiavone had observed the landscape. The black forests, the bursts of gravel vomited downhill from the rocky slopes like rivers of milk. At least one good thing, during that endless climb: around Brusson, the snow had stopped falling and the moon, riding free in the dark sky, reflected off the blanket of snow. It looked as if someone had scattered handfuls of tiny diamonds over the countryside.

Rocco got out of the car wrapped in his green loden overcoat and immediately felt the chill of the snow bite through the soles of his shoes.

"Commissario, it's up there. They're coming to get us with the cat now," said Pierron, pointing out the headlights partially concealed by the trees halfway up the slope.

"The cat?" asked Rocco, his chattering teeth chopping his breath into little puffs as it fogged up in the cold air.

"That's right, the tracked vehicle that works the slopes."

Schiavone took a breath. What a fucked-up place to come die in.

"Italo, explain something to me. How could it be that no one saw a dead body lying in the middle of the piste? I mean, weren't there skiers on that run?"

"No, Commissario," Pierron said, then corrected himself. "Excuse me, Deputy Police Chief. They found him in the woods, right in the middle of a road they use as a shortcut. No one takes that road. Except for the snowcats."

"Ah. Understood. But who would go bury a body way up there?"

"That's what you're going to have to find out," Pierron concluded, with a naive smile.

The noise of a jackhammer filled the cold, crisp air. But it wasn't a jackhammer at all. The snowcat had arrived. It stopped at the base of the cableway with the engine running, dense smoke pouring out the exhaust pipe.

"So that's the cat, right?" asked Rocco. He'd seen that kind of thing only in movies or documentaries about Alaska.

"That's right. And now it's going to take us up, Commissario! Deputy Police Chief, I meant to say."

"Listen, just do this—you're not going to wrap your head around it no matter how hard you try. Call me whatever you want, I don't give a damn anyway. Plus," Rocco went on, looking at the treaded vehicle, "why do they call it a cat if it looks more like a tank?"

Italo Pierron limited himself to a shrug in response.

"Well, okay, let's get aboard this cat. Come on!"

The deputy police chief looked down at his feet. His Clarks desert boots were dripping wet, the suede was drenched, and his feet were starting to get wet, too.

"Dottore, I told you to buy a pair of suitable shoes."

"Pierron, stop busting my balls. I'm not putting on a pair of those cement mixers you people wear on your feet—not as long as I'm still breathing."

They set off through snow piles and potholes created by the skiers' power slides and oversteers. The snowcat, with the lights mounted on the roof, standing motionless in the middle of the snow, looked like a giant mechanical insect poised to seize its prey.

"Here, Dottore, step up on the tread and get in," shouted the snowcat driver from inside the Plexiglas cabin.

Rocco obeyed. He took a seat inside the cabin, followed immediately by Pierron. The driver shut the door and pushed the gearshift forward.

Rocco caught a whiff of alcohol mixed with sweat.

"I'm Luigi Bionaz, and I'm in charge of the snowcats up here in Champoluc," said the driver.

Rocco just looked at him. The guy had a couple of days' whiskers, and his eyes were lit up with an alcoholic gleam. "Luigi, are you okay?"

"Why?"

"Because before I go anywhere in this contraption, I want to know if you're drunk."

Luigi looked at him, his eyes as big as the snowcat's head-lights. "Me?"

"I don't give a damn if you drink or smoke hash. But the one thing I don't want is to be killed in this thing up at an elevation of five thousand feet."

"No, Dottore, everything's fine. I only drink at night. The odor you smell is probably from some youngster who used the vehicle earlier this afternoon."

"Of course it is," said the deputy police chief skeptically. "Fine. Come on, let's get going."

The snowcat made its way up the steep ski slope. Illuminated by the headlights, Rocco saw a wall of snow straight ahead of him, and he couldn't believe that that pachy-derm could successfully climb such a nearly vertical incline.

"Hey, tell me something! We're not about to go head over heels, are we?"

"Don't worry about a thing, Dottore. These behemoths can climb slopes steeper than a forty percent grade."

They took a curve and found themselves in the middle of the woods. The blade-like beam of the headlights lit up the soft blanket of snow and the black trunks of the trees that were suffocating the groomed run.

"How wide is this piste?"

"Fifty yards or so."

"And on a normal day, how many people come through here?"

"That's something we'll have to ask at the head office. They know how many daily ski passes they sell. So we could get a count, but it might not be all that accurate."

The deputy police chief nodded. He stuck his hands in his pockets, pulled out a pair of leather gloves, and put them on. The run was veering to the right. Pierron said nothing. He was looking up, as if searching for an answer among the branches of the larches and firs.

They went on climbing, accompanied only by the engine's roar. At last, in a broad clearing, they saw the beams of the floodlights arranged around the site where the body had been found.

The snowcat left the piste and cut through the woods. It bounced over a few tree roots and hummocks.

"Listen, who found the body?" asked Rocco.

"Amedeo Gunelli."

"Can I talk to him?"

"Sure, Commissario, he's down at the cableway station, waiting. He hasn't really recovered yet," Luigi Bionaz replied as he braked the snowcat to a halt. At last, he switched off the engine. The minute he set his shoes down on the snow, Deputy Police Chief Rocco Schiavone understood just how right his co-worker had been to recommend he wear heavy boots with insulated soles, the kind of shoes that Rocco called cement mixers. Because they really did resemble a pair of cement mixers. The chill gnawed at the soles of his feet, which were already tingling from the cold, and the feeling jangled his nerves from heels to brain. He heaved a breath. The air was even thinner than it had been at the bottom of the hill. The temperature was well below freezing. The cartilage in his ears was pulsating and his nose was already dripping. Inspector Caterina Rispoli approached him, light-footed.

"Deputy Police Chief."

"Inspector."

"Casella and I went up to secure the location."

Rocco nodded. He looked at Inspector Rispoli's face, which he could barely glimpse under the hat crammed down over her head. Her mascara and eyeliner were oozing down as if off a wax mask.

"Stay here, Inspector." Then he turned around. Far below, he could see the lights of the village. To his right was the snowcat that Amedeo had been driving, still parked in the middle of the woods where that poor devil had abandoned it hours ago.

Walking through nearly knee-deep snow, Rocco drew closer to the monster. He examined the front of the vehicle. He ran his hand over it, sized it up carefully, as if he were thinking of buying the thing. Then he squatted down and looked under the tracks, covered with fresh snow. He nodded a couple of times and headed over to the place where the body had been found.

"What were you looking for, Dottore?" asked Italo, but the deputy police chief didn't reply.

A policeman with a pair of skis thrown over his shoulders came toward them, striding easily, even though he was wearing ski boots with stiff, heavy hooks. "Commissario! I'm Officer Caciuoppolo!"

"Fuck, another native!"

The young man smiled. "I secured the crime scene."

"Good for you, Caciuoppolo. But tell me, where did you learn to ski?"

"At Roccaraso. My folks have a place there. Are you from Rome, Commissario?"

"Yep, Trastevere. What about you?"

"Vomero, Naples."

"Excellent. Let's go see what we have here."

What did they have here? A half-frozen corpse under five or six inches of snow. To call it a corpse was a euphemism. It might have been one once. Now it was a mess of flesh, nerves, and blood that had been pureed by the snowcat's tillers. All around it, goose feathers. Everywhere. The deputy police chief wrapped his overcoat tighter. The wind, though it was light, penetrated beneath the lapel and caressed his neck, leaving a wake of hairs standing at attention like soldiers saluting a general. Rocco's knee already hurt, the one he'd crushed when he was fifteen, playing the last match of the season with his team, Urbetevere Calcio. Bent over the dead body was Alberto Fumagalli, the medical examiner of Livorno, who was using a pen to poke at the hems of the poor man's down jacket.

The deputy police chief went over without saying hello. In the past four months, since the day they'd first met, he'd never said hello to him yet. So why start now?

"What are all these feathers?" asked Rocco.

"The filling of the down jacket," replied Alberto, bent over the corpse.

The poor man's face was unrecognizable. One arm had been sheared off neatly, and his rib cage had popped open under the vehicle's weight, spewing forth its contents.

"What a mess," said Rocco in a low voice.

Fumagalli shook his head. "I'm going to have to do an autopsy in a proper facility. I'll get a good look and let you know. Just by the sight of him … I don't know! That thing crushed him. You can imagine the work it'll take just to reassemble him! But right now, since I'm frozen and pissed off, I'm just going to head back down and get something hot to drink. Well, anyway, it's a man—"

"I'd gotten that far myself."

Alberto glared at Rocco. "Would you let me finish? It's a man, around forty. His watch says seven thirty. That's when I think that tank must have run over him."

"I'm with you."

"He has no ID. He's wounded, all cut up. Still, you know something, Schiavone?"

"Why don't you tell me, Fumagalli."

"There's blood everywhere."

"Maybe even too much blood. So?" asked Rocco.

"You see? Blood with all its components, water and cells, already freezes at zero degrees Celsius. But just to be safe, in the lab we keep it at minus four degrees centigrade. But the thing that should give you pause is the fact that up here, we're at zero degrees, understood? Zero degrees centigrade. But this blood is still nice and liquid, I'd say. Which tells me that he hasn't been dead long."

The deputy police chief nodded in silence. He'd found himself staring at the corpse's left hand. Big. Gnarled. It reminded him of his father's hands, damaged by years and years of inks and acid solvents in the printing plant where he worked. The dead man's left hand was missing three fingers. The right hand lay about thirty feet away from the remains of the still unidentified body.

"I've seen hedgehogs on the highway in better shape than that!" said Schiavone, and a billowing cloud of condensation emerged, fat and compact, from his mouth. Then he finally turned to look at the area that the officers had secured.

It was a mess.

Aside from the deep tracks cut by the snowcat, there were footprints everywhere. Thirty feet away, at the edge of the woods, there was even an officer taking a piss on a tree. He had his back turned, so Rocco couldn't tell who it was.

"Hey!" he yelled.

The guy turned around. It was Domenico Casella.

"What the fuck are you doing?" Rocco shouted at him.

"Taking a piss, Dottore!"

"Nice work, Casella. Just think how happy the guys from forensics are going to be!"

Fumagalli shot a glare at Casella, and at Caciuoppolo, who was standing with his skis over one shoulder at a nice safe distance so he wouldn't have to look at the mangled remains. "You're all just a herd of pathetic cocksuckers!" the Livornese doctor grumbled.

"I gotta say. Didn't they teach you guys anything?"

Casella zipped up his pants and walked over to the deputy police chief. "No, it's just that I couldn't hold it any longer. Plus, Dottore, we don't have any proof they even killed him here, right?"

"Ah, we have our own homegrown Sherlock Holmes! Fuck off, Casella. Get the hell away from here and stick close to the snowcat, where you can't screw things up. Down there, by Inspector Rispoli. Move! Did you touch anything else?"

"No."

"Good. Get over there, don't move, and try to stay out of trouble." Then Rocco spread his arms wide in exasperation. "You want to know something, Alberto?"

"What?"

"Oh, you're going to hear from the Aosta forensics team before long, once they find fingerprints from our men, and urine, and pubic hair, and head hair. Once you guys are through with the place, even if the killer took a dump on the ground, they wouldn't be able to find an uncompromised piece of evidence. Thanks to imbeciles like Casella ... and you, too, Caciuoppolo! You say that you secured the crime scene, and then what?"

Caciuoppolo dropped his head.

"Look what you've done! Here are your footprints all around the corpse, on the road, everywhere! Holy Mary, mother of God! A guy could just give up and go home after this!"

His shoes were sopping wet. The cold was increasing exponentially as the minutes crept by. Fumagalli's zero degrees Celsius was just a fond memory by now, and the wind continued to torment him, even under his warm woolen undershirt. Rocco wished he were at least four hundred miles away from here, ideally in the Gusto Osteria, on Via della Frezza, "Da Antonio," just a stone's throw from the Lungotevere, eating fritto misto and beef tartare, washed down with a bottle of Verdicchio di Matelica.

"Do you think he could have been a skier?" asked Officer Pierron, to break the tension; up till then, Pierron had been keeping a safe distance from the corpse.

Rocco looked at him with all the contempt he'd been accumulating in four months of exile from Rome. "Italo, he's wearing boots! Have you ever seen anyone go skiing in a pair of rubber-soled calfskin boots?"

"No, I couldn't see them from here. Sorry!" Italo replied, hunching his head down between his shoulders.

"Well, then, instead of spouting bullshit, take two steps forward and look for yourself! Do your job!"

"I'd have to decline that offer, Commissario!"

A wave of depression swept over Rocco. He looked the medical examiner in the eyes. "These are what they give me, and these are all I have to take with me when I work a case. Okay, Alberto, thanks. Give me a call the minute you have something. Let's just hope he died of a heart attack, fell down, and got covered up with snow."

"Sure, let's hope," said Alberto.

Rocco shot one last glance at the corpse. "Give my regards to the forensics squad." And he turned to go.

But something struck him, like an insect when you're riding fast on a moped with no windshield. He spun around again.

"Alberto, you're a man of the world. Would you say this guy was wearing technical gear?"

Alberto made a face. "Well, his pants were padded. His windbreaker was the right stuff, no question: North Face Polar. Couldn't have been cheap. I bought one just like it for my daughter. Only in red."

"So?"

"It cost more than four hundred euros."

Rocco bent over the half-frozen corpse again. "No gloves. I wonder why."

Alberto Fumagalli spread his arms in bafflement. The deputy police chief stood back up. "Let's think this one over. Let's think on it."

"Well, Commissario," chimed in Caciuoppolo, who had been leaning on his ski poles and listening, "maybe he's someone who lives in one of the huts up in Crest. You see? Just two hundred yards from here."

Rocco looked at the little cluster of houses hidden in the snow.

"Ah. There are people who live up there?"

"Yes."

"In the middle of nowhere? Huh ..."

"If you love the mountains, that's the place for you, right?"

Rocco Schiavone grimaced in disapproval. "Maybe so, Caciuoppolo, maybe so. Nice work."

"*Grazie.*"

"But he also could have died somewhere else and been carried up here. No?"

Caciuoppolo stood lost in thought.

"Even though ..." Rocco added, "... that means they put the down jacket on him afterward. Because a person's hardly likely to die indoors wearing a down jacket. Or else—why not? Maybe he was about to go out, and then he died? Or else he went to see someone, only had time to get his gloves off, and then died?" Rocco looked at Caciuoppolo without seeing him. "Or else no one killed him at all, he just died on his own, and I'm standing here spouting bullshit. No, Caciuoppolo?"

"Commissa', if you say so."

"Thanks, Officer. We'll look into this, too. In any case, I don't know if you read the memos that circulate, if you keep up with these things, but they've abolished the rank of *commissario* in the police force. Now we're called deputy police chief. But I'm just keeping you informed. I really couldn't give a damn, personally!"

"Yes sir."

"Caciuoppolo, why would someone born in Naples, with Capri, Ischia, and Procida just a half-hour ferry ride away, along with Positano and the Amalfi Coast—why would you come up here to freeze your ass off?"

Caciuoppolo looked at him and flashed a southern smile, with all his gleaming white teeth accounted for. "Commissa'—excuse me, Deputy Police Chief, sir. What's that old expression? There's one thing that pulls a cart stronger than a team of oxen, and that's ..."

"Understood." Rocco looked up at the black sky, where racing clouds covered and uncovered the stars. "And you met her up here in the mountains?"

"No. In Aosta. She has an ice cream shop."

"An ice cream shop? In Aosta?"

"Sure. You know, they have summer up here, too."

"I wouldn't know that yet. I got here in late September."

"Trust me, Dotto'. It'll come, it'll come! And it's beautiful, too."

Rocco Schiavone started walking toward the snowcat, which was waiting to take him back to town. By now his feet were like two frozen flounder fillets.

When the snowcat let Schiavone and Pierron out at the base of the cableway, the crowd of rubberneckers was smaller, thanks to the leverage of the snow and the cold. Only the Brits were still there, a small knot of people singing "You'll Never Walk Alone" at the top of their lungs. The deputy police chief looked at them. Red-faced, eyes half shut from the beer they'd swilled.

Suddenly he couldn't take it anymore.

He still remembered May 30, 1984, like it was yesterday. Conti and Graziani kicking the ball at random while Liverpool beat Rome and took home their fourth European Cup.

"Pierron, tell them to shut up!" he shouted. "There's a corpse up there—a little respect, for fuck's sake!"

Pierron walked over to talk to the Brits. They very civilly begged pardon, shook hands, and fell silent. Rocco only felt worse. First of all because now he was pissed off, and a nice rowdy brawl would have been just the thing. And second because Pierron spoke English. Schiavone barely knew how to say "Imagine all the people," a phrase that was unlikely to be particularly useful, either in Italy or in far-off Albion.

"Do you speak English, Italo?" he asked him.

"Well, you know, Dottore ..." replied the officer in an apologetic tone of voice, "in the valleys here, we all speak French, and they do a good job of teaching English in the schools. The thing is, we live on tourism. See, the schools in Val d'Aosta are first-rate. We learn languages, banking, and we're pretty much in the vanguard when it comes to—"

"Pierron!" the deputy police chief broke in. "When you people were living in caves and scratching your fleas, in Rome we were already decadent faggots!" and he hastened over to the waiting car.

Pierron shook his head. "What are we going to do, head back to town?"

"I want to have a talk with the guy who found the corpse," Rocco replied, and turned toward the cableway administrative offices. Italo followed him like a bloodhound.

The offices of Monterosa Ski were deserted at that time of night. Aside from a young woman in a skirt suit and a policeman dressed for skiing, both seated in the lobby. The fluorescent lights made their faces look worn. But while the policeman had the handsome tan of someone who spends hours on the slopes, the shapely young woman looked pale and exhausted. *Slightly overweight, but not someone you'd kick out of bed*, thought Rocco as soon as he saw her, coming in through the double glass doors with Pierron. The skiing policeman snapped to attention. At his feet was a small puddle of water, evidence that the snow clinging to his Nordica ski boots had melted. And an unmistakable sign that the officer had been sitting there for quite some time now.

"Officer De Marinis."

Rocco looked him up and down. "So why aren't you with your Neapolitan colleague, Caciuoppolo, guarding the scene of the murder?"

"I was here with Amedeo, the one who found the corpse," the cop explained.

"What are you, a babysitter? Get your skis and go on up and lend a hand."

"Right away, Dottore."

With the loud clapping of ski boots on the floor, De Marinis left the building.

"Where is he?" Rocco asked the young woman.

"Come this way; Amedeo's in there," the clerk replied, pointing to a shut door behind her. "I brought him a cup of hot tea."

"Good work … Margherita," said Rocco, reading the name on the badge pinned to her lapel. "Good work. Could you bring a couple more for the two of us, please?"

The young woman nodded her head and left.

Amedeo was sitting in a Naugahyde chair. His eyes were puffy, and his hair was flattened to his head. He'd set his cap and gloves down on the table, and he was staring at the floor. Rocco and Italo grabbed two office chairs with wheels and sat down facing him. Finally Amedeo looked up. "Who are you?" he asked in a faint voice.

"Deputy Police Chief Schiavone. Do you feel up to answering a couple of questions?"

"Christ on a crutch. I still can't believe it. I heard a crack and—"

Rocco stopped him with an upheld hand. "Do me a favor, Amedeo. Let's take things one at a time. So, now, you work on the thingies, the ... snowcats, right?"

"Yes, for the past few months. Luigi, my boss, got me the job. He's a good friend of mine."

"He's the one who took us up, Dottore," Italo added. Rocco nodded.

"I'd just finished doing the piste near the top. There was a wall and—"

"A wall?" Schiavone asked with a grimace.

"When the slope turns really steep, that's what we call it. A wall. Or a black piste," Italo offered, coming to his aid.

"Go on, Amedeo."

"The wall is just too steep. You can't take it. It's dangerous, and narrow, and if you're not super-skillful and experienced, it can end badly. Luckily my boss, Luigi, gave me a call and told me I could head down and finish the last part of the piste, where it comes into town."

"And?"

"And so I headed back. It's just that to go back down to town, we don't drive over the runs we've just groomed. We take the shortcut, the Crest shortcut."

"Do all of you use it?"

"Use what?"

"This Crest shortcut," replied Rocco.

"When our shift is over, yes. Otherwise we'd ruin all the work we've done. I got done early, because basically I'm the one with the least experience. So you take the shortcut through Crest, which is that little village of just a few houses. From there, at the fountain, the shortcut runs through the woods and downhill."

"And that's where you ran over the corpse."

Amedeo said nothing. He looked down.

"And then from the shortcut where do you go?" Rocco asked.

"You wind up in the middle of the piste that runs down to town. Which is the last one we do. And then our shift is over."

"Understood. You go through one at a time, and the last one down grooms it so it's ready for the next day's skiing," Rocco concluded. "So if it hadn't been you, somebody else was bound to run over the corpse. You just had the bad luck to be first, Amedeo."

"Yeah."

"Fine. That's all clear," said Rocco, just as Margherita walked into the room with two small steaming plastic cups. Rocco took one. "Thanks for the tea, Margherita," he said and gulped it down.

It tasted like dish soap. But at least it was hot. Margherita was about to leave when Rocco stopped her. "Tell me something, Margherita."

The young woman turned around. "Certainly, Dottore."

"How many people live in Champoluc?"

"Leaving out the tourists?"

"Just residents, I mean."

"Not even four hundred."

"Just one big family, right?"

"Right. We're practically all related, really. For instance, me and Amedeo are cousins."

Amedeo nodded in confirmation. Margherita, seeing that the deputy police chief had no other questions, left with a smile.

Rocco slapped the snowcat driver on the knee. This was the first time Italo had ever seen his boss make an affectionate gesture toward a stranger. Amedeo jerked in fright. "All right, then, Amedeo, now it's time for you to head home. Get some sleep if you can. In fact, you want some advice? Get drunk—tie one on. And don't ever think about it again. After all, it wasn't your fault, was it?"

"No. That's the truth. I was driving, then all of a sudden I heard this super-loud cracking sound and I slammed on the brakes. I didn't know what it was. A root, or a rock. But when I got out, all that blood ... I hadn't seen the body at all!"

Rocco tilted his head slightly to one side, then reached one hand out toward the breast pocket of the young man's windbreaker. He inserted two fingers and pulled out a pack of Rizla cigarette papers.

"You didn't see it—unless you had smoked yourself blind," Rocco said, sniffing the papers. "Grass. At least grass keeps your spirits up. How many joints did you smoke while you were up grooming the snow?"

"One," Amedeo muttered with a groan.

"Plus you can throw in a couple of jiggers of grappa for good measure, and then that poor sucker might have been trying to cross the road and you would never have seen him, would you?"

"No, Dottore! No! I swear that I just didn't see that person at all. The snowcat has seven spotlights bolted to its roof; if he'd been crossing in front of me, I'd definitely have seen him!"

Wide-eyed, Amedeo looked first at Rocco and then at Italo, in search of an understanding gaze. "When I got out, I thought I'd run over a chicken, or a turkey, even if there are no chickens or turkeys up here. But there were feathers and down everywhere, a sea of feathers."

Rocco smiled faintly. "It could have been a down comforter from Ikea, no?"

"Believe me, Dottore. I didn't see him!"

"How the fuck do you know it was a man?" Rocco snapped, and the sudden shift in mood frightened even Italo Pierron.

Amedeo seemed to shrink into his chair. "I don't know. I just said that, for no reason."

Rocco stared at the young man in silence for at least ten seconds. Amedeo was sweating. The fingers of his hands gripped the little table, shaking.

"Amedeo Gunelli, believe me, if I find out that he was out walking and you ran him over, it'll be manslaughter at the very least. You'll be looking at a nice long stretch in lockup, you know that?"

"When the deputy police chief says 'lockup,' he means prison," Italo translated. Having spent the past four months listening to Rocco, he was starting to understand the way people talked in Rome.

Amedeo's jaw dropped as if someone had just pulled a string.

"Remember one thing, Amedeo," said Rocco as he got up from his chair. "The police can be your friend or your worst nightmare. That's up to you."

Outside, the wind slapped the two cops in the face with its icy palms. Italo trotted over to the deputy police chief. "Why did you say that to him? Do you think he ran him down?"

"I wish he had. The case would be closed. No, he's not the one who did it. The snowcat up there has no dents or scrapes on the front section. If he'd hit him straight on, there would have been something. But there's nothing."

"Well?" asked Italo, who was baffled.

"You see, Italo, if you scare them, they'll always be eager to help. He's a good kid—he might turn out to be useful. It's always better for them to be afraid of us, trust me."

Italo nodded with conviction.

"But there is one thing we'll need to keep in mind: even with those blindingly powerful spotlights, he didn't see that poor guy's body lying on the ground. That's something we need to give some thought to."

"A sign that the body was covered with snow?"

"Nice going, Italo. You're starting to catch on."

* * *

Rocco and Officer Pierron were about to get into the car when a dark blue Lancia Gamma screeched to a halt thirty feet away.

Rocco rolled his eyes. There was no mistaking it: dark blue Lancia equals attorney general's office.

A man got out of the car, five foot six tops, bundled in a down coat that hung below his knees. He wore a fur hat that almost covered his eyes. He strode rapidly over to Rocco Schiavone, right hand extended. "Name is Baldi. Pleased to meet you."

Rocco shook his hand. "Schiavone, deputy police chief of the mobile squad."

"Well, can you tell me what we're looking at here?"

Rocco looked him up and down. The man looked like a veteran of the Italian army in Russia, but he was the investigating magistrate on duty. "Are you the investigating magistrate?"

"No. I'm your grandmother. You bet your ass I'm the investigating magistrate."

This is beginning well, thought Rocco.

Dottor Baldi seemed to have an even shorter fuse than Rocco did. He was on duty and now he too had landed this tremendous pain in the ass. In a way, it made Rocco happy—it meant he wasn't the only one who'd been dragged out of a warm bed on a quiet night at home and sent rudely out into the snow at an elevation of five thousand feet above sea level.

"Well, there's a corpse up there. A man. Between forty and fifty years old."

"Who is it?"

"If I knew that, I would have told you first name and last."

"No ID?"

"Nothing. We're just guessing that it's a man. I don't know if I convey the idea."

"No, you don't convey it at all," the magistrate replied. "Why don't you stop beating about the bush. Get to the point. Dottor Schiavone: how can you tell that it's a man? Describe clearly exactly what we're dealing with, because I'm already pissed off."

Schiavone cleared his throat. "Because the snowcat ran over him and churned him to bits with its tillers. You see, the head was crushed, with resulting expulsion of brain matter; from the thoracic cavity there was a generalized and random expulsion of shreds of lung particles and other visceral matter that even Fumagalli, our medical examiner, was hard put to identify. One hand lay thirty feet from the body, an arm was ripped loose, the legs were bent in a manner that defies nature roundly, and have, therefore, clearly been shattered in numerous places. The stomach has been twisted into an array of bloody coils and …"

"That'll do!" shouted the magistrate. "What, is this your idea of fun?"

Rocco smiled. "Sir, you requested a detailed description of what we have up there, and I'm just providing you with it."

Maurizio Baldi nodded repeatedly, looking around him as if in search of a question to ask or an answer to give. "I'll be at the courthouse. I'll see you around. Let's hope that this was an accidental death."

"Let's hope so, but I don't believe it."

"Why not?"

"Because I have a sense about it. I haven't had a lot of luck in a while now."

"You're telling me. The last thing I'm looking for is a murder case underfoot."

"Ditto, exactly."

The investigating magistrate glanced at the deputy police chief. "Can I give you a piece of advice?"

"Certainly."

"If what you say is true and this is not an accident, you'll have to work up here. Dressed the way you are, there's a good chance you'll develop frostbite, then gangrene, and we'll have to amputate your hands and feet."

Rocco nodded. "Thanks for the advice."

The magistrate looked Rocco in the eye. "I know you, Dottor Schiavone. I know lots of things about you." Then he narrowed his eyes. "So let me warn you: avoid pulling any of your bullshit."

"I've never pulled any."

"I happen to have different information."

"We'll see you on the banks of the River Don, Dottore."

"Don't make me laugh."

Without bothering to shake hands with the magistrate, Rocco went back to the car, where Pierron was waiting for him. Maurizio Baldi, on the other hand, walked to the base of the cableway. Still, under that fur hat, a faint smile had played briefly across his face.

"That's Dottor Baldi, isn't it?" asked Pierron. Rocco said nothing. He didn't need to. "He's half crazy, did you know that?" asked Italo as they got into the car.

"You feel like putting this thing in gear and getting me out of here, or do I have to call a taxi?"

Pierron obeyed immediately.

It's forty-five minutes past midnight. A person can't come home half-frozen at forty-five minutes past midnight. The minute I open the door I realize that I left the lights on. In the hall and in the bathroom. Forty-five minutes past midnight and I look down at my half-frozen feet. Shoes and socks aren't worth keeping. It doesn't matter; I have three other pairs of desert boots. My big toe is still black. That idiot D'Intino. I'll have to get him transferred, get him transferred as soon as possible. It's a question of my psychophysical equilibrium. If I've ever had such a thing.

I turn on the water. I slip my feet into it. It's hot—boiling hot. Only it takes a good three minutes before I can even tell how hot it is. I run hot water over my ankles, between my toes, and even over my black toenail. At least that doesn't hurt.

"Keep that up and you'll get chilblains."

I turn around.

It's Marina. In her nightgown. I think I must have woken her up. If there's one thing that annoys me (one thing? there are thousands), it's when I wake up my wife. She sleeps like a rock, but she seems to have a sixth sense when she hears me up and about.

"Ciao, my love."

She looks at me with her sleepy gray eyes. "You woke me up," she says.

I know. "I know. Sorry."

She leans on the doorjamb, arms folded across her chest. She's ready to listen. She wants to know more. "We found a corpse in the middle of a ski run, buried in the snow. In Champoluc. A tremendous pain in the ass, my love."

"Does that mean you're going to be staying up there for a while?"

"Not on your life. It's an hour's drive. Let's just hope it turns out to be a case of accidental death."

Marina looks at me. I keep my feet submerged in the bidet, which smokes like a pot of spaghetti. "Sure, but tomorrow morning you're buying yourself a pair of decent shoes. Otherwise, in a couple of days they'll have to amputate your feet for gangrene."

"The investigating magistrate said the same thing. Anyway, if there's one thing I hate, it's sensible shoes."

"Have you eaten?"

"A piece of stale pizza on the way."

Marina has vanished behind the door. She's gone to bed. I dry my feet and go into the kitchen. I hate this furnished apartment. The kitchen is the only decent room in the apartment. I wish I could understand the way other people live. Most of their apartments and homes are furnished in a way that evokes pity, nothing else. Only in the kitchen do they spend vast sums, furnishing the place with electric appliances of all kinds: ovens, microwaves, and dishwashers like something out of the Starship Enterprise. Instead, in the living room, arte povera and paintings of clowns hanging on the walls.

It's a mystery.

Every once in a while, I compare it with my home, in Rome. On the Janiculum Hill. I look out over the city, and on a windy day, when the air is clear, I can see St. Peter's, Piazza Venezia, and the mountains in the distance. Furio suggested I should rent it out. Instead of leaving it empty. But I just can't bring myself to do it. I can't stand the idea of strangers walking over the parquet floors that Marina chose, or opening the drawers of the Indian credenzas that we bought years ago in Viterbo. To say nothing of the bathrooms. Strangers' asses planted on my toilet, in my bath, strange faces admiring their reflections in my Mexican mirrors. It's out of the question. I get myself a bottle of cool water. Otherwise I'll wake up in the middle of the night with a throat and tongue that resemble two pieces of sandpaper.

Marina is under the blankets. As always, she's reading the dictionary.

"Isn't it a little late for reading?"

"It's the only way I can get to sleep."

"What's the new word for today?"

Marina has a little black notebook that she keeps in her lap with a pencil. She opens to her bookmark and reads. "Stitch—transitive verb: To sew or embroider something. It can also be used of one who sews with no particular enthusiasm." She sets down her notebook.

The mattress is comfortable. It's called memory foam. A material developed by NASA for astronauts in the sixties. It envelops you like a glove because it remembers the shape of your body. That's what it says in the pamphlet that came with it.

"Could you say that I'm stitching in Aosta?" I ask Marina.

"No. You're not a tailor. I'm the one who knows how to sew."

The mattress is comfortable. But the bed is cold as ice. I wrap myself around Marina. Looking for a little heat. But her side is as cold as mine.

I close my eyes.

And I finally put an end to this shitty day.

FRIDAY

The telephone drilled through the silence that double-pane windows and the absence of traffic gave to Deputy Police Chief Schiavone's apartment on Rue Piave. Rocco leaped like a hooked bass and opened his eyes wide. Despite the scream of the cell phone on his nightstand, he was still able to gather his thoughts: it was morning, he was at home, in his own bed after spending the night out in the snow. He wasn't actually lying underneath Eva Mendes, and she wasn't actually wearing nothing but a pair of dizzyingly high stiletto heels and dancing like a sinuous serpent, tossing her hair to and fro. That image was nothing but a cobweb that the telephone had scorched with its deranged shrieks.

"Who's busting my balls at seven in the morning?"

"Me."

"Me who?"

"Sebastiano!"

Rocco smiled as he ran one hand over his face. "Sebastiano! How you doing?"

"Fine, fine." And now his friend's croupy voice had become recognizable. "Sorry if I woke you up."

"I haven't heard from you in months!"

"Four months and ten days, but who's counting?"

"How are you doing?"

"Fine, fine."

"What are you up to?"

"I'm coming up north."

Rocco shifted comfortably on the memory foam mattress. "You're coming up? When?"

"Tomorrow night. I'll be on the seven o'clock train from Turin. Are you going to be around?"

"Of course I will. I'll meet you at the station."

"Excellent. Will it be cold up there?"

"What can I tell you, Seba? Bone-chilling cold."

"All right, then I'll wear a down jacket."

"And insulated shoes—take my word for it," Rocco added.

"I don't have those. What kind of shoes do you wear up there?"

"A pair of Clarks desert boots."

"Are they insulated?"

"No. Which is why I'm telling you to wear a pair of insulated shoes. My feet are like a couple of ice cubes."

"Then why don't you get yourself a pair?"

"I can't stand the things."

"Well, you do what you like. I'm going to swing by Decathlon and get a pair. So—see you tomorrow?"

"See you tomorrow."

And Sebastiano hung up the phone.

Rocco dropped his cell phone on his down jacket. If Sebastiano Cecchetti, known to his friends as Seba, was coming to Aosta, then matters were becoming distinctly interesting.

When Rocco walked into police headquarters at 8:15 a.m., Special Agent Michele Deruta walked up to him immediately. He was moving his tiny feet as fast as his two-hundred-plus pounds allowed him, and he was panting like an old steam locomotive. His chin was sweaty and his thinning white hair, combed specially to conceal his bald spot, was glittering, oiled by who-knows-what pomade.

"Dottore?"

Rocco stopped suddenly in the middle of the hallway. "Your face and hair are damp. Why damp, Deruta? Did you stick your face into a barrel of oil?"

Deruta pulled out his handkerchief and tried to dry himself off. "I wouldn't know, Dottore."

"But still, you're damp. Do you take a shower in the morning?"

"Yes, of course."

"But you don't dry off."

"No, it's just that before coming to work, I help my wife at her bakery."

Officer Deruta, getting close to retirement age, started talking about his wife's bakery just outside of town, the work in the predawn hours, the yeast and the flour. Rocco Schiavone paid no attention to a word he said. He just watched his damp, loose lips, his hair streaked with white, and his bovine, bulging eyes.

"What's surprising," said the deputy police chief, interrupting his special agent's monologue, "is not that you work at your wife's bakery, Deruta. It's that you have a wife at all— that's what's truly extraordinary."

Deruta fell silent. It wasn't as if he expected special praise for his daily sacrifice of working a double job, but a kind word, something like "You're wearing yourself out, Deruta. What a good man you are," or, "If only there were more people like you." Instead he got nothing. A scornful lack of consideration was all his superior officer could offer him.

"Aside from your double shift, is there anything important you need to tell me?" asked the deputy police chief.

"The chief of police has already called three times this morning. He needs to speak to the press."

"So?"

"First he wants to hear from you."

Rocco nodded and turned away, leaving Deruta there; still, the officer chased after him on his dainty feet. To watch the heft of his 225 pounds bounce along on his size 7½ men's shoes, you'd expect him to roll headlong across the floor at any moment. "The chief of police isn't in town, Dottore. There's no point in you going up to see him. You'll have to call him."

Rocco stopped and turned to look at Officer Deruta. "I see. Well, now, listen to me and listen good. Two things. First of all, start getting some exercise and put yourself on a diet. Second: later on, I've got an important job for you." He

furrowed his brow and looked Deruta in the eye. "Very important. Can I rely on you? Do you feel up to it?"

Deruta's eyes opened wide and became even bigger than
usual. "Certainly, Dottore!" he said, and flashed him a bright,
thirty-two-tooth smile. Actually, a twenty-four-tooth smile,
because there were several gaps. "Certainly, Dottor
Schiavone. You can trust me blindly!"

"Why don't you find yourself a dentist!"

"You think?" asked Deruta, covering his mouth with one
hand. "Do you know how much they cost? On my salary?"

"Tell your wife to give you the money."

"That money goes to my daughter, who's studying in
Perugia to be a veterinarian."

"Ah. I get it. You're training your own family doctor. Good
thinking!" and he finally walked into his office, slamming the
door behind him and blocking out the baffled face of the
officer, who stood there, still chewing over what the deputy
police chief had meant by his last comment.

In his long-ago high school days, Rocco had read that some
philosopher, possibly Hegel, had described the newspaper as
"the realist's morning prayer." But his version of the realist's
morning prayer was to roll a fat joint to put his mind at peace
with the world and the fact that he'd been forced to live all
this distance from Rome for the past four months. And the
knowledge that there was no way to get back there.

Not that he had anything against Aosta. Quite the opposite.
It was a lovely city, and the people were all nice and polite.

But it wouldn't have been any different if they'd stationed him in Salerno, or Mantua, or Venice. The end result would be the same. It wasn't a matter of the destination. What he missed above all was his native city, his existential stomping grounds, his home base.

He pulled the key out from under the framed photograph of Marina on his desk and pulled open the top drawer on the right. Inside sat a wooden box with a dozen handsome fatties, all ready to go. He lit one and, as he twisted the key shut in the drawer lock, took a long, generous drag that went straight to his lungs.

Funny how this small everyday gesture helped to soothe his brain. With the third puff, he gained a sense of lucidity and started planning out his day.

First thing: call the chief of police.

Then the hospital.

And then Nora.

He laid the half-smoked joint down in his ashtray. He was just reaching out for the receiver when the phone started to ring.

"*Pronto, sì?*"

"Corsi speaking!"

It was the police chief.

"Ah, Dottore, I was just about to call you."

"That's what you always say."

"But this time it's the truth."

"Then you're saying all the other times you were lying to me?"

"Sure."

"All right, Schiavone, go ahead."

"We still don't know a thing. Neither who he was nor how he died."

"So what am I supposed to tell those guys?"

It wasn't that the chief of police had forgotten the word. It was just that he never named the city's crew of print journalists. He always called them "those guys." As if he weren't willing to soil his lips with the common noun. He hated them. As far as he was concerned, they were a life form just one step up from the amoeba, the one flat note in the symphony orchestra of creation. That was how he felt about the print journalists. "Those other guys," television reporters—he didn't even consider them to be living entities.

That hatred was rooted deep in his personal history. It had been almost eighteen years since his wife left him for an editorialist at *La Stampa*, and since then Corsi had been waging a senseless crusade against every member of the guild, irrespective of race, religion, or political creed.

"Dottore, that's what we know. If they would be patient—if the gentlemen of the press would be so good as to patiently await the developments of the investigation … Otherwise, unfortunately, I have nothing to add."

"Those guys won't wait. They're lying in wait, eager to bite me in the ass."

"That's what you think, Chief. The press around here loves you," Rocco said seriously.

"What makes you say that?"

"I hear what people say. They respect you. They need you."

There was a pause. The police chief was mulling over what his underling had just told him. And Rocco smiled, delighted to go on tangling the threads of the relationship between his boss and "those guys."

"Cut the bullshit. I know those guys. Listen here, Schiavone, would you rule out categorically the possibility that last night's death might have been accidental?"

"With my luck? Yeah, I'd rule it out."

Andrea Corsi took a deep breath. "When are you going to give me more comforting information?"

"In, let's say, forty-eight hours?"

"Let's say twenty-four!"

"Okay, we make it thirty-six and not another word on the subject."

"Schiavone, what do you think this is, the flea market at Porta Portese? If I give you twenty-four hours, you have twenty-four hours."

"I'll call you this time tomorrow morning."

"I'll believe it when my team Sampdoria wins the national championship."

"If I haven't called you back in twenty-four hours, then I swear I'll get you free tickets for the Genoa–Sampdoria match."

"I'm the police chief. I don't need your free tickets."

And he hung up the phone.

"What a pain in the ass!" shouted Rocco, stretching his aching arms. He was looking at a mountain of work, work, work. That's the way life was up here in Aosta. Serious folks, serious city, inhabited by serious people who work hard and mind their own business. And if they got high, at the very most it was with a round of *grolle*, local multi-spouted mugs of grappa and coffee, passed around communally. The days of Rome were over, a city where dope was processed as if on an assembly line. The days of decent opportunities, lucky breaks—those days were over. How much longer would he be forced to languish in this purgatory? He lived in the richest city in Italy, with a per capita income to rival Luxembourg's, but after four months he had nothing to show for it. Then he thought about Sebastiano. Who would be coming up north tomorrow. And if Sebastiano was willing to take a plane all the way to Turin and then a train, in the middle of winter, there must be a reason, and a very good one.

That thought electrified him to the point that he found himself on his feet, rubbing his hands together. Only when his hand was on the door handle did he remember the joint with a homemade filter sitting in his ashtray. He went back, slipped it into his pocket, and finally left his office.

The streets were deserted. The cloudy gray sky promised more snow to come, and the black lava rock mountains seemed ready to swallow the landscape all around them. Italo Pierron drove, eyes on the road, while Rocco was on his cell phone.

"And yet it's not that hard, D'Intino! Listen to me carefully." Rocco spoke slowly and clearly, as if he were addressing a none-too-bright child. "Find out whether, in the city or province of Aosta, especially in Val d'Ayas, there have been any missing-person reports, people who didn't come home, you see what I mean? Not just since yesterday; let's say in the past month." Rocco rolled his eyes. Then, with infinite patience, he repeated the concept: "D'Intino, listen: for the past month. Is that clear? Over and out."

He punched the OFF button and looked at Italo, whose eyes were glued to the road ahead. "Tell me, is D'Intino playing with me or is he really that dumb?"

Italo smiled.

"Where's he from?"

"He's Abruzzese. From the province of Chieti."

"Doesn't he have any pull down there? No connections? Couldn't he go back down there and stop busting our balls?"

"I don't know, Dottore."

"Everyone in Italy has a connection. I had to wind up with the one brain-damaged mental defective who doesn't even have a relative or friend who can pull some strings for him."

They left the car in a parking space at the hospital, even though a security guard had told them not to because that was the chief physician's spot. Schiavone did nothing more than pull out his badge and shut up the zealous functionary of the Health Ministry.

They walked downstairs and past the laboratories until they finally reached the double glass doors where Fumagalli worked. The morgue.

"Dottor Schiavone?" asked Italo in a faint voice.

"What is it?"

"Do you mind if I wait here for you?"

"No. You come on in with me and enjoy the show. Didn't you choose to be a policeman?"

"Actually, no, I didn't. But it's a long story." He dropped his head and followed his boss.

There was no need to take off his coat, because the autopsy room was more or less the same temperature as outside. Under Fumagalli's lab coat Schiavone could see a turtleneck sweater. He wore latex gloves and a sort of green apron spattered with brown splotches. "And to think I complain about my shitty job!" Rocco said to him.

As usual, Fumagalli didn't bother to say hello, limiting himself to waving his hand in the two policemen's direction and leading them to the second room, which was a small waiting room. There the doctor gave both policemen a surgical mask, plastic shoe covers, and a strange paper smock.

"All right, the two of you come with me."

In the middle of the room was a nice big autopsy table, and on top of the table lay the corpse, mercifully covered with a white cloth.

In the room you could hear a faucet drip, along with the continuous hum of the recycling air vents, which were spreading a mixture of ferocious stenches as they circulated the air in the morgue. Disinfectant, rust, rotten meat, hard-boiled eggs. Italo Pierron felt as if he'd been punched in the solar plexus, bent over and clapped his hands to his mouth, then hurried away to lose the breakfast that had just come surging up his esophagus.

"All right, now that we're alone," said Rocco with a smile, "have you had a chance to work on him?"

"I've tried to reassemble all the pieces. I've done easier jigsaw puzzles," the doctor replied, and uncovered the corpse.

"Fuck!" came out of the deputy police chief's mouth, clear and loud and straight from the heart.

There was no body. There was just a series of shredded pieces of flesh, more or less reassembled to form an object that only remotely resembled anything human.

"How can you work with this?"

Fumagalli cleaned his lenses. "Nice and slow. Like doing art restoration."

"Sure, but those guys are fixing a masterpiece, and it's a pleasure to look at."

"This is a masterpiece too," said Fumagalli. "It's God's handiwork, or didn't you know?"

In the deputy police chief's head, the suspicion that lengthy and involuntary interactions with human corpses had finally undermined the Livornese physician's mental equilibrium finally became a certainty.

"Can I smoke in here?" asked Rocco, slipping his hand into his pocket.

"Of course. You want me to get you a whiskey, or maybe something a little lighter? Shall I put on some lounge music? Would you like that? All right, let's get to work."

The medical examiner pointed to a point on the corpse's right pectoral: "He has a tattoo."

Some writing and signs that Rocco couldn't decipher. "What's it say?"

"*Maa vidvishhaavahai,*" said Alberto. "Luckily, I was able to read it."

"But what is it?"

"It's a Hindu mantra. It means roughly: 'May no obstacle arise between us.'"

"And how do you know that?"

Alberto smiled behind his thick-lensed glasses. "I'm a guy who knows how to find out things."

The dead man's face was crushed. Out of the red-and-black mush, which reminded Rocco of a painting by a major Italian artist whose name he couldn't quite recall, jutted teeth, bits of lips, yellowish filaments.

"This is the first strange thing," Alberto began, lifting a piece of handkerchief that must once have been a bandanna.

"Indeed, how very strange," said Rocco, "a piece of hand-kerchief. Never seen anything like it."

"All right, let's cut out the cheap irony, if you don't mind."

"Okay. But you started it when you brought up the whiskey and the lounge music."

"So the dead man has this red handkerchief in his trachea."

"In his what?" asked Rocco.

"In his trachea."

"Is there any way that the snowcat shoved it in when it ran over his face?" Rocco hypothesized.

"No. It was crumpled up. And when I unfolded it, look at the treat I found inside." Alberto Fumagalli pulled out a sort of metal cup in which a slimy purple thing lay, with what appeared to be two little mints beside it.

"What's that? A piece of rotten eggplant?"

"The tongue."

"Oh, Jesus fucking—"

"And there were a couple of teeth to go with it. You see? They look like two Tic Tacs." The doctor continued, "The snowcat crushed the poor man's head, and the pressure pushed in this piece of handkerchief. It was in his mouth."

"It made him swallow it?"

"Or else he swallowed it himself."

"Sure, but if he swallowed it, then he was still alive!"

"Maybe so, Rocco. Maybe so." Alberto took a deep breath. "So then I expressed the hypostases."

"Translation, please."

Fumagalli rolled his eyes in annoyance.

"Why are you getting pissed off? I studied law, not medicine! As if I were to ask you to define *usucaption*."

"*Usucaption* is a Latin term for 'acquisitive prescription,' in which ownership of property can be gained through continuous possession thereof, beyond a specified period of time—"

"Enough!" Rocco interrupted him. "Let's get back to these hypotheses."

"Hypostases," Alberto corrected him. "Now then, hypostases form when the heart stops beating. Blood pressure drops, and the blood flows by gravity to the lowest areas of the corpse. And since the body was lying in a supine position … there, you see?" Fumagalli gently lifted the poor wretch's torso. There was a squeaking sound, as if he'd dragged a jellyfish across the floor. "You see these reddish-purple spots?"

They were barely visible. They looked like very faint bruises.

"Yes," said Rocco.

"When the heart stops pumping, then what happens? The blood follows its most natural path, that is, wherever the force of gravity tends to pull it. Are you with me?"

"I'm with you."

"Good. The body was lying supine, and therefore the blood flowed to the back. Yesterday when I got there, they were just starting to form."

"Which means what?"

"These things form three or four hours after death. That means this poor sucker died more or less three hours before I got there. So I got there at about ten, and he died between six and seven. More likely seven than six, I'd say."

"He didn't die. He was *killed* between six and seven."

"If you want to be exact. That's right."

Rocco Schiavone went on staring at those mangled remains. "Also in an attempt to be exact, could you tell me *how* someone killed him?"

"I'll have to take a look at the internal organs. To rule out poisoning or suffocation. That'll take me a little while. Come with me." The doctor moved away from the autopsy table. But Rocco stood there a little longer, staring at the mass of flesh and blood that had once been a man's face. "The more I look at it, the more I'm reminded of a painting by an artist— doesn't it remind you of that painter? The one who used to make black burn marks on a red background and who—"

"Burri," Alberto replied as he pulled open a drawer in a cabinet next to the door. "I was reminded of him myself."

"Burri, that's right. Exactly." Rocco caught up with the doctor. "No, it's just that if a person tries to remember a thing and he can't quite get it, he might wind up killing a bunch of neurons. Burri. What's that?" he asked the medical examiner, who was holding out another plastic bag.

"In here is the rest of the handkerchief. It was hanging out of his mouth."

"Did the snowcat cut it? Weird. That seems pretty odd to me."

"My job is to analyze corpses. Yours is to understand how they got that way."

Rocco pulled away from the wall and grabbed the door handle.

"Wait! There's one last thing that will interest you." The doctor picked up two plastic bags. One contained a glove. The other held a pack of cigarettes. "Now, then. These were found in the inside pocket of the down jacket. An empty pack of Marlboro Lights, and this glove. Black. A ski glove. Colmar brand."

"Ah. Okay, good. We've found one glove. What about the other?"

"No idea."

"You know something, Alberto? This is a pain in the ass, number ten on the scale, summa cum laude."

"Which means?"

"The mother of all pains in the ass!"

Cursing under his breath, Rocco walked through the door and left the doctor with his patients.

*   *   *

Italo was outside the hospital smoking a cigarette. Rocco walked past him. "You're so damned helpful, Italo."

The officer flicked away his cigarette butt and followed the deputy police chief. "It was because of the taste in my mouth."

"Fine, but now that you're sure to have the breath of a cesspool, do me a favor and don't talk in the car."

"I've got chewing gum."

"Well, chew it," Rocco ordered him as he got into the car.

They hadn't gone fifty yards before Rocco's cell phone started ringing.

"Who is it?"

"Dottore, it's me, Officer D'Intino."

"To what do I owe the honor?" asked Rocco, lighting yet another of Italo's Chesterfields.

"Did you call me 'your honor'?" D'Intino replied, in confusion.

Rocco sighed and, with endless patience, replied, "No, D'Intino, I didn't. It's just a figure of speech. What can I do for you?"

"Ah, yes, I didn't think so. Well, I called you to say ..." And with that the line went dead.

"Hello? D'Intino, hello?"

Static and sighs from the other end of the line.

"Officer D'Intino, hello?"

"Yes? I'm listening, Dottore!"

"You're listening, my ass! What is it? Why did you call me?"

"Ah yes, in fact. I was looking, as you ordered me, to see if there were any missing-person reports, people who fail to come home, in other words, that kind of thing."

"And?"

"There was no need. Just a little while ago, Luisa came into the police station."

Rocco, struggling to control himself, held in the curse of all curses he was about to utter. "Officer! Who is Luisa?" he shouted.

"Luisa Pec. She says that her husband never came home last night. Or this morning, for that matter."

"So where is this Pec?"

"Who even knows where he is, Dotto'? Luisa says the man's disappeared!"

"Where's Luisa Pec! Not her husband!" shouted Rocco at the top of his lungs. Italo was barely able to stifle his laughter.

"Ah ... she's here ... Hold on, should I put her on?"

"What are you talking about? Put who on, D'Intino?" Rocco stared at Italo. "I'm going to kill him. I swear to all the saints in heaven, I'm going to kill him. Listen to me, Officer D'Intino, are you there?"

"Yes, Dottore!"

"All right." Rocco took two quick breaths and tried to calm down. "Now do me a favor and tell Signora Luisa Pec to wait for me in the police station, and tell her we'll be there soon. Is that all clear?"

"Yes, Dottore. Certainly. You'll be here any minute. Now, if I can stop looking for missing persons, then I can start organizing the files in the personnel office, because today Officer Malta is sick, so I could—"

"No. Go on looking. We don't know for sure that this Luisa Pec is the right person, do we?"

"True. You have a point, Commissario."

"Oh, go fuck yourself, D'Intino!"

"Yes sir."

Rocco hung up. He looked at Italo. "Her husband hasn't come home and first thing, people assume the worst. For all we know, the guy's holed up with some chippie."

Italo nodded as he accelerated toward the police station. "Dottore, listen, if you want I can have a word with D'Intino and tell him not to call you anymore."

"Let it be. He wouldn't understand. He's my nemesis. You know, when you've done a few things that are just so-so? There's such a thing as divine justice. And I'm paying it. D'Intino is just a tool that God Almighty is using to punish me. A man's got to accept his fate!"

"But why? What did you ever do?"

Rocco crushed out the cigarette in the ashtray and looked at Italo. "One or two things you already know. You've been looking through the papers."

Italo gulped.

"The most normal thing in the world. I'd have done the same thing. Let's just say that it was best for me to make myself scarce down in Rome. Decisions from on high."

"I see."

"No, you don't see. But let it suffice."

*   *   *

Luisa's eyes were the first thing he noticed. Big baby blues. Along with the oval face and copper blond hair that made her vaguely resemble an Italian-English actress.

"Greta Scacchi," Rocco whispered to officer Pierron as he approached Luisa, who was sitting waiting on a bench.

"Huh?" asked Italo.

"She looks like Greta Scacchi. The actress. You know the one?"

"No."

The deputy police chief extended his hand to the woman, who had risen to her feet and was holding out hers.

"Deputy Police Chief Rocco Schiavone."

"Luisa Pec."

The woman's hand was hard and callused, in sharp contrast with the softness of her face and the curves of her body. On her cheeks, a faint blush made her look hale and healthy.

"Please follow me to my office, Signora Pec."

Luisa and Rocco walked off down the hallway. "So last night your husband didn't come home?"

"No. He didn't come home last night."

"*Prego*, take a seat," and Rocco opened the door.

He immediately noticed a whiff of cannabis and hurried to throw open the window. He gestured to Luisa Pec, who took a seat in front of the desk. Now Rocco could take a closer look at her. Her eyes were dull, marked by circles as deep as trenches. Luisa was the very picture of anxiety, but she still managed to be pretty.

Rocco sat down in his high-backed leather chair. "Tell me all about it," he said, and placed both elbows on his desk.

"Last night my husband didn't come home."

"Well, that's a concept I think we've thoroughly examined. What is your husband's name?"

"Leone. Leone Miccichè."

"Miccichè. Not a native of these mountains, unless I'm guessing wrong?"

"Quite right. He's from Catania."

"Where do you live?"

"Leone and I have a chalet in Cuneaz."

"Where?"

"On the pistes, about three hundred yards past the end of the cableway. There are a few houses up there, practically a village, I guess, and it's called Cuneaz. Well, that's where we have our hut. Last night Leone went down to town. He always goes down on foot. Then he comes back by the cableway."

"And you haven't seen him since last night?"

"Since last night."

Schiavone opened the desk drawer. He had a sudden urge to smoke another joint, maybe just a couple of quick puffs, but instead he opted for a more official Camel. "Mind if I smoke?"

"No. I don't smoke myself, but Leone does and I've gotten used to it."

"What was your husband going to do in town?"

"He generally went down every other day. He'd just head down, see some people, drop by the bookstore, pick up a novel. That kind of thing."

Rocco lit his cigarette. "But last night he didn't come home …"

"No. I heard about what happened and I couldn't sleep all night long. The person you found, did he have any ID?"

Rocco halted her with a wave of his hand. "Signora Pec, unfortunately we don't know the identity of the person we found last night."

Luisa gulped and swallowed a bundle of anxiety. Then tears welled up in her eyes.

"Maybe your husband slept in town last night, don't you think? He might have had too much to drink and ..."

"He'd have called me this morning!"

Schiavone smiled. "Signora, when a guy's had way too much to drink, the next morning he won't even know where he is, take it from me."

"You see, Dottor ..."

"Schiavone."

"Schiavone. Before coming here today, I went to all the places Leone usually goes. Last night, nobody saw him."

A tear slid down Luisa's cheek. Rocco sat there looking at her face. He was attracted by the slightly downturned lips, which gave her an expression that was at once surprised and sensual. Tears and sadness looked out of place on that healthy, vital complexion. And that odd counterpoint, so unmistakable, aroused the deputy police chief to a surprising degree. Luisa wiped the tears from her eyes with the sleeve of her Patagonia sweater.

"Would you like a glass of water, signora?"

Luisa shook her head. "No. I wonder if I can go take a look at the man you found. At least that way I could set my fears to rest, no? I can't stay up at the hut all alone. Not as anxious as I feel."

Rocco stood up and went to the window. He tossed the cigarette butt into the street, then pulled the window shut. "Tell me something: this hut, this chalet, exactly what is it? A lean-to of some kind?"

"No, Dottore. It's a small bar and trattoria up in the mountains. There was a time when huts were just huts. Now they're chalets, did you know that? We serve food and drinks, and the place is furnished better than a boutique in Milan."

"Ah. And does it make money?"

"If the season is successful, yes. It makes plenty of money."

Rocco leaned his forehead against the glass and watched the sidewalks, dotted with snow. A woman holding a child by the hand crossed the street. "How much can you make with a chalet?"

"Why? Are you thinking of finding a new line of work?"

Rocco laughed. "That'd be nice." Then, at last, he turned around and looked at Luisa Pec, sitting across the desk from him. "No. It's just to help me understand. I've only been here a few months. I come from Rome, and let's just say that the mountains and me are as distant as … as Rome and the mountains."

A small smile broke the worry lines on Luisa's face; it lit up as if someone had touched a lit match to a lamp wick inside. "Well, now, what can I tell you? Enough to earn a perfectly decent living."

Rocco sat back down in his chair. "Do you really want to see him, Luisa? It's not a pretty sight, you know."

The woman bit her lip. Then she nodded briskly, three times.

Rocco stood up. "The face, if you know what I mean, is no longer recognizable. Maybe if ..."

"Leone has a tattoo. On his chest."

Rocco looked down, as if he were searching for a precious object that had just fallen on the floor. The woman sensed that something wasn't right. A gray, invisible veil once again fell over Luisa's pretty face. "What is it, Commissario? What's wrong?"

"I'm not sure that ... Oh well, forget about that. What does the tattoo say?"

"I have the same tattoo. We got them together. It's a Hindu mantra. *Maa vidvishhaavahai*, which means—"

"May no obstacle arise between us," Rocco finished the sentence for her, head bowed.

Luisa's pupils dilated like two oil patches. "But how ... how did you ...?" Then Luisa understood.

And she burst into tears.

He'd managed to avoid the procession to the hospital. He'd let Officer Casella accompany Luisa Pec to see Fumagalli and take care of all the administrative details. He'd delegated the official phone calls that had to be made to the investigating magistrate and the chief of police to Inspector Rispoli, one of the few officers on whom he relied almost blindly.

Now Rocco was sitting at his desk. In front of him, spread out like a sheet, was a map of Val d'Ayas. Across the desk, on the other side, was the raw material the state had provided him with: Officer D'Intino, looking at him blank-eyed, and Special Agent Deruta, still damp, his hair combed back. Inspector Caterina Rispoli with her lively blue eyes was sitting some distance from the pair of them, as if pointing out that her IQ was much higher than her colleagues'. The deputy police chief looked at his two male officers. He knew perfectly that the task he was about to assign them went well beyond their skill sets, but he also knew that the task would keep them busy for a long time, and the thought of not seeing D'Intino and Deruta wandering around police headquarters put him in a good mood.

"All right, listen up. As Deruta was saying, I have a very important job for you."

Deruta gulped with excitement.

"It's going to be a time-consuming, nerve-jangling, challenging task. But it's a job that only two smart, bold, and completely discreet officers can complete."

"Go ahead, Dottore," Deruta broke in, his chest swelling with pride and eagerness.

"D'Intino. Deruta. Now I want the two of you to make the rounds of all the carabinieri barracks, hotels, pensiones, and rentals in"—and here the deputy police chief shot a glance at the map—"Champoluc, Brusson, Antagnod ... In other words, let's include all the townships close to Champoluc in a range of thirty miles or so."

"That'll take forever!" said Deruta through clenched teeth.

"Yes," said Rocco, "but that's exactly why I chose the two of you."

"I don't understand," said D'Intino.

"That's nothing new. So what am I asking you to do? I want the identity details of all the people who registered in any of these places. And I want first and last names of everyone who rented a house, a room, a stable, or a grotto in the past week."

"Who are we looking for?" asked Officer Deruta.

"If I knew that, I'd give you their first and last name and tax number, no? All right, then, D'Intino! Deruta! The two of you get going. And remember: Inspector Rispoli is in charge, from headquarters. Is that clear?"

"Yes sir," replied Rispoli.

Deruta and D'Intino exchanged angry glances. Inspector Rispoli had enlisted only a year ago, and already she was in charge.

"So, Rispoli," the deputy police chief continued, "I want you to man the phone, the fax, and the computer and take down all the information that comes in from our officers. You're in charge of the whole operation."

"Very good."

Rocco looked at the two male cops. "Something wrong? You look like you have questions."

Finally Deruta screwed up his nerve. "No, it's just that, well, I was wondering if—"

"You're not being paid to wonder. You're being paid to do what I tell you. Now, here's one important thing." Rocco picked up the map and tried to fold it. Unsuccessfully. In the end he crumpled it into a ball and tossed it onto the floor. "How the fuck are you supposed to fold up these piece-of-shit maps! So—I was telling you something important! You can skip families with children and excursions and field trips or any groups that have to do with the church. Everyone else, get me the names as quickly as you can. Go in peace."

Deruta and D'Intino rushed to the door and vanished. Caterina Rispoli followed them. Rocco called her back. "Keep an eye on Laurel and Hardy."

Caterina smiled. "All right. Don't worry."

For four months, as far as Deputy Police Chief Schiavone was concerned, Caterina Rispoli had been just a uniform with short hair. But when he saw her smile for the first time after 120 days, he understood that, under the collar badges and regulation shoes, there was a woman. Twenty-four years old, with big eyes and somewhat droopy eyelids, her cheeks sprinkled with freckles and her mouth, small and sensuous. On her nose, a tiny hump, a slight imperfection that suited her. Her body, bundled into its uniform, was an exotic land awaiting discovery. But the deputy police chief's gaze, more penetrating than an X-ray, was capable of guessing that there, too, Inspector Rispoli acquitted herself with distinction.

Her tits must tilt up, Rocco decided.

There was only one detail left to examine. "Very well, Inspector. You can go."

Caterina Rispoli turned around, and Rocco's appraising eye immediately shot, like a hawk pouncing on a mouse, to the firm and shapely buttocks of the young police functionary.

He'd have to find out if she had a boyfriend. He hoped she did. Fewer headaches that way.

* * *

Sitting at the bar and sipping an espresso, Rocco Schiavone heard a church bell ring the hour of noon. He didn't feel like going home. He wasn't hungry. He limited himself to watching the gray sky where the clouds raced after one another in layers, in a competition without meaning.

"Dottore, do you want something to eat?" Ugo, the proprietor of the bar across from police headquarters, asked him. Rocco shook his head no. He just sat there, looking up at the sky.

How much longer could he stand living in this city? There was nothing familiar here. Everything about Rocco Schiavone was in Rome. And had been for forty-five years.

A handkerchief in the mouth, he thought.

The last thing they needed was a settling of accounts among Sicilian families at the foot of Monte Rosa.

"Can a guy surrender?" Rocco asked the glass pane of the window overlooking the street.

But it was Ugo's voice that answered him. "Of course he can. But I'd rather go on fighting than let myself be taken prisoner."

Rocco smiled. And at that very moment, a piercing, unpleasant sound from his cell phone informed him that he'd just received a text.

You going to come see me?

It was Nora. He'd forgotten about her.

He had a choice between going to her apartment in Duvet and going to Champoluc to start doing his job.

He opted for the first choice.

* * *

"Can I make a phone call?" Rocco asked as he got up from the bed.

Nora watched his ass. It was a nice ass. Muscular, firm, round. A little less nice where the legs were concerned. Too skinny for a man, they would have been nicer on a young lady. But at least they were straight. Perhaps Rocco Schiavone would benefit from a little diet and some exercise. Not so much for the love handles—Nora knew that after a certain age you just can't get rid of them, and also, according to a study done by one of the usual American universities somewhere in the Ohio hinterland, it was also a genetic issue if a man couldn't achieve a sculpted six-pack. And the biceps weren't bad, either. But a diet and the occasional workout would have toned him up nicely, along with his chest muscles. They were starting to droop. "Why don't you go to the gym every once in a while?" she asked him.

Rocco looked himself over. "I never have before. Why should I start now?"

"I don't know."

"So can I make this phone call, yes or no?"

"You know that you have a nice nose?" Nora asked, pulling the blankets up to cover her breasts. "It's long and pointy. Funny. And look at all that hair! How did that song go?" Nora started singing: "Gimme a head with hair. Long, beautiful hair. Shining, gleaming, streaming, flaxen, waxen ... *Hair*."

"Oh! I'm standing here freezing to death! Can I or can't I make this phone call?"

"Certainly, you can make a phone call," Nora replied. Rocco yanked the quilt off the bed, leaving Nora covered with nothing but sheets, wrapped the quilt around himself, and headed off to the living room.

"Ugh!" Nora cried.

Rocco turned around and looked at her, baffled.

"With that blanket on, you look like an Apache."

The deputy police chief caught a glimpse of his reflection in the mirror next to the door. He smiled. He brushed back his hair. "More like a Huron, actually."

Then, without another word, he vanished through the bedroom door, the Ikea quilt trailing after him.

That's the way it always was. After sex, Rocco Schiavone's mood always turned blacker than a cave's mouth. After four months of going out with him, Nora understood that. What she hadn't yet figured out was that man's timing: before making love, he was intractable. Afterward, even worse. It was only during sex that there was a gap in the clouds and it was possible to glimpse daylight—what Rocco could have been if life had smiled at him just a bit more often.

But Nora could hardly spend the rest of her life naked and clinging to Rocco Schiavone's body just for a moment of serenity! No, this was definitely an affair destined to end soon. She knew it.

And he knew it, too.

"Dottor Corsi? Deputy Police Chief Schiavone."

"Ah! Excellent. You're actually calling a little ahead of the twenty-four-hour deadline. Do you have good news for me?" The police chief's voice was vigorous and vibrant.

"I don't know if it's good. The name of the corpse was Leone Miccichè. He owned a hut, a chalet up at Cuneaz, above the Champoluc pistes, along with his wife, Luisa Pec, thirty-two years of age, looks a little like Greta Scacchi."

"Margherita Buy."

"What?"

"She looks like Margherita Buy, not Greta Scacchi," the police chief replied.

"You know her?"

"Of course. I'm a man who likes to ski, and I often go to eat at the Belle Cuneaz. They make a barley soup that's to die for. I knew them both, you know? Damn it to hell, though, Leone Miccichè. You've just given me some bad, bad news."

"I'm sorry," said Rocco, feeling like an idiot. "Anyway, for now the autopsy hasn't been completed, but judging from the preliminary analyses, Fumagalli is leaning toward a hypothesis of murder."

"Oh, mother—!" cursed the police chief, biting back the second word in the phrase. "Would you mind telling me how he can be so certain?"

"Of course. Leone Miccichè had a balled-up handkerchief in his mouth."

"A handkerchief in his mouth?"

"And a section of that handkerchief was found in his trachea. Inside it was a piece of tongue and two teeth. He'd swallowed it, because the trachea is intact. If the snowcat had crushed it in, then the trachea would be shredded, too."

"That makes sense."

"Right. And death can be placed around seven in the evening. Fumagalli will be more accurate after he checks body temperature against exterior temperature and so on and so forth. Well, I've told you everything I know. For now. You have plenty of material to give the reporters."

"I'd like it if you'd come with me to talk to those guys."

"I'm going up to Champoluc. I don't have any time to waste, Dottore," Rocco said, dodging the request.

"Of course. Right. You go. Last night the forensics team came up from Turin. They're on the site. You go take a look." And the police chief hung up without saying good-bye.

Rocco stood up from the armchair. Nora was there, leaning against the door frame, her face fresh with the complexion of the newly awakened.

"Everything you just heard? You never heard it," said Rocco.

"I sell wedding dresses. I'm no lawyer."

"Good. Now I have to go. Up. To the village."

"Of course. Tonight?"

"Tonight I'll definitely be late. I'll be heading home."

"If you change your mind …"

"If I change my mind I'll give you a call; that is, if you still feel like it. I know that sooner or later you're going to tell me to go to—"

"You're wrong there. I wouldn't tell you that. At least not today. And I'd like to see you tonight."

"Good. And forgive me. Maybe someday I'll make peace with myself."

"So you'll call me?"

"I'll call you, Nora."

"I don't believe you."

Rocco Schiavone had been staring at the magistrate's closed office door for more than fifteen minutes. By now he knew the pattern of the mahogany grain by heart, and he'd already found in the twisting grain surrounding the knots two elephants, a sea turtle, and a woman's torso, complete with belly button.

He was starting to get annoyed.

He hated being summoned by magistrates, he hated the courthouse, he hated the climate, and above all he hated the fact that it would be more than 3,650 days until he turned fifty-five.

Age fifty-five was the goal he had set for himself.

No longer so young that he could burn the candle at both ends like he had in his twenties, but also not yet so old that he was confined to a wheelchair, drooling soup into his lap and swallowing pills all day long.

He'd already selected the location six years ago, after extensive study and discussion with his wife, Marina. Not far from the sea, because he loved salt water, but deep in the country, because Marina loved the country. The Maremma would have been perfect, but it was definitely not a good idea to stay in Italy. In the end, they'd chosen Provence. And he'd take his weary old bones up there to bleach in the sun until death finally separated him from that earthly paradise.

Another 3,650 days.

A farmhouse. In the heart of the country. With at least twenty-five acres, so that he could be sure that there was no asshole sleeping within a stone's throw of him. The farmhouse would need to have at least six bedrooms for his friends from Rome. And a pool. Looking through the listings for properties available under four million euros, there was nothing even remotely resembling that. He was still considerably short on cash. He was thinking about Sebastiano Cecchetti's scheduled arrival when the door to the magistrate's office swung open and Maurizio Baldi appeared. In a jacket and tie, his appearance improved considerably. He no longer looked like one of Rigoni Stern's fellow soldiers lost in the snow of the Ukrainian steppes, as he had the night before. In fact, there was even the hint of a smile on his relaxed face. Rocco had assumed he was hairless under the Russian bearskin hat he'd been wearing at the foot of the cableway; but instead he had a lush head of blond hair, a fine, smooth shock of it dangling over his eyes, which made him look like a member of Spandau Ballet.

"Schiavone," said the magistrate as he extended his hand.

Rocco stood up and shook hands, then the magistrate showed him in and pointed him to a chair.

The office was small. The usual Italian tricolor, a photograph of the president, diplomas, certificates, and a couple of glass-front bookcases with dozens of tomes that no one had opened in years. On the desk, a code of criminal procedure and a framed photograph, turned facedown.

"We started off on the wrong foot yesterday, Dottore," said the magistrate, his face finally relaxing into a smile. "But I'm working on a major case of tax evasion, and this corpse arrives at a very inconvenient time." He stared Rocco in the eye. "I know a lot of things about you. I know why you're here, but I also know that you have an unusually high percentage of solved cases. Is that right?"

"Yes, that's right." Rocco was being cautious. The man he was looking at might have been the brother of the magistrate he'd met the night before. He didn't seem like the same person at all.

"Well, then. Have you looked into this Miccichè?"

Rocco nodded. "There's no smoking in here, is there?"

"No."

"Miccichè, Leone. Forty-three years of age. His family lives in the province of Catania, Sicily. They own a major vineyard and winery."

"Have they been informed?"

"Yes. They're coming north tomorrow."

"Yesterday I was really on edge," said the magistrate, suddenly veering off topic.

"There's no need to explain. I was, too."

"Listen to me, Schiavone. Do you like your job?"

Where is he heading with this? Rocco wondered.

"No. Do you?"

"Yes, I do. And there are certain days when I feel like telling everyone to go to hell and starting over on an island in the Indian Ocean, just eating coconuts all day."

"The Indian Ocean is a dangerous place. Tsunamis and seaquakes are everyday events," said Rocco, who knew all about it. It had been one of the first destinations he'd studied in detail with Marina. "Plus health care is mediocre at best. You should choose a clean, civilized country."

"Civilized …" Baldi said under his breath. "Civilized, sure, you have a point. You know what I was thinking about this morning?"

The question was rhetorical, and Rocco didn't bother to reply.

"I was thinking about soccer teams."

"And?"

"And, so, just think about it with me. For instance, do you know what a soccer team does to achieve better performance?"

"They practice?" Rocco guessed.

"That's not all. They buy players. Foreign players. Agreed?"

"Sure. It's true—just take a look at the Inter team roster."

"Exactly. You put together a team with the best players from around the world and you win national and international championships. Correct me if I'm wrong."

"You're not wrong."

"Fine, Schiavone. Now let's transfer this concept to our country."

Rocco crossed his legs. "You've lost me."

"Let's imagine that, in order to achieve the best results, we—that is, Italy—go around the world buying the best players."

"No, here you have a problem," Rocco objected. "The Italian national soccer team has to be made up of only Italian players."

"I'm not talking about soccer anymore. Soccer is nothing but a metaphor. I'm referring to politics. So what would I do? I'll buy a nice Swedish prime minister, say a Reinfeldt; then we put a German in charge of the economy, a Brüderle; then a French culture minister, say, Christine Albanel; a Danish minister of justice; and there you go! Just think what a dream team you'd have! And finally this country might stop being such a joke. You get what I'm saying?"

The likelihood that the magistrate might be suffering from some form of bipolar disorder surfaced powerfully in Rocco Schiavone's mind. "Loud and clear. A good old-fashioned shopping spree," he replied, because agreeing wholeheartedly seemed like the safest approach.

"Exactly!" and the magistrate slammed his fist down on his desk. "Exactly, Schiavone. It would be great, don't you think?"

"Yeah."

"I'm kidding, obviously. I hope you didn't take me seriously, did you?"

"A little bit, yes."

"No. In part because it's not enough to put new people in the top positions. In Italy, we need to send half our ruling class into house arrest. But don't worry about me; I'm just a little disgusted at what I see and read in the newspapers every day. Take care of yourself and keep me informed." He suddenly stood up and extended his hand. Rocco imitated him. As soon as he shook the magistrate's hand, Baldi winked at him. "Let's find this killer, agreed?"

Rocco nodded as he pumped the magistrate's hand up and down. Then his gaze fell on the photograph lying facedown on the desk. The two men stood there, hands clasped, staring at the silver frame. Rocco asked no questions. Baldi offered no information. He shot Rocco a false smile through clenched teeth and released the deputy police chief's hand. Rocco turned on his heels and left the office without another word.

Walking down the courthouse steps, he decided that, mourning or no mourning, he needed to go have a nice long chat with Luisa Pec.

Italo Pierron drove smoothly through the switchback curves that ran from Verrès to the Val d'Ayas. Rocco sat there in silence the whole way, looking out the window. Only a tiny patch of blue sky had appeared to break the monotonous gray field of clouds. When the sign warned them that they were entering the township of Brusson, the deputy police chief finally spoke. "Are you married, Italo?"

"No, Dottore."

"Engaged?"

"No, not engaged either. I had a girlfriend, but we broke up three months ago."

"Why?"

"I saw her in a restaurant with another man. An old boyfriend of hers."

"So?"

"So it hurt my feelings."

Rocco looked at Italo. He still had the features of a boy, but his mouth, which looked like a cut slashed across the face with a scalpel, aged him by several years. As an old man, he'd definitely have a beard or a mustache to conceal his lip deficit. His head was small and moved jerkily. His slightly prominent nose seemed always to be on the alert. His eyes were dark and deep. Wide awake. Officer Pierron sensed he was being watched. He shot a glance at the deputy police chief, smiled, and resumed his focus on the road ahead.

When Rocco was a boy, he had an encyclopedia of animals, which, along with the *Junior Woodchucks' Guidebook* and the *Quindici* boys' encyclopedia, constituted the entire household library. The last volume of the encyclopedia of animals, volume five, consisted of plates of illustrations done by first-rate artists from the nineteenth century. It was his favorite. Curled up on the carpet in his bedroom, he'd spend whole afternoons at a time poring over those illustrations, one by one. He'd wondered more than once how those artists had managed to do those paintings of animals. In the first half of the nineteenth century, they didn't have photography at all. And even when they did, it wasn't as if toucans and bats would perch there, obedient and still, happy to sit for their portraits. Then it dawned on him that the painters had worked with stuffed animals as their models. Dead ones. And yet those illustrations endowed the animals with a vitality and a movement that made them seem vividly alive, more alive than any photograph. He loved the colors, the species, especially the ones that had already gone extinct. If it weren't for those pictures, he always thought, we'd now have no idea what a thylacine, or Tasmanian wolf, was even like; and the same applied to the quagga, a subspecies of the African plains zebra. Ever since, whenever he met anyone in real life who reminded him of one of these illustrations, he'd immediately catalog them, like a zoologist with a mental notebook. Italo Pierron was a *Mustela nivalis*. A weasel. He'd met plenty of weasels in his time, but never in the police.

"Italo," he said suddenly, and the officer's Adam's apple jerked up and down a couple of times. "Italo, do you like your job?"

The other man's eyes opened wide. A faint hint of a smile appeared on the lipless mouth. He shrugged. "It's a job."

"How much does a police officer make every month?"

"Not much, Dottore. Not much."

"And no real schedule, right? Hard to start a family."

"I'm not interested in a family. I'm fine the way I am. But why are you asking me these questions?"

"To get to know you better. You're a good cop. You know it. But if you ask me, you could do more."

"More than what I'm doing now?"

"No. Something else. You could really up your game. Take it to another level." And Rocco fell silent, letting the officer mull over the last thing he'd told him.

"Listen," he went on, "before we go up to see Luisa Pec, we should swing by the post office."

"All right. But at this time of day it'll be closed."

"Don't you worry about that. Just take me there."

When they pulled up outside the post office, there was a man in his early fifties waiting for them outside the front door. He was wearing a broad-ribbed wool sweater. His cheeks were red, and he was rubbing his hands. Italo stopped the car. As soon as Rocco got out, an icy gust of wind buffeted him. Even if it was broad daylight, the temperature was well below freezing. "Jesus fucking Christ, it's cold as a bitch out!" the deputy police chief muttered under his breath. "You wait here for me!" he said to Italo, closing the door of the BMW behind him. Then he went over to the man on the steps, who immediately extended his hand.

"I'm Riccardo Peroni. The postmaster here. I received a phone call from police headquarters ..."

"Yes, yes," said Rocco, shaking his hand. "Deputy Police Chief Schiavone. Shall we go in? It's freezing out here!"

The postmaster opened the glass door and let Rocco in.

"Go ahead and lock up behind us," the detective said to him once they were inside.

Peroni did as he was told. "What can I do for you?"

The empty office had no lights on except for the "next customer in line" lights over the service windows; the trash cans were full of ripped-up forms and receipts. On a set of shelves were the products that the post office sold but that had nothing to do with the postal service: cookbooks, children's books, a couple of best sellers, pens and markers.

Even the post office moonlights on the side to make ends meet, Rocco mused. It reminded him that he still needed to pay last month's electric bill. He felt a stab of regret. He could have remembered and taken care of at least this one small husbandly duty.

"I read something in a book and it stuck with me."

"What's that?" asked the postmaster with a courteous smile.

"The post office is like your fingernails and hair. When you die, they keep on growing. Same thing with letters and bills. They keep on being delivered, even if the recipient is already dead and buried. True, no?"

Peroni thought it over for a minute. "I'd never considered it in those terms."

"So from today on, all the mail that should have gone to Signor Leone Miccichè? You'll forward it to me at police headquarters. As quickly as you possibly can."

The postmaster turned serious. "What? Leone? He's dead?"

"You have the gift of observation."

"But when?"

"Yesterday. Up on the ski runs."

The postmaster turned pale. "That was the corpse you found?"

"All his. Head to foot, every bit of it."

"Poor Luisa ..."

"Yes, it's a shame. So you understand? And listen to me: not a word to a soul. Have I made myself clear?"

Peroni looked at the floor, still upset by the news.

Schiavone brought him brusquely back to the real world. "Hey! Did you understand what I said?"

"Eh? Ah, yes. I understood. Leone's mail—"

"Should be forwarded to me. That's right."

Peroni opened his eyes wide, an indication that his brain had started to work again. "But I'm not sure about this. Is it strictly legal?"

"No. I really don't think it is," the deputy police chief replied calmly.

"Then what you're asking me to do is ...?"

"Leone's mail. Forwarded to my office, at police headquarters, strictly personal."

"I'll have to see whether ... That is, I have certain duties. I can hardly promise you that ..."

Peroni didn't see it coming. He only felt the pain on his cheek at the same time that his head swiveled around in a thirty-degree arc to his left. He put his hand up to touch his cheek right where Rocco had punched him unexpectedly. "Now, then," the deputy police chief said calmly. "I'm going to repeat it politely. Are you going to let me have Miccichè's mail or am I going to make your life a living hell?"

The postmaster nodded in fright. Then Rocco handed the man his card. "It's all written down right here. And thanks for your help." He took a couple of steps toward the glass door, seized the handle, but then stopped. He stood there as if a thought had suddenly crossed his mind. He turned around and looked at Peroni, who was standing forlorn with Rocco's card in one hand while the other hand tenderly caressed his cheek. "Peroni. Not a word about this understanding of ours to a soul. If not, I'll be back. Have I made myself clear?"

"Yes."

"Have a good day."

*　*　*

To get up to the slopes, they had to take a six-seat cable car. It looked something like a pea pod attached to an enormous steel cable by a metal hook. Rocco and Pierron got into pea pod number 69, which shot off uphill at top speed, taking them straight up to an elevation of 6,500 feet. The man running the cableway had stared intently at Rocco's clothing, so completely out of place, focusing on his Clarks desert boots for a good ten seconds at least, but then, locked up in his work and his mountain man's tendency to remain silent, he had said nothing. He'd simply double-checked the closure of the double door and then turned to help the next passengers.

"Wait, are people skiing today?" asked Rocco, peering out of the Plexiglas windows.

"Only on the higher-up pistes. The one farther downhill, where we found Miccichè, is closed."

The cabin was already brushing over the tips of the fir trees below. The forest, wrapped in a dense and impenetrable drizzly fog, seemed to have come out of a Celtic saga. Rocco looked down at the blanket of snow between the rocks and trees. There were pine needles, but especially tracks. Large and small.

"Birds, hares, ibexes, and chamoix," said Italo Pierron, "all of them on the hunt for food."

"Are there weasels too?"

"Sure. In the winter, they turn white. Why?"

"I was just wondering."

"Yeah, weasels are clever. They camouflage themselves."

"Really?" asked Rocco, staring into Italo Pierron's eyes intensely until he blushed, unable to fathom his superior officer's intentions. Rocco was studying him, that much was clear. But he couldn't piece together reason.

"It's important to camouflage yourself, Italo. If you want to survive in a world of predators."

Suddenly the sooty slush around them fell away, and a bright, blinding sun lit up the landscape. Rocco stood open-mouthed. They'd emerged from the clouds, as if in an airplane. Now the sky was blue, and all around the snowy alpine peaks surrounded them like a crown. They looked like so many islands jutting up from the grayish, foamy waters of a lake. Rocco squinted to see through the dazzling light. "So pretty," he said spontaneously, "so pretty."

"Right?" agreed Italo.

The snow, like an immense lava flow of whipped cream, covered the high plateaus, the cliffs, and the boulders. To look down on it like this, the snow didn't even seem particularly cold. In fact, Rocco felt the urge to jump in and roll around in it for fifteen minutes. Even pick some up and eat it. It must be soft and sweet. It glittered with a thousand sharp-edged points of light, and if he stared too hard, he felt stabbing pain in his eyes and his head began to spin. The black slate roofs of the little huts and cottages were submerged in snow, and if it hadn't been for the smoking chimney pots, it would have been impossible to see them at all. They lay buried in that sea of white, as absolutely clean and candid as so many flocks grazing happily, lazy and somnolent.

At last the cable car reached its destination. Rocco got out, pleased that he hadn't felt even a hint of vertigo.

Outside the cableway station, the snow was deep, and the sun had melted it a little. Skiers dressed in a dizzying array of colors, so that they resembled a cluster of carnival masks, were sprawled out at the tables of a chalet bar, drinking in the day's last rays of light, sipping foamy goblets of beer. Others headed down to the slopes with skis, snowshoes, and helmets thrown over their shoulders, walking like so many golems in large, noisy snowboots. Rocco was reminded of the damned souls in some Dantean circle of hell.

"Are you saying they pay for all this?" he asked Italo.

"Deputy Police Chief Schiavone," said Pierron, unbelievably nailing Rocco's correct rank, "have you ever tried skiing?"

"Never."

"Then take it from me that if you tried even once, you'd understand. Just like a little while ago on the cableway. Did you see? Suddenly sun and sky and snow. The same thing on skis. The same sensation."

But Rocco wasn't listening anymore. He was comparing the snow on the ground with his shoes, so ill suited to the situation.

"Don't worry, Dottore, we only have to walk about a hundred yards. Luigi is waiting for us."

"Who's Luigi?"

"The head snowcat operator. The one who took us up last night. Luigi Bionaz. He's going to take us to Cuneaz. You see that valley down there?"

Rocco looked. Four hundred yards ahead, in the midst of runs busy with overjoyed skiers, there was a collection of snow-covered humps. "Yes, I see. What of it?"

"Cuneaz is down there, behind those rises in the slope. In the summer, you can walk it. But in the winter you'd need snowshoes."

"You'd need what?"

"Snowshoes … those rackets on your feet. You know what I mean?"

"Ah. Like Umberto Nobile?"

"Who?"

"Forget about it, Italo. Let's go see Luigi."

Barely fifty feet outside the cableway station, there was an enormous rock-and-timber structure off to one side. This was the snowcat garage. In the distance, outside a glass door with the ski school logo, the instructors were loitering on wooden benches in the sun, all of them wearing red jackets and black pants. Italo raised one hand to catch someone's attention. Rocco, on the other hand, looked down at his Clarks desert boots, which resembled two waterlogged sewer rats.

"Hey there!" shouted someone Rocco couldn't really see because of the glare.

"Look, there's Luigi. Let's go," said Italo, "he's waiting for us."

Walking laboriously through the deep snow, dressed in his loden green overcoat and gray corduroy trousers, under the inquisitive gazes of the skiers, Rocco finally made it to the door of the garage. Luigi Bionaz was there, waiting for them.

"*Buon giorno*, Commissario, don't you remember me?"

The night before, Luigi's face had been nothing but an indistinct mass beneath a heavy cap with earflaps. Now, in the light of day, Rocco was finally able to make out his features.

The first thing Rocco noticed was his eyes, such a pale blue that they looked like those of a sled dog, a husky. High cheekbones, a strong jaw, and clean white teeth that seemed to be reflecting the surrounding snow. If Luigi Bionaz had been born in America, he could have become an action movie star. He had the face and he had the body—everything necessary to drive the women of half a hemisphere mad with desire.

"I heard. Leone. I'm so sorry. Was it an accident?" he asked as he rolled himself a cigarette.

Rocco didn't say a word, and Luigi understood that this was not the time to ask any other questions. So he smiled and slapped his hand down twice on the seat of a 4x4 all-terrain vehicle. "No snowcat today. We're going on this."

It was a quad, a sort of four-wheeled motorcycle. Rocco had driven one many years before, on the dunes of Sharm el-Sheikh, in the famous motorcade through the desert. He'd overturned the quad and broken the phalanx bone of his wife's middle finger.

"It's faster," Luigi added. "Theoretically, we aren't allowed to take this thing onto the pistes." He lit his cigarette, and the tip glowed red and dropped burning ashes onto the snow. "But you're from the police, no? So who's going to tell us what to do?"

"True. But you could have come all the way down and picked us up at the cableway terminal, no?" said Rocco. "My feet are drenched from walking up here!"

Luigi laughed merrily. "Dottore, you're going to have to get some proper equipment for the mountains!" replied the head snowcat operator as he climbed onto the quad.

"So that I can look like a clown, the way they do?" and he pointed to the skiers with his nose. "Oh, give me a break."

He got on behind Luigi. Pierron got on, too.

"Luigi, will this thing carry three people?"

Luigi ignored the deputy police chief's question. He started the engine and, with a half smile and his cigarette clenched between his teeth, he revved it and took off.

The four studded tires got their teeth right into the snow and, leaving a huge spray of slush in the air behind them, shot the vehicle uphill toward the ski runs at a dizzying velocity. Rocco watched the vehicle narrowly miss skiers as needles of ice stung his face. The wheels drifted, then came back into alignment, only to veer suddenly as the vehicle slid across a sheet of ice. He could feel the quad wobble, career off to one side, roar, plunge into the snow, and then recover, only to lurch forward again in a terrifying plunge, worse than the pitching and yawing of a speedboat in an ocean squall.

Two minutes of breathtaking speed and they were at Cuneaz.

Rocco got off, brushing the snow off his overcoat. Then he looked at Luigi, who still had the cigarette dangling from his lips. "On the way back, I'm driving!" he said, pointing a finger at his chest.

"Why?" Luigi asked innocently. "Were you scared?"

"Scared? Of what? This is incredibly cool!"

Pierron felt quite differently about it. He merely shook his head in disapproval.

Cuneaz was a perfect little mountain village, with the small central piazza, the houses, the firewood cut and stacked neatly outside the homes. There were three huts. The finest was definitely the Belle Cuneaz, property of the unfortunate Leone Miccichè. It was closed. Luigi knocked on the door. Not thirty seconds had gone by before Luisa Pec's sad face appeared in the glass window of the door, right behind the Visa and PagoBancomat credit card decals. Those were essential, because they allowed Rocco to keep his feet securely planted on the ground; otherwise, what with the lack of oxygen, the snowy dreamscape, the silence, the smoking chimney pots, and the wooden houses with their mysterious words written in gothic characters, he could easily have given in to the belief that he had fallen into a story by the Brothers Grimm.

Luisa welcomed Rocco and Pierron in and directed them to two Chesterfield settees.

"Now I'll get you a little something to drink. It'll warm you up, and it tastes good, too," she said without a hint of a smile, as if she were reciting memorized lines.

The hut, as they called it up here, looked as if it had come straight out of an interior design magazine. The light pine boiserie on the walls, the stone floors interspersed with a time-burnished salvaged parquet, the vintage woodstove with the andirons. The lights, diffuse and warm. The stripped wooden tables and the excellent paintings on the walls, of late-nineteenth-century mountain landscapes. The bar was an antique Venetian apothecary's counter, with shelves for bottles made from the traditional straw drying racks used in those valleys. Everything, from large to small, clearly stated: This renovation was hugely expensive!

And the result was spectacular.

The mistress of the house returned with a bottle of juniper berry grappa and two glasses. "But is it true that the police never drink when they're on duty?" she asked.

"Yes," Rocco said as he poured himself a glass of the liquor. Pierron, on the other hand, turned down the offer.

Luigi had lingered, standing, by the window, like a faithful servant. He was rolling a second cigarette and was running his tongue down the edge to seal it. Rocco looked at him. "Listen, Luigi, do you mind taking a walk? We have some things to talk about that are strictly between us."

Luigi drank the grappa down with a jolt and left the chalet, striding briskly.

"This place is fantastic," said Rocco, taking in the great room at a glance.

"Thanks," Luisa replied. "Upstairs there are six bedrooms, and the restaurant's through that door. I'll show it to you later—it's a nice dining room, especially because it has a plate-glass window that directly overlooks the valley."

"It's enormous," Rocco noted. "A person would hardly think that up in the mountains ..."

"This used to be the school. Until the war. Then the people abandoned Cuneaz, they moved down to Champoluc, and then ..."

"Did you buy it?"

"Me? No," Luisa replied with a smile. "It belonged to my grandparents. Let's just say that it was a hovel; they used it as a stall. Hold on." She got up, went to the facing wall, pulled down a black-and-white photograph that was hanging there, and brought it back to the deputy police chief. "You see? That's how it was before we did the work."

Rocco looked at the picture. A broken-down stone-and-timber hovel, vomiting straw out of the unglazed windows.

"Well, it's unrecognizable. I can't imagine how much money you spent."

Luisa grimaced. "Don't even mention it. Anyway, it was around four hundred thousand."

The deputy police chief whistled like a teakettle.

"Look, before you ask, I'll tell you myself. Anyway, everyone in town already knows. It was Leone's money. It's all due to him that the place looks the way it does." Her chin began to quiver, her epiglottis emitted a rattle, and a fountain of tears poured out of Luisa Pec's pretty blue eyes. Italo immediately lunged forward and offered her a handkerchief.

"Sorry ... forgive me."

"No, we owe you the apology. Unfortunately, this is the horrible work I do. I'm worse than a vulture. Oh, well ..." and, with a smile, Rocco tossed back his glass of juniper berry grappa.

It was good. It slid like a caress down to his stomach and his icy feet.

"Luisa, I have to ask you something. Did Leone ever have problems with, let's say, people from down south?"

Luisa sniffed, dried her tears, and handed the handkerchief back to Pierron. "What do you mean, 'problems'?"

"Did he or his family, as far as you know, ever have any unclear dealings with Sicily? I'm talking about organized crime."

Luisa Pec turned red. Her eyes opened wide. "Ma ... Mafia?"

"You can call it that."

"Leone? No, oh my God, no. His family makes wine. They've been in the wine business for a hundred years. A solid company. You see? That's theirs," she said, turning slightly to point to a wine rack full of bottles with a distinctive label. "Nice people. Never fought with them once."

"Are you certain? Did he ever seem worried about anything? Ever get any mysterious phone calls?"

"No. I swear he didn't." Then a shadow passed over Luisa Pec's face. Rocco knew how to read nuances, to say nothing of things marked with a highlighter. "What is it, Luisa?"

"A few days ago he talked on the phone to Mimmo ... Domenico, his older brother. They argued. But I don't know what it was about; maybe it wasn't anything serious."

"Maybe not."

"But you can ask him yourself. They're coming up for the funeral."

"I know. In fact, they ought to be here already. It was a pleasure to see you again."

"I'm here if you need me. Don't you want to see the restaurant?"

"No. Too many beautiful things, one after another, can really do a number on your self-esteem," Rocco replied with a smile and stood up. Pierron followed suit and gripped Luisa Pec's hand.

"Buck up," was the only thing Italo said.

"Buck up?" the deputy police chief asked Italo as soon as they left the Belle Cuneaz. "Seriously? How do you come up with these things, Italo?"

"Poor thing. She was so upset, she seemed—"

"Whatever she seemed to you, you can keep it, think about it, swallow it, and take it home with you. *Buck up*. Would you do me a favor! Come on, Luigi, let's get this hunk of metal and take it back down the hill."

"So you're going to drive?" said the head snowcat operator, a dead cigarette butt in his mouth.

"You bet."

A minute and forty-five seconds later, the quad driven by Deputy Police Chief Rocco Schiavone braked to a halt in front of the snowcat garage.

"This thing is amazing."

"When we hit the bump at the end of the piste, I'm pretty sure my feet went higher than my head," said Italo Pierron, brushing snow off his down jacket.

"Because you lack confidence."

"Well, see you around?" said Luigi as he headed off.

"See you around."

Italo and Rocco were heading for the cableway station when a voice shouted out: "Dottore! Dottor Schiavone!"

Rocco turned around. From the little knot of ski instructors lounging on the benches he saw Caciuoppolo's uniform emerge—Caciuoppolo, the skiing Neapolitan. He was waving one hand in the air to get his attention and smiling with his gleaming white teeth. He hurried up in his ski boots, his skis thrown over his shoulder. The deputy police chief walked toward him, both hands in his pockets—after the motorcycle ride at 6,500 feet above sea level, they felt like two blocks of ice.

"Caciuoppolo!" he shouted back, and a billowing puff of dense steam emerged from his mouth. "Why aren't you with the forensics team?"

"Dottore!" The young man raised one hand to his forehead in a rough approximation of a military salute. "They weren't crazy about my presence. It seems that we made a huge mess on the location." Officer Caciuoppolo's smile vanished, and his face turned sad, in spite of the burnt-sienna suntan. "Commissa', I need to speak to you."

"What about?"

"Not here."

"Then where?"

"Were you heading back down to the village?"

"Yes."

"Then I'll come with you. Inside the cable car would be better."

The first one in the cabin was Pierron, followed by the deputy police chief and, last of all, Caciuoppolo, who got in after securing his skis to the external rack. The cabin attendant checked to make sure the doors were securely shut, and the little shell began its descent.

"All right, then, what do you have to tell me?"

"There are things you ought to know. Leone Miccichè, the corpse …"

"Well?"

"Well, he'd been with Luisa Pec for three years. And they were expecting a baby."

Rocco looked into Caciuoppolo's dark eyes. "How do you know that?"

"I know because Omar told me so."

Italo Pierron nodded.

"Do you know him?" Rocco asked him.

"Sure. Omar is one of the ski instructors. Or maybe we should say the chief ski instructor, really," Italo replied.

"Well, what the hell is it to Omar? Instead of teaching people how to ride on those gadgets, what do they do? Gossip like a bunch of housewives?"

"No." Caciuoppolo laughed. "No, you see, Dottore. Omar Borghetti was Luisa Pec's boyfriend. Before she started seeing Leone. So that means he knows everything."

"Boyfriend?"

"Right."

Rocco looked outside. The sun was smashing down onto the mountains, drenching them in orange and making them look like so many enormous caramel Mont Blancs.

"The boyfriend. Is that what you wanted to tell me?"

"That's not all, Dottore," Caciuoppolo went on. "There's something that I think you might need to know. Omar Borghetti was very upset when Luisa broke up with him. He couldn't get over it. They had planned on fixing up the hut together. Omar had applied for loans and everything. Then the dream vanished in a puff of smoke. I mean, you've seen Luisa Pec, no?"

"Good work, Caciuoppolo. You've already identified the person of interest. *Bravo.*"

"*Grazie.*"

The cable car slipped between sky and clouds. Mountains and sunset both disappeared, swallowed up by the milky glaze. The deputy police chief started thinking aloud. "In other words, he found out that Luisa was pregnant and he just saw red. Could be, eh? I don't say no, Caciuoppolo. Let's leave no stone unturned."

The downhill station came closer and closer. Rocco saw the men of the forensics team loading plastic crates onto their parked pickup trucks. He rolled his eyes skyward. "There are the guys from the forensics squad," he said. Italo and Caciuoppolo pressed their faces to the windows to see. "You know how you can recognize them? When they walk, they look as if they're afraid they're going to step on shit. An occupational hazard. You see the guy with the green jacket?" He pointed his forefinger at a man waiting with folded arms next to the pickup. "That one is an assistant commissioner. And he's the team leader."

"How do you know that?" asked Italo.

"Because I know him. His name is Luca Farinelli. He's a tremendous pain in the ass, but he's also the best there is. In particular, he's got one thing that could make anyone go a little apeshit."

"And what's that?" asked Caciuoppolo.

"His wife. A terrifyingly hot babe. Olive skin, curly hair, green eyes. Nobody understands how she could have fallen for Farinelli. You can't really see him from here, but he's the most uninteresting man I know. You know that kind of face you see and immediately forget?"

Rocco's cell phone played the first few notes of the "Ode to Joy." "What's up, Deruta? Tell me all about it."

"Ah, Dottore, we're hard at work. But there's a bunch of English names. What should we do, check them all out?"

"All of them, Deruta, check them all. Do you have anything else for me?"

"D'Intino."

"Well?"

"He collapsed."

Rocco burst out in a liberating peal of laughter. "And how is he?"

"He got a look at Miccichè's corpse. First he turned white, then purple, then he slammed to the floor. Now he's at the hospital, but they say they're only going to keep him overnight."

"All right, Deruta. All right. It strikes me as an excellent piece of news."

"You think?"

"I do. Take care of yourself," Rocco said, and, cackling to himself, put his cell phone back in his pocket. Pierron was looking at him inquisitively, but he saw no reason to satisfy the young officer's curiosity.

* * *

The cable car lurched to a halt and vomited out the three policemen.

"All right, Italo, now you go with Caciuoppolo to the bar and exchange telephone numbers. I'm going to talk to Farinelli. Have a good time. Ah, no, wait a second. Italo, give me a cigarette."

Pierron pulled out his pack of Chesterfields and offered his superior officer a cigarette.

"Why don't you buy Camels, Italo? I don't like Chesterfields." Rocco put the cigarette in his mouth and lit it while the two young officers headed off toward the metal staircase that led down to the main street of Champoluc. The deputy police chief twisted the cricks out of his neck and started walking toward the parking lot, where the assistant commissioner of the forensics team was waiting for him.

"How's it going?"

"It's going," Rocco replied. "What do you say?"

"You guys made a mess."

"Farinelli, come to the point. My right leg hurts, my feet are frozen, I'm smoking a cigarette that tastes like iron, and I have no time to waste. Is there anything I would be interested to know?"

"This."

He pulled a plastic baggie out of his pocket. Inside were a number of indistinct particles, small and black. They looked like gnats smashed onto a windshield.

"What's that stuff?"

"Tobacco. There was a fair amount of it, you see?"

"Tobacco?"

"Now we're going to look into it and try to find out more."

"Okay, fine, whatever." Rocco knew that that kind of analysis took forever—biblical amounts of time. And he also knew that if you don't catch the killer in the first forty-eight hours, then it's too late. "Marlboro Light. The corpse had a pack in his pocket. He smoked it."

"Ah. Well. He smoked it. In that case ..." and he put the baggie back into his pocket. "Someone peed on the tree next to the crime scene. We collected the urine."

"Throw it away."

Farinelli looked at Rocco, tilting his head to one side, as if he hadn't heard him right.

"That was Officer Casella."

Farinelli looked crestfallen. "There were a bunch of footprints, but I'll bet that if we run it all to ground we'll find it was all your guys' shoes."

"Mine are easy to identify." Rocco lifted his foot and pointed to it. "I'm the only one wearing Clarks desert boots."

"Those are Clarks?"

"Yeah, they used to be."

"They look like your feet are wrapped in rags. I'm going to have to report to the judge."

"Do as you think best."

"Do you want to come, and we can report together?"

"No, I've got things to do."

"Listen, Schiavone, I don't give a damn about how you do things. I like to follow procedure."

"Good for you, go on following it. But did you happen to take a look at the corpse?"

Farinelli nodded a couple of times while Rocco discarded his cigarette butt. "I cleaned under his fingernails," the assistant commissioner said.

"*Bravo*. And what did you find?"

"Nothing. There was no struggle, no fight. Just traces of a black fabric, but …" Farinelli bent over. He had a black combination-lock briefcase on the ground. He opened it. "We found all kinds of things under the snowcat's tillers. Shreds of clothing, blood, vomit, a couple of teeth, and even this stuff here."

He pulled out another plastic bag. Inside it was the finger of a black glove. The man from the forensics team stood up and showed the exhibit to the deputy police chief.

"What's left of a glove. And I'm pretty sure that the fibers that the guy had under his fingernails belong to this one. It's leather. Now I'm trying to find out the model and brand."

"Don't bother; I already know. This is a leather ski glove, made by Colmar. We found the other one next to the corpse."

"Is it important?" Farinelli asked, looking Rocco in the eye.

"It's fundamental."

He'd turned off his cell phone. Now, under a dark, starless sky, wrapped in his loden overcoat, with a new pair of Clarks desert boots on his feet, Rocco Schiavone was in Piazza

Manzetti, outside the train station. He'd left his car double-parked and had shouted at a traffic cop who wanted to point out the fact to him. Sebastiano's train was coming in about half an hour late.

He finally heard the sound of train wheels screeching on the rails. He flicked his cigarette away and walked into the station. There weren't many people. The Café de la Gare was empty and was about to lock up for the night. But that didn't matter: he had no desire to drink anything, not even an espresso. He just wanted to wrap his arms around Sebastiano, take him somewhere to have some dinner together, and talk about the good old days.

He saw him climb down from the passenger car. Powerful, tall, with the briefcase of a traveling salesman, his beard still full and his hair curly and unruly. Sebastiano, in Rocco's mental zoological classification, was an *Ursus arctos horribilis*, an ugly scientific name for the grizzly bear. He was placid, handsome, and big, but he was also very, very dangerous. Rocco stood under the streetlight, in plain sight, and waited for him. As soon as Sebastiano recognized him, he smiled and hastened his step, even though he'd bought himself a pair of boots that must have weighed about 150 pounds.

They hugged without a word.

Sebastiano insisted on going to the Trattoria degli Artisti Pam Pam. It was recommended by the Gambero Rosso restaurant guide, the one book he always carried with him, and there were plenty of positive comments online. Over a cutting board of salumi with mocetta goat ham and a bottle of Le Crete, Sebastiano and Rocco finally caught up.

"So how are you?"

"You see, Seba, I'm feeling like the guy who has three of a kind playing against someone with a royal flush."

"Like shit," Sebastiano summed up.

"That's right. How about you?"

Sebastiano popped a slice of prosciutto into his mouth and swallowed it. "Rome just isn't Rome anymore. It's been a while since it was last Rome. I hate it. We all hate it. Speaking of which, Furio and Brizio and Cerveteri all send their regards."

"How are they?" asked Rocco, a sweet smile of homesickness on his lips.

"Brizio's struggling with alimony payments and a pack of lawyers, Furio's opened two places that have slot machines, and Cerveteri seems to be on to something good in America."

"Still dealing in Etruscan shit?"

"No. Now he's moved over to paintings. After the whole episode with the stolen vase by Euphronios that was sold to that American museum with all the ruckus in the press, that's a risky line of business, and you can't make a euro in it anymore."

"Sure." Rocco forked a slice of speck and shoved it straight into his mouth. "Why do you say Rome isn't Rome anymore?"

"Why? The people. When we were little and we used to play in San Cosimato, when it was time for lunch or dinner you'd hear: 'Mario! Come home and eat! And if you don't get up here this very minute we're going to have a serious conversation, damn it to the place you know well!' "

"That's right. And if I skinned my knee, Mamma gave me something to cry about."

"These days there are no more kids out in the street. And if their mother has to call them, she'll say: 'Enrico, fucking hell! If you don't get up here right this second, I'll smash your face in!'" Sebastiano gave his friend a sad look. "You understand? A mother who tells her son that she's going to smash his face in. It's just depressing. And you know why? Because no one has a penny anymore. Everyone's pissed off, choking on debt, asphyxiated by all the cars and the tour buses that park in front of your windows with the engine running. While if you try to park your own car but you don't have the special permit, then the next thing you know you've got a hundred-euro ticket under your windshield wiper. Then there's another thing that's just heartbreaking." Sebastiano poured himself half a glass of wine and drained it at a single gulp. "Old men. You go to a market. Any one you care to name: Trastevere, Campo dei Fiori, Piazza Crati. And wait for closing time to roll around. Even before the trash trucks, they show up: the old men. Some of them dressed in a suit and tie, can you believe it? They come around with their plastic shopping bags and collect the fruit and vegetables, still edible. And these aren't bums, Rocco. They're retired people. People who worked their whole lives. People who ought to be home playing with their grandchildren, reading, watching TV. Instead, there they are, rain or shine, gathering up old cabbages and fennel."

Rocco nodded. "I know, Sebastiano, I know." He tossed back the wine in his glass. "I know all that. I haven't been gone all that long, you know? It's been four months."

"And another thing, Rocco, my friend: the ones who are in charge these days are the gypsies. But not the ones who live in trailers. The ones with villas in the country and penthouse apartments in the center of the city."

"They've always been in charge," Rocco replied, looking into his friend's eyes—bovine, calm, and untroubled. Seba was a guy who never stopped complaining. Not since they'd first met, the very first day of elementary school. The bow on the front of their school uniform was made of nylon, and it smelled bad. The collar was too tight and cut into his neck. The covers of their textbooks came off. The blue pen and the red pen both ran out of ink. And even the Our Father Who Art in Heaven, which they had to recite every morning before lessons, was just too long—plus the "we forgive those who trespass against us" part had never made sense to him. But now Rocco could see an odd nostalgia in his friend's eyes. *Maybe it's his gray hair*, he thought, *or maybe it's something else I'll find out about tomorrow*. But it struck him as the expression you'd see on the face of someone about to give up and surrender. Someone about to throw in the towel.

"I want to get out," Sebastiano went on, "but now is still too soon. What about you?"

"For now I'm here. I'm waiting. It'll be a while yet. But if nothing shakes loose, maybe we're going to have to start doing the shaking ourselves."

"At least this is a nice, quiet little city, isn't it?"

"That's what it looked like. But just now, a corpse popped out of nowhere. A Sicilian. Someone killed him up on the ski slopes."

"Was it an accident?"

"Not on your life. Murder."

"Well, that's a pain in the ass."

"A first-class pain," Rocco agreed. "You staying at my place?"

"No. I reserved a hotel. I'll just be here for a couple of days."

Rocco didn't ask. He already knew that as soon as Sebastiano was done pouring the wine, he'd talk.

And in fact his friend started telling the story.

"All right, Rocco, it's all pretty simple. It's a truck that crosses the border. It's transporting exotic furniture. It comes from Rotterdam and it's heading for Turin."

"When?"

"At night, the day after tomorrow. There's going to be a crate in the truck. I have the measurements. On it is written CHANT NUMBER 4. That's very close to the name of a song by Spandau Ballet."

"So what's inside this crate?"

"Mary Jane."

"How much marijuana?"

"A few kilos."

Rocco added some numbers in his head. "Where did you get the information?"

"From Ernst."

"And you trust the German?"

"Not much. But what do we have to lose?"

"So how's this going to go? What do you have in mind?"

"Simple. Let's say we stop the truck, we check the cargo, we discover the shit, and you take the guy in. And a certain amount of it makes it to police headquarters. It's not like they're going to stand there and weigh it, right?"

"Where are we going to put the leftovers?"

"I'll take care of that. I'll take it down to Rome."

"How much would come to me?"

"Thirty thousand euros."

"Net?"

"Net. Like always. I'll give the money to the lawyer and he'll take care of it."

Rocco nodded. "Sure, sure. I'd gladly skip all this shit, but … fine. You and me?"

"You and me. In plain clothes," Sebastiano replied.

"How many drivers?"

"I don't know, Rocco."

"If it's coming from Rotterdam, there's a chance that there'll be two of them. On long trips, they drive in shifts."

The waiter came to the table and Rocco and Sebastiano fell silent. With a smile, the young man removed the cutting board, now empty, on which he'd brought the salumi. "Have you gentlemen made up your minds?"

"Yes," said Sebastiano, who'd studied the menu and memorized it. "Two Valdostana veal chops and a polenta concia, which we're going to do in two."

The waiter gave him a blank look. Sebastiano clarified the point: "We're going to do in two—that means we're going to split it."

"Ah. Very good."

"For the wine, bring us a relaxed red. But dry. Otherwise, what with the fontina, the butter, and the eggs, it'll never cut through the flavors."

"Understood," said the attentive waiter. "I'll bring you an Enfer d'Arvier."

"Excellent!" said Sebastiano with a smile. With a slight bow, the waiter disappeared. "If the way they cook is as good as the salumi and the wine, then this place is heaven on earth."

"It's not as good, Sebastia'. It's better!"

"Back to us," Sebastiano resumed. "So, you say that there might be two drivers. So what do you suggest?"

"I thought a uniform could do the trick."

"We need someone we can trust. You have someone?"

Rocco thought it over. "Maybe I do. Can we spare thirty-five hundred?"

"I can put in fifteen hundred and you put in two thousand?"

"Done. I'll let you know by tomorrow."

They drank to their agreement. Then they got started on the more serious business.

"How's the pussy around here?" asked Sebastiano.

"Good. There's plenty."

"So what am I going to do tonight?"

Rocco reached a hand into his pocket. He pulled out his wallet, opened it, and took out a card. "Here. When I first moved here it was useful. They cost 150, and they'll come to your room."

Sebastiano took the card. "But are they Italian girls?"

"It depends. If you're lucky, yes. If not, usually Moldovan."

"Good. They won't talk. You say 150 euros? That seems fair."

Ten o'clock. It's ten o'clock at night, and I feel as if it's three in the morning. I even left the television going and all the lights on. What a mess.

"Nice! In this photo you're magnificent. You have the sensual charge of a real top model."

There's a woman on TV, black, beautiful, with smooth hair. If you ask me, it's a wig. A famous ex-model. Her name is Tyra Banks. I sit on the sofa and watch her. It's a competition of some kind. There's a group of breathtaking babes who want to become America's next top model.

"Nice, Jeannie … you gave it your all."

What a fucked-up show. One ex-top model, a transsexual, and a couple of assholes deciding who wins. Jesus, it's ridiculous. "Why are you watching it?" I ask Marina, who's sprawled in the armchair. Marina smiles at me, but she doesn't say a word.

"I saw Sebastiano. He's here on business, but he has to leave right away."

"You could have invited him to stay with us," Marina says to me.

"He got a room. He said he'd rather stay in a hotel."

Marina shrugs. She doesn't ask. She doesn't want to know. She's never wanted to know.

"You see, Elizabeth? In this photo you didn't give it your all," Tyra Banks says to one of the competitors. "You look dull, no energy."

"How's Sebastiano?"

"Excellent. Big and taciturn. He wants to leave Rome."

Marina smiles. She knows that bear will never leave its den. Sebastiano will die in Rome.

Marina looks at me. Now she wants to know. So I tell her.

"He was named Leone Miccichè. Someone killed him. For now I have nothing. Only that he was Sicilian and that he had a handkerchief in his mouth."

"A handkerchief in his mouth?"

"I know what you're thinking. But this has nothing to do with the Mafia or some fucked-up vendetta."

"Why not?"

"For two reasons. First, if the Mafia kills you, either the corpse is never found or else, if they're trying to send a message or make a point, you'll find the dead man in the middle of a street or on a sidewalk or under a bridge. Everyone's supposed to see it, no? They're not going to leave it in the middle of a forest, on a shortcut used only by snowcats."

"What's the second reason?"

"They don't leave a neckerchief, a bandanna, in someone's mouth. They put a rock, which means someone talked too much, or else they just put the guy's own cock in his mouth. No. Whoever killed him is from here. In fact, it's someone from Champoluc."

"Nice, Eveline," says Tyra Banks as she looks at a photo of an anorexic girl as tall as a lamppost. "Here you're finally yourself!"

"I'm sick of this program," says Marina. "Change the channel, see if there's anything else on."

"Then why were you watching it?" I ask.

Marina smiles. "Because the girls are pretty. Stupid, but pretty. They remind me of when I was their age."

"You were pretty, but you weren't stupid."

Marina looks at me. "Correct that. 'You were pretty, but you aren't stupid.' It sounds better, no?"

"It's true, you aren't," I tell her. Then my eyes fill up with some kind of liquid. I have to squeeze them once, twice, three times, otherwise I can't even see the sofa I'm sitting on.

"Don't cry, Rocco. It's not worth it. I'm going to bed now."

She gets up, collects her legal pad, and heads off down the hall. "Will you turn off the lights?"

"Sure," I say. "What do we have today?"

"Today the word is sanious. It's an adjective for a discharge of purulent pus."

"Who's discharging purulent pus, Marì?"

"Usually someone who's been stitching and pricks themselves."

Stitching. Wasting time. Sanious. A discharge of purulent pus. "Is that me, Marì?"

But she's already gone to the bedroom, to bed, to sleep.

I turn off the television, and silence falls over the apartment, like a half-ton of lead. I turn off the lights, too. I stand there, looking at the living room. It's strange. The television's off. But it still emits a faint halo of light, illuminating the darkness. And in the end it becomes clear to me: either I toss out this television set or I have to get another one. One of those new *ones, plasma, HD. But I'm just too fond of this set. It reminds me of lots of things.*

Memories.

Those are the things that have always failed me.

There was a German poet who said that the past is a dead person without a corpse.

It's not true.

The past is a dead person whose corpse never stops coming to see you. By night and by day. And you're even happy that it does. Because the day that the past doesn't show up at your front door is the day that you belong to the past. You yourself have become the past.

Maybe I need to get more sex.

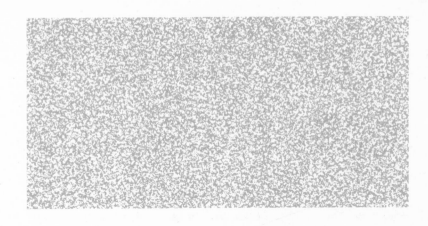

SATURDAY

Domenico and Lia Miccichè, the dead man's brother and sister-in-law, were sitting in the green-velvet-upholstered lobby of the Hotel Europe. Domenico was fat. So was his wife. And they both wore sad expressions. But it was that slightly generic sadness, a cheap one-size-fits-all sadness that's as suitable for a child's bad report card as it is for a car so badly damaged in a crash that it's not worth repairing.

As soon as they saw Rocco Schiavone, they introduced themselves. The policeman didn't miss the whiff of alcohol on the sister-in-law's breath. Domenico Miccichè announced his name through clenched teeth. As if he were ashamed of it. He'd already been to the morgue. He'd taken care of the bureaucratic procedures, and he seemed to be eager to get back to his vineyards. They talked about the cold and the snow, until Domenico asked: "Why?"

Rocco shook his head. "For now, all I can tell you is when and what time of night. For *why* and *who*, I'm not ready yet."

Domenico Miccichè sat down in the velvet armchair, and his wife followed suit. Rocco had no choice but to do the same thing. "Still, I have a couple of things I'd like to ask you."

"If it can help with the investigation," said Domenico. His face protruded from his turtleneck sweater, as red as a buoy. On his forehead, at the exact beginning of his curly head of hair, there was an oily patina. It might have been sweat, or it could have been hair oil. His watch was a Rolex with a stainless steel case. And wedged among the black hairs of his wrist was a gold bracelet.

"Your brother Leone had been here three years. He'd moved into a chalet with—"

"Luisa." Lia finished the sentence, caressing her double chin and jingling a necklace that she wore over her white cardigan.

"Right. Luisa Pec. Financially, it appears that things were going just fine. But there's something I'd like you to help me understand. According to what his wife told me, you and your brother had a fight on the telephone a couple of days ago."

Domenico huffed. "It's always the same thing. You see, I bought out his part of the company years ago. Now we still jointly own a couple of properties. Leone wanted to sell them."

"What kind of properties?"

"A *maso* that needs renovation, outside of Erice, and a *dammuso* on Pantelleria."

"How much money are we talking about, Signor Miccichè?"

"A million, roughly. Between us, obviously."

"Obviously."

Domenico settled comfortably into his armchair. "Listen, Dottore. My company invoices more than six million euros a year, as you can verify on our tax returns. You're not suggesting that for less than 500,000 euros I would—"

Rocco stopped him with a simple wave of the hand. "I'm not suggesting anything, Signor Miccichè. I just want to understand what happened. And by providing me with this information, you'd be saving me a little time. So your brother wanted to sell and you didn't?"

"That's not exactly how it was."

"That's what Luisa says," Lia Miccichè broke in.

"Please, Lia. Would you let me talk? This is about my brother!"

Lia dropped her eyes.

"Excuse me, Dottore. Now, as I was saying, that's not exactly right. I'd have been willing to sell, but at the right price. Or else buy back the other half. You see, Leone wanted 500,000 euros, and I don't know what he intended to do with it. It's just that we couldn't come to an understanding. You know how it is between brothers."

"No. I don't. Why don't you tell me."

"Stratifications, Mr. Deputy Police Chief. Stories going back years, things that rot and develop gangrene, until you can't even remember how or when they got started. I'm five years older than Leone. And he was always the hothead in the house. When Mamma and Papà died, if I hadn't been there, he would have run through the whole company. Well, that was

Leone. He just put his head down and ran, without considering the pros and cons. That's the way he lived, chasing after whatever he most liked at that instant."

"Do you know how much money he had left when he died?"

"No. I don't know."

"Knowing the way he was, I doubt it was much," Lia broke back in. "In fact, I wouldn't be surprised if there were debts to pay."

Rocco looked at the woman, with her small mouth and moist lips set in a pale, buttery face. "A *dammuso* and a *maso* ought to be more than enough, don't you think, Signora Miccichè?"

"No. Because those properties are not inherited by Leone's wife. I'm surprised that a policeman like you wouldn't know about such basic matters of the law!"

"Maybe you'll be even more surprised to learn, signora, that a wife does inherit property—and not only that, but debts. So that will be a problem for Luisa Pec, don't you think?"

Lia Miccichè closed her mouth. Her husband glared at her moodily. If his eyes had been daggers, Lia Miccichè would already be a ghost, and for some time now.

Rocco couldn't take sitting there with those two any longer. His underwear was prickly, and he wanted to give himself a good hard scratch, take a walk, smoke a cigarette.

"My brother and I were never very close," Domenico suddenly said. "Never. I hoped that maybe one day, who knows, that things might take care of themselves. But nothing took care of itself at all. And now it's too late."

"Yeah, it's too late," admitted Rocco, "and by the way, it's pretty late for me, too."

The café at the foot of the cableway had been poor Leone Miccichè's favorite place in town. It was the haunt of snowcat drivers and ski instructors. The dead man had spent his evenings there talking with Mario and Michael, who ran the place. At that hour of the morning, only Mario was there. Rocco had taken a seat on the wooden bench, placed both elbows on the counter—a single length of tree, carved and shaped—and proceeded to look out at the street through the large, fogged plate-glass window, still decked with Christmas decorations on the sill. Mario had his back to him as he filled the coffee grinder with fresh beans. Ignoring the man who'd been sitting at the counter for a while now, with his loden overcoat and his weary face.

"Does a person have to issue a subpoena to get an espresso?" said Rocco, still looking out the window. Mario turned around, smiled, and went over to the bar. "*Buon giorno*, what'll it be, an espresso?"

"No, three ounces of aged prosciutto. Of course I want an espresso. This is a café, isn't it?"

Mario smirked and went over to the Faema espresso machine.

"Are you Mario?" asked Rocco. The man nodded his head as he set an espresso cup under the arm of the espresso machine.

"You knew Leone, didn't you?"

"Yes. He was in here all the time. Poor guy. What a nasty way to die."

"Make it strong. What was he like?"

"Who, Leone?"

"Exactly."

"He was a guy with plenty of energy, you know?" He set the espresso down on the bar. Rocco put in half an envelope of sugar. "When he got here, he'd never seen a mountain in his life. Nevertheless, after not even a couple of years he was skiing, and climbing in the summer. There's lots of great climbs around here, did you know that?"

"Listen, though. Who had he pissed off?"

The barman gave the deputy police chief a blank look.

"Was there anyone who hated Leone?" Rocco drank the espresso. It was good and foamy.

"Ah, no. No one. And why would they? He always minded his own business. He was always courteous. He lived with Luisa, and they opened that wonderful hut up at Cuneaz."

"Any business competitors?"

"Here in Champoluc? No. There's plenty of money for everyone, you know. No, they were nice and everyone liked them, both him and Luisa. They were going to start a family. Poor things. And they'd almost done it, did you know?"

"Almost done what?"

"Luisa's expecting Leone's baby. She discovered it a month ago, Deputy Police Chief Schiavone."

"How do you know who I am?"

"I've seen you before. The night of the murder. Luigi took you up to Crest with the snowcat. Luigi Bionaz is one of my best friends, and he's also the cousin of my partner, Michael. We're all sort of related here in Champoluc. We natives, I mean to say—you understand."

Rocco licked the little spoon. "Excellent espresso, this. *Grazie.* Listen, Mario. What's the cheapest ski shop in town?"

"You go out, continue another hundred yards, and on the same side of the street there's a store. It's excellent, and it's the cheapest one in town, you know?"

"Is the woman who runs it your cousin?"

Mario laughed. "No. She's just a friend of mine."

"You're all sort of related here, no?"

"Nearly all of us, you know?"

"Well, then, would you explain to me why, if you're all related, someone decided to kill Leone?"

"Who says it was someone from here? It could have been someone from the outside, no?"

"No, it's someone from here, trust me. I just have to figure out why."

Rocco took a euro out of his pocket and put it on the bar, got up off the barstool, and left the place without saying good-bye.

The air was thin, and it burned his lungs. The deputy police chief looked at the houses with their pitched roofs and the icy, dirty snow lining the street. A car went past, its chains jangling on the asphalt. A little supermarket was packed with English shoppers, each of them with two beers in hand, lining up at the cash register. The plate-glass window of Mario's friend's shop was decorated with fake polystyrene snowflakes covered with glitter. On display was an array of brightly colored skis. Rocco was impressed by the prices. It was hard to find anything for less than eight hundred euros.

He walked in.

A bell jingled to alert the shopkeeper that a customer had just come in. Rocco looked around, but there was no sign of the proprietor. There were shelves, a counter with a cash register, sweaters, fleeces, hats, gloves, pants, ski suits, and ski boots.

"Hello! Is anyone here?"

Nothing. No reply. He thought about what would have become of that unguarded store on any street in Rome. They would have sucked it dry as a chicken bone. He went over to the cash register. At least that wasn't lying open. The air was filled with a pleasant scent of wood and resin. And if he sniffed carefully, there was also a faint aroma of cherry marmalade. His footsteps creaked on the wooden floor. A nice hardwood parquet. That bright, light-colored floor would have been nice in a beach house.

Oak, Rocco mused, *without knots. A nice choice.*

Next to the cash register was a laptop computer, turned on. The latest Vaio, the first thing that would be stolen in Rome, without a second thought. On the screen, the deputy police chief recognized the picture of the cableway terminal, up at 6,500 feet. He could see a corner of the large garage where the snowcats were parked, as well as the office used by the ski instructors. Rocco walked over to the computer. The browser was showing the Monterosa Ski website.

He was looking at the still image when the bell on the door jingled. A woman about thirty-five years old, tall, with short brown hair and jutting cheekbones, came in with a smile. "*Buon giorno*. What can I do for you?"

Rocco took an immediate liking to the proprietor. He moved away from the counter. "Hi. Just take a look at these shoes of mine," he said and pointed to the Clarks desert boots, which by now were shoes only in name. "Your friend Mario told me that you have the lowest prices in Champoluc."

"He told you the truth. The best prices and superior quality. That's my motto. I have lots of different models—what size do you wear?"

"Forty-fours."

The woman vanished behind a pillar lined with mirrors plastered with decals.

"Come on back," said the proprietor of the shop from behind a screen, and Rocco walked over.

She had bent over to get a couple of styles of boots that were on the lowest shelf. As she did so, her tight black trousers slid down, revealing the elastic band of her panties. Floral-patterned.

A thong, Rocco decided.

"Here, I can show you the various styles of shoe. Do you prefer leather or technical materials?"

"Please, no plastic."

The woman smiled. She showed him two pairs of snow-boots. One pair was big and solid and black with red laces. "These are very popular."

Rocco gazed at the boots skeptically. "More like they *were* very popular. They remind me of the shoes the Alpine troops wore on the Tofane Mountains in the First World War!"

The woman laughed heartily and showed him another pair of boots. They were a little more understated. Brown leather. A pair of ugly city shoes.

"Okay, I prefer these."

"Come try them on," said the proprietor, and Rocco followed her.

He sat down and unlaced his Clarks. For a moment he was afraid there might be a hole in his sock. He couldn't afford to look like a bum in front of the barista's pretty friend. Not because she was a friend of Mario's, but because he didn't even know her name yet, and he'd already started to make plans that involved that lovely specimen of womanhood.

He took off his shoe. The sock was intact. He heaved a deep sigh of relief.

"Have you heard about what happened up at Crest?" asked the proprietor of the shop as she extracted the crumpled paper from the interior of the boot.

"Yes. I'm in charge of the investigation."

"Ah," said the woman drily, as if she'd just clucked her tongue with her mouth open. "You're a policeman."

"Deputy Police Chief Schiavone," he said, standing up and extending his hand.

"Annarita Pec."

"Pec? Like Luisa, poor Leone's widow?"

"Yes. We're third cousins, though. You know, here in Champoluc—"

"I know. You're all related."

"But Luisa and I don't see each other. Oh, Lord, of course we say *buon giorno* and *buona sera*. That doesn't mean that I don't love her, don't misunderstand. She's still a cousin of mine. But what actually happened?" asked Annarita, her eyes glittering with curiosity. "Was it an accident, or else ..."

"Or else," the deputy police chief replied abruptly.

The proprietor of the shop nodded and handed Rocco the boot. "Here, try it on."

Rocco sat back down and put on the boot. The minute he slipped it on, he had the sensation that there was an incinerator roaring away inside it. "They're hot," he said with a smile. He stood up. He took a few steps. Comfortable.

"Fine, I'll take them." He reached out and took the other boot out of Annarita's hands, sat down, and started putting it on.

Annarita stood there, looking the deputy police chief in the eye. "Where are you from?" she asked.

"Rome," he said, leaning on the *R* as hard as he could, in the distinctive Roman pronunciation. "Ever been?"

Annarita shook her head no.

"Ouch ouch ouch, that's not good. It's a wonderful city. If someday you decide to go, I'll show you around. I know Rome pretty well," he said and turned on the best smile in his repertoire. The half smile, the one that stretched his facial skin and made crow's-feet form around his eyes. He'd first seen it when he was a boy, on Clint Eastwood's face, and he swore that when he grew up he'd use it. It usually worked wonders.

"The city must be wonderful. Will you take offense, though, if I tell you something?"

"Not at all."

"It's the Romans I can't stand. And in Rome there are at least a couple million of them." She concluded the lunge with a smile. A beautiful smile, tight and bright, that seemed to make her hazel eyes glow even more. Annarita Pec was a woman who knew the art of self-defense. If he was going to have a chance with her, it would take weeks of hard work. But what with Leone's corpse and Sebastiano in Aosta, the deputy police chief wasn't going to have time.

Too bad, Rocco said to himself and got to his feet. "Well, message received, Annarita, loud and clear."

"I know you didn't take that the wrong way."

"Absolutely not. And I even have to agree with you. A good eighty percent of the Roman population are absolutely intolerable people."

"I'm sure you're part of the good twenty percent."

"And that's where you're wrong. I'm part of the very worst two percent." He said it without smiling, but still staring Annarita right in the eye. "Let's get back to serious business. I need a pair of gloves."

Annarita shook her head, as if trying to shake off sleep. "All right. What kind of gloves, Gore-Tex or leather?"

"No, listen, I'm looking for a very special kind of gloves. You may have them. They're ski gloves. Colmar. Black leather."

"That's a model that was popular a couple of years ago. Still, in the bargain bin, maybe … Let me take a look." She moved quickly over to a light fir bin that was full of ski gloves. She started pulling out pair after pair. "Are these for you?"

"You're Luisa's cousin. So you must have known Leone."

Annarita turned to look at the deputy police chief. "Certainly, why?"

"Let's just say that the gloves are for him."

The woman smiled and shook her head slightly. "I don't get it."

"He must have worn about the same size as me, no?"

The proprietor of the shop looked at his hand. Then she nodded sadly. "More or less." And she started rummaging through the wooden bin again. "Here you are. Are these all right?"

Rocco looked at them. "Excellent. I'll take these, too. How much?"

"Huh? Oh, well, then. The Tevas are one hundred ninety euros. The gloves are eighty."

Rocco didn't blink an eye. He pulled out his wallet, walked past Annarita, and went straight to the cash register. Annarita moved quickly and got behind the counter.

"Do you take credit cards?"

"Of course, of course."

The woman punched the total into the cash register and the credit card terminal, then swiped the card.

"Where is that video camera?" asked Rocco, pointing to the computer screen.

"Oh, that? It's on a terrace overlooking the pistes. It's so we can see what the weather is like on the slopes. It's over the Internet."

"And is it always on, twenty-four hours a day?"

"Always. But it takes stills, not actual video."

"Who installed it?"

"The people up at Monterosa Ski. They control it from their offices."

Rocco took back the credit card. He signed the receipt, turned around, and picked up his old Clarks desert boots, and put them in a bag. "May I?" he asked Annarita, pointing to the trash can.

"You want to throw them away?"

"Yep," and he tossed the old Clarks into the shop's trash can. "Thanks very much. You've been more than kind."

"Don't mention it. It's been a pleasure, Deputy Police Chief. Can I ask why you bought a pair of gloves for poor Leone?"

"They're not for poor Leone. They're for me. Have a good day."

On his way up to the offices of Monterosa Ski, Rocco looked at his new boots. Ankle high, with insulated soles, they were warm enough to poach his feet. They were big, but at least they were an acceptable color, and they were tight around the ankles, so his pants could fit around them and hang normally. He wasn't forced to tuck his pants into his shoes and look like some sucker with a flooded basement. The gloves were warm, too. They wrapped his hands in a warm, cozy interior that was made of some nasty synthetic material but did its job. The only problem was the fingers. Enormous, like yeti fingers.

And they made it impossible to do any coordinated action except to clap like an orangutan.

Pierron had parked right in front of the cableway offices. When he saw the deputy police chief arrive, he immediately took note of the change in apparel.

"At last!" he said. "Now those are some real shoes!"

"They cost one hundred ninety euros. Did I pay too much?"

"That depends. What brand are they?"

"You've got me. They're made of leather, and they have a cleated sole. Ah, here it is, it says Teva."

"Teva brand? One hundred ninety euros? Nice price."

"While we're going to the offices, you call whatever the hell his name is—Luigi, the chief snowcat operator—and tell him to come down here. I need him to take us up."

"We can ride the cableway."

"Italo, you're a good guy, but when I tell you something, there's a reason for it."

"Got it. Sorry," said Italo, grabbing his cell phone and trailing after Rocco, who was heading for the glass-and-wood offices of Monterosa Ski.

Rocco was sorry not to find Margherita, the young woman from the night before, waiting for him. Instead, there was a guy who was as bald as an egg, slowly chewing a wad of gum. He had a long face, and, as if that weren't enough, he'd grown a whitish pointed goatee that made it look even longer. His eyes were round and distant, dull and lifeless. The only sign of any presence of cerebral activity was the continual and incessant chomping of teeth and jaws on the chewing gum. Rocco immediately cataloged him as a *Connochaetes gnou*, or white-tailed gnu, an African bovine ruminant, the ones that in documentaries are always being massacred by cheetahs and lionesses.

When the young man reached out his hand to introduce himself as Guido, the office manager, Rocco was almost amazed to find human fingers instead of an ungulate's hoof.

"We put the images up on the Internet and they remain in the computer for a few days. Then every once in a while we delete them, because if we don't, the hard drive fills up. We haven't deleted any files lately. You're in luck," the gnu said, and stood there placidly ruminating and gazing at the deputy police chief.

"Do you have the image files here?"

"No. They're in the technical office."

And the bovid stood there, motionless, gazing at the two policemen.

Rocco smiled. "Which is where?"

"Down the hill."

"Down the hill where?"

"Down the hill next to the equipment sheds."

The deputy police chief looked at Italo. "What do you think, is he putting us on or is it real?"

"No, if you ask me, this is real," Italo replied.

Rocco was impressed with himself for having managed to keep his nerves under control. "If you, Guido, don't show me the way, how will I know where the sheds and the technical office are located?"

"I don't know if I can take you there."

The deputy police chief took a nice deep breath. "Guido, let's put it this way. Either you take me to that technical office or I'm going to kick your sorry ass all the way down to police headquarters in Aosta." Then he pointed to Pierron: "And he'll help."

No light flickered on in the eyes of the ruminant. Neither alarm nor fear, anger, or defiance. Nothing. An expressionless black hole. Guido extracted the chewing gum from his mouth, a pink bolus the size of a Ping-Pong ball, stuck it to the bottom of his desk, and finally walked out of the room. Throwing his arms wide, Rocco followed him.

The technical office looked like an empty garage, with a couple of computers and an armchair with threadbare upholstery. The reek of mold and other unknown fungi assailed his nostrils.

"There, that's the computer," said Guido, pointing to something that looked like a vintage radiator. "That's the hookup to the video camera, and that's where it sends the images out over the Internet."

"Do you know how to use it, Guido?" asked Rocco, looking at the putrescent walls while Italo stared intently at the PC.

"No."

"In that case, can you get someone who does?"

"I can do it," said Italo. "It's an old PC. How hard could it be?"

"Then go ahead, Italo. I want to take a look."

The police officer went over to the desk, pulled out the chair, and lightly touched the mouse, causing the screen to light up. Guido remained standing at a good, safe distance from the computer, as if he were afraid it might be about to blow sky-high at any minute.

There were twenty or so folders, all of them identified by dates.

"You see what a mess it is? We could be sitting here until nighttime," said Guido.

"What's in those files?"

Instead of answering, Italo opened one at random. There were dozens of photographs. All framed identically. Pictures from the webcam overlooking the slopes. Hour by hour. The month chosen was May, and instead of snow and lowering clouds, there were flowering meadows and the sun high overhead. To the left was the large garage with the ski instructors' school, in the middle the cableway entrance to the pistes, and on the right the hill that concealed Cuneaz, the little village in the gorge where Miccichè had his hut.

"Good, Italo. Look for the pictures from the day before yesterday. Thursday."

"But at night you can't see a thing."

"Well, then, show me the ones for four in the afternoon and so on."

Italo found the file. "Here it is. Thursday, February fifth. Let's see, now …"

There were dozens of photographs. All the same. The only thing that changed was the color of the sky.

"Listen," said Guido, "I can see that you know what you're doing. I'm going to leave you here; I can't be away from the office for too long."

Rocco was looking at the photographs on the desktop; he nodded without replying.

"When you're done, will you come and let me know?"

Then Guido slowly left, heading out the door of the basement office.

"Get up a second," said Rocco, and Italo vacated the chair so the deputy police chief could sit down.

He started looking at the photos for Thursday. Taken hour by hour. He lined them up. The movement of the sun from morning to evening created a nice effect. He looked most closely at the pictures from 5:30 and 6:00 p.m. He hoped against hope for a piece of luck. That he'd spot something or someone that could prove useful. But there was nothing. Nothing but snow. And in the 6:00 p.m. photo, a treaded snowcat going past, heading uphill. "That might be Amedeo's snowcat, the guy who found the corpse," said Italo.

The two policemen kept their eyes glued to the screen. Rocco clicked on the mouse and opened the folder that contained the photos from earlier in the week. These, too, were arranged according to time. He picked the same time for each day, 5:30 p.m., and pulled those files out of the folders. He dragged them onto the desktop and started comparing them with Thursday's files.

"What are you doing?" asked Italo.

The deputy police chief worked away with the mouse. "I'm arranging the photos so we can compare them. Let's see if we find something. Do you know that brain teaser they have in the weekly puzzle magazines: Sharpen Your Eye?"

"Of course! Discover the twenty details that are different in the two drawings."

"Exactly, Italo. Concentrate."

The blue light from the computer screen lit up Rocco's and Italo's faces, so focused on what they were doing that they were blinking only occasionally, and slowly. Reflected on their pupils were dozens of photographs. All identical.

They couldn't find any differences. Always the same thing. The snow. The snowcat garage. The ski instructors' school. The base of the cableway. The beginners' slopes. The hill behind which Cuneaz lay hidden. Not a shadow. No one going by.

"Here!" Rocco suddenly shouted, making Italo jump.

"What?"

Rocco went back to the photos from the day of the murder: Thursday, February 5, 6:00 p.m. There was something that didn't add up in that picture. He compared it with the photo from Wednesday. Again, from 6:00 p.m. He put them one next to the other. No difference. The garage, the cableway …

"They all look the same to me," said Italo.

"The ski school. Look closer!" And Rocco pointed to it with the cursor of the mouse. "You see?"

Italo leaned in. On the photo from the day of the murder, the door of the ski school was open. "It's open!"

"Right," said Rocco, "and now look at the photo for Wednesday."

The door of the ski school was closed.

"Now I'm going to open the photos from the previous days."

All of them at 6:00 p.m. All of them framed identically. And the door of the ski school was always closed.

"You see it? At 6:00 p.m. the door is closed. Except for the day of the murder." Then Rocco stretched out in the chair. He put both arms behind his head and smiled. "I'd like to take these photos with me to police headquarters."

"That's no big deal. I'll go buy a flash stick and I'll copy them to it," said Italo, getting to his feet.

With the usual noise of jangling hardware, the snowcat pulled up at the base of the cableway, snorting smoke and snow.

"There it is!" said Italo.

"I'd noticed," Rocco replied.

Luigi Bionaz got out, waved to the policemen, and gestured for them to come closer.

No comparison. Walking with those two kayaks on his feet instead of the Clarks desert boots was a decided improvement to his lifestyle. Now Rocco was practically having fun crushing the piles of snow underfoot, the same piles that until today he'd avoided as if they were his mortal enemies.

"*Buon giorno*, Commissario!"

Rocco didn't bother to correct him. He was sick and tired of the whole thing. And for that matter, decades of literature and television series, from Maigret to Cattani, had driven that word into the minds of the Italians: *commissario*. What it made him think of was the show trials in the Soviet Union under Stalin. He climbed up into the snowcat, followed by Pierron. Luigi put the machine in gear and started uphill, along the main piste.

"Where are we going?" asked Luigi.

"Where we found Leone."

"Got it," he said and took a curve, clenching the usual dead cigarette butt between his teeth.

Rocco looked at Italo. "I'm going to need to talk to you later."

Italo nodded, with a worried look in his eyes. "Did I fuck up?"

"No. The reason I need to talk to you is that I've noticed that you tend *not* to fuck up."

"You've lost me."

"You wouldn't be able to follow me. Because you don't know what I need to talk to you about."

Luigi had taken an interest in the conversation between the two cops. "And now you've got me curious," he said, shifting gears as he drove.

"What the fuck!" Rocco replied. "Just do your best not to turn this thing over and I'll be happy."

Luigi Bionaz burst out laughing, banging his hand down on the steering wheel. "You Romans are just too much fun!"

"You think?"

"Yes. You seem like rude, nasty people—instead here you are making jokes all day long."

"If that's how you see it," said Rocco.

* * *

Someone had strung a white-and-red-striped tape around the whole area where the body had been found. There was a man bent over the snow, picking something up. He was wearing a white jumpsuit and overshoes. A woolen cap on his head kept off the cold.

Italo looked at him intently. "Is the forensics team still at work?"

"Yeah."

The man in the white jumpsuit turned around. Rocco waved his hand, and from a distance the man nodded his head in response. Then he went back to searching for who knows what. Rocco and Italo went around the tape while Luigi waited by the snowcat, relighting the cigarette butt.

The deputy police chief went over to the exact spot where the body had been found. The snow was still stained with brown blood. He looked around. Before him, at the top of a small hill, was Crest, the village with six houses and a hut. The shortcut was clear and visible, running down toward them and continuing on past to the large piste that ran to town. On his right, trees. On his left, trees and an abandoned hovel. In the distance, the roof of a house. The chimney was emitting smoke.

"Down there, an old woman lives alone. She's eighty," Italo started up, as if he'd read Rocco's thoughts. "We talked to her, but she's half-deaf and it's a miracle if she can remember her own name."

"Why was Leone here?"

Rocco's words vanished into the air, along with the puffs of his breath. "If he was heading to town along the big piste down there, why on earth would he have come up here?"

"Maybe he went down by way of Crest."

"Did anyone see him?"

"No one. There are six guests staying at the hut, along with the waiter, the cook, and two young people who work there. No one saw him that night. And all the houses are abandoned."

"To go to Crest, he'd have had to make a detour. So if he had gone, he would have had to have a reason. And he had no reason. So I say he came down from his house straight down along the main run. But I don't understand why he was here, in the middle of the shortcut, far from the piste. It makes no sense."

"No. It makes no sense. Unless someone carried him there."

"But there are no signs of a body being dragged. Does that mean he was alive when they brought him?"

"And then they killed him there?"

Rocco looked down at the wide groomed section once again. The marks of the snowcat that had run over Leone's corpse on Thursday night were unmistakable. He measured the distance with his eyes. "Between here and the big piste is about forty yards. It would be hard to drag someone through the fresh snow for forty yards. A footprint, at least one, ought to be there, no? It's not like the guy fell out of the sky!"

Italo had nothing to say. Rocco nodded a couple of times. "He came up here of his own volition. There was someone up here that he knew. Someone who had called him or with whom he had an appointment, even. They smoked a cigarette together, and probably that person killed him. I don't have any real doubts on this case." He took a deep breath and felt the cold, clean air penetrate into his lungs. "All right, let's go join Luigi. I'm going to go pay a little call on the ski school. You wait for me at the terminus of the cableway."

He was walking toward the large structure that served as a garage for the tracked vehicles, at the far end of which, behind a glass door, stood the ski school. Women wrapped in fur coats sat waiting for their skiing children. They looked like turtles, each woman's head almost entirely retracted into its furry carapace and their hands shoved into their pockets. They looked like they had fox terriers wrapped around their ankles. Rocco took a quick look behind him. He saw the station of the cableway that was transporting people up the mountain from the town. Italo had lit a cigarette and was enjoying a little sunshine. Above the station, set on a terrace that everyone was avoiding like the plague because of the icy cold, there was a bar. Concealed behind a flagpole that flew the Italian flag was the webcam. The deputy police chief waved at the lens, secretly hoping that at that moment the camera might have snapped the half-hourly weather photo, capturing him for posterity. Then he headed for the ski school.

One of the instructors was sprawled out on a lounge chair with a pair of mirrored Ray-Bans on his face and his arms behind his head. His face was dark from the sun. Rocco walked past him and went into the office. He was immediately knocked back on his feet by a whiff of stale *vin brulé*, or mulled wine. There were two instructors, a man and a woman. The man was in his mid-twenties, a good-looking, curly-haired athletic type. The woman was sitting behind the desk. As soon as she saw the deputy police chief, she stood up. She was considerably overweight.

"*Buon giorno,*" she said.

"*Buon giorno,*" Rocco replied.

"Did you want to schedule a lesson?" the tanned whale asked politely.

"No. I'm here for another reason."

"If it's to get information, go right ahead and ask."

The young man in his mid-twenties was about to move off, but Rocco stopped him with a gesture. "No, hold on, please. I'd like you to stay, too. You could be useful. In fact, as long as he's here, why don't you go get your co-worker from outside." The young man knit his brow. Rocco smiled at him. "Deputy Police Chief Schiavone, mobile squad of Aosta. Police. *Compris?*"

The young man nodded rapidly and went to summon his co-worker, who came in, immediately bringing with him from outdoors the cocky attitude of someone who's not afraid of anyone or anything. "What's this about?" he asked. "What happened Thursday night?"

"*Bravo.* You're good. You should come work for us," Rocco said, shutting him down. Then he stood face-to-face with the three instructors and stared hard at them for ten seconds or so. Ten seconds that to those three wizards of the ski slopes must have seemed like an eternity. The woman was the one who broke the metaphorical ice. "What can we do for you?"

"What time do you close?"

"Four in the afternoon. The lessons last an hour, and at 4:45 they close the slopes and the cableways, so the last slot to schedule a lesson is at 3:30."

"Who locks up?"

"That depends. We take turns."

"Who locked up Thursday?" Schiavone asked.

"Day before yesterday, I locked up," replied the twenty-five-year-old.

"At four forty-five?" asked the deputy police chief.

"Yes, more or less. Actually, a little earlier than that, because when I left, the cableway was on its last run."

Rocco took a quick look around. He looked at the poster of that season's full team of instructors. There were at least twenty people there. All of them smiling. "Is the person who locks up at night the same person who opens up the next morning?"

"Yes. It's always the same person," said the young man. "In fact, yesterday, Friday, I opened up."

"And how did you find the office door?"

"Locked. Why?"

Rocco pointed to the group photo. "Who else out of this crowd would have the keys to the place?"

"The one whose shift it is to lock up and Omar, who runs the school."

"Omar Borghetti, right?"

The arrogant ski instructor took off his mirrored Ray-Bans. He was cross-eyed. It was all Rocco could do not to break out laughing right in his face. "Do you know him?" asked the instructor.

"I've heard about him. Where is he?"

"He's teaching a group."

Rocco turned his gaze to the younger instructor. "After you locked up, what did you do?"

"I put on my skis and I went down the mountain."

"On the piste, or did you take the Crest shortcut?"

"Are you crazy, Dottore? On the piste! On that shortcut, with all the rocks it has, I'd ruin my surface and my edges. When my workday is done, I take my own skis to go home, not the ones they give me here."

"And then?"

"And then nothing. I went home. Took a shower, smoked a cigarette, went out for dinner. When I left the pub at ten, I ran into all that mess."

"So we can say that from four thirty to seven you were at home. Is there anyone who can verify the fact?"

The young man looked at the policeman with some embarrassment and looked down just as the big woman raised her hand. The cross-eyed instructor burst out laughing.

"What are you laughing at?" Rocco barked at him.

"Sorry, it's just that this is a new one on me." Then he looked over at his co-workers. "How long has this been going on?"

"What the fuck do you care? Mind your own damned business," said the big woman, who had turned redder than her team jersey.

"Can you call this Omar Borghetti for me?" Rocco interrupted.

"Sorry, Dottore, he's with a group of Swedish skiers at Gressoney, which is on the far side of the valley. He won't be back for at least a couple of hours."

Rocco shook his head. "My bad luck, eh? As soon as he returns to base, tell him to get in touch with police headquarters in Aosta. I need to talk to him. You all be well." He gave them a half smile, then looked at the curly-haired young man. "So long, Ahab." And, leaving the kid to mull over that strange farewell, Schiavone left the three instructors.

As soon as he got off the cable car that had taken him and Italo back into town, Rocco pulled out his cell phone. "Inspector Rispoli, this is Schiavone." The clear-timbred voice of the police functionary rang out from Rocco's cell phone: "Right here, Dottore ..."

"How long would it take you to get me Omar Borghetti's address?"

"Champoluc?"

"I don't know, but I think so."

"I'll call you back in a minute. Uh, listen, D'Intino and Deruta aren't giving any signs of life. They aren't calling me back and they aren't answering their phones. What should I do?"

"Forget about them. Ignore them. Consider them missing in action."

Rocco hung up. He put on his Colmar ski gloves. He looked at Italo. "With these fucking oversize gloves, you could slap somebody in the face, but nothing else."

"Are those the same as the victim's gloves?"

"Same brand and more or less the same size."

The sun was shining, and the steam rose from the roofs of the houses. A smell of good things to eat spread into the air. Everything was calm and quiet. Descending the iron steps that led down onto the main street, for a moment Rocco thought that it might not be so bad after all to live in a place like this. It was nice and peaceful. But it couldn't be the refuge for his old age. It had three fundamental defects: there was no sea, it was too cold, and it was in Italy.

"It's a pity, I was just starting to like you," he said, addressing the town, but the phrase was overheard by Italo, who hadn't said a word the whole way.

"Me? What did I do wrong?"

"I wasn't talking to you. I was talking to the town."

Italo said nothing.

They were heading to the car when Deruta's unmistakable voice made them turn around. "Dottore! Dottore!"

Deruta and D'Intino were right behind them, just fifty yards away. Their faces were blue with cold. D'Intino's teeth were chattering, and Deruta had swollen, purplish ears. At the sight of that pathetic vision of weariness and exhaustion, Rocco smiled, congratulating himself. The two policemen hurried forward, taking small steps, and the closer they got, the more Rocco noticed that their uniform shoes, trousers, and jackets were drenched.

"They look like a pair of vaudeville comedians, don't they?" Italo laughed with a smirk.

"Wow, it's cold, isn't it?" said Deruta once he'd caught up to the deputy police chief.

"Not in my opinion," replied Rocco, showing off his nice new gloves. "Well, then, D'Intino, you feeling better? I heard about your little fainting spell yesterday."

"Yes, I feel better. They even put me on an IV drip."

"Good for you. And how is the search coming along?"

D'Intino pulled out his notepad. "We're collecting all the names, just like you told us, and—" The notepad fell face-down on the snow. Its owner picked it up, but the snow was already washing away the ink, and soon the whole page would be illegible.

"D'Intino, what the fuck are you doing?"

The officer tried desperately to dry off the first page, but he succeeded only in smearing the stain of blue ink over the entire page. Rocco tore it out, crumpled it calmly into a ball, dropped it on the ground, and kicked it out into the middle of the street. Then he looked at the two officers. "Back to work, you two. We're not here on vacation, have I made myself clear?"

"Certainly, Dottore. There's something you might be interested in."

"Let's hear it."

"At that hotel there"—he jerked his head in the direction of a sign reading HOTEL BELVEDERE on the side of a house, directly beneath a painting of a honeysuckle bush—"we found two people, a couple, who checked out in a big hurry the night of the murder. The day before yesterday."

"Good. Did you get their names?"

"Yes."

"Report them to Inspector Rispoli."

Deruta looked down at the ground.

"What's the matter, Deruta?"

"What's the matter is that, really, Dottore. Rispoli has been on the force only two years. D'Intino and I have been on the force since 1992. It doesn't seem right to us that—"

Rocco interrupted him. "What is this, now you're arguing about orders? If I say Rispoli's in charge, Rispoli's in charge. Have I made myself clear?" And he turned on his heels and started walking to the car, followed by Pierron. Just then, the deputy police chief's cell phone rang. "Go ahead, Rispoli."

"All right, then, Omar Borghetti's exact address is in Saint-Jacques, number two, Chemin de Resay. Before you ask, I looked up the map on the PC. I'll tell you how to get there."

"Go ahead."

"Head out straight along the road from Champoluc, go past Frachey, then at a certain point you come to a village. In fact, that's Saint-Jacques. There's a hotel there. That's where you turn onto the street in question. Borghetti's house is at number two."

"*Grazie*, Rispoli. Look, I just ran into Laurel and Hardy here in Champoluc. They're fine. Alert their families."

Caterina Rispoli laughed over the phone. And that sincere, crystalline laughter restored Rocco Schiavone's good mood.

With the heat cranked to high, Rocco and Italo left Champoluc and headed for the village of Frachey. The road ran up into the belly of the mountains, which loomed over the landscape and seemed ready to swallow them and their car at any moment. Rocco looked up at them in silence. The sensation they were giving him wasn't one he liked in the slightest. Boulders ready to fall and crush you. And it was almost an automatic reflex to have the usual perception of how tiny human beings are, the fragility of life, and that sort of thing. Luckily, Sebastiano's phone call arrived just in time to interrupt the deputy police chief's thoughts, as dark as they were pointless.

"Sebastiano! How's it hanging?"

"You were right, Rocco. They sent me a Ukrainian girl who made me want to howl at the moon."

"You have fun?"

"Yes. And it didn't even cost that much. Where are you?"

"Up at Champoluc. I'm following up some trails."

"Ski trails?" Sebastiano said, misunderstanding.

"Seriously, Sebastia', ski trails? Can you see me on a pair of skis? Listen, I still haven't talked to the uniform that we need." He shot a furtive glance at Italo, who was keeping his eyes fixed firmly on the road. "But I'll take care of that later. We'll get together at the restaurant and make our plans."

"That sounds great. I'm going to go get some lunch now, and in the afternoon I'll call that girl again."

"Don't fall in love."

"Rocco, the blow jobs she gives ought to be classified as UNESCO cultural treasures of mankind!"

Rocco smiled as he hung up. He'd have preferred to spend a nice quiet afternoon under the covers with some Ukrainian girl, or with Nora.

"Here we are," said Italo.

The sign for Saint-Jacques snapped him back to his shitty duties as a cop.

"What a beautiful building!" Pierron exclaimed. "It's a *rascard*."

"A what?"

"A *rascard*," Italo explained. "They're characteristic houses you find around here, and also in France. In the old days, they had stalls for cattle and horses on the ground floor, and living quarters only upstairs. Now, of course—"

"The architects have taken over," Rocco concluded. "Well, it's beautiful, all right."

"But Omar's not here. What are we going to do?"

"You stay put here in the car."

"What about you?"

"I'm not staying put. Do we have a screwdriver?"

Italo pulled open the glove compartment and pulled out a little red-handled screwdriver. He handed it to the deputy police chief.

"What do you need that for?"

"Italo, did your mother ever tell you that you ask too many questions?"

"No, she died when I was just a baby."

"Then take it from me."

Rocco opened the car door and got out.

He shot a look around. The houses and the street in the village of Saint-Jacques seemed deserted. He approached Omar's front door, which opened onto an alley shielded by a house under construction, the scaffoldings covered with snow, the cement mixer and bricks abandoned there by the masons at the end of fall.

The *rascard* was concealed from the street and prying eyes. The deputy police chief eyed the little front door. There was only one simple door lock. It wasn't reinforced. It was the kind of keyhole you'd find on a bathroom door.

They're certainly trusting folk up here, he thought.

He approached the side window. It was a small, double-hung sash window, less common in Italy than elsewhere. The wood was old, and cracked in a couple of places. He tried to peer inside, but a filmy curtain blocked his view. What he wanted to know was the exact location of the sash lock. It was in the middle. He pulled on the lower sash slightly, creating a tiny gap between the two sashes, just enough to insert the tip of the screwdriver. He moved it two or three times quickly, until he heard a click. He pushed the screwdriver toward the exterior. Then he slowly pulled up the lower sash. The window opened. Rocco clambered over the sill and slipped into Omar Borghetti's house.

* * *

The place was small, the walls lined with wood. On one wall was a bookshelf stuffed with novels. A table and four chairs, two armchairs upholstered with green velvet, a small television set. The small galley kitchen stood in a far corner. Just one bedroom, a bathroom, and, last of all, a floor-to-ceiling storage cabinet packed with ski equipment. Four hundred and fifty square feet, a cozy little hideout. A haven where a man could pull the plug and be alone, with no contact with the outside world.

Rocco had no idea of exactly what he was looking for. But he knew that rummaging through someone's possessions is a better way of finding out about them than having a nice conversation. Objects don't lie.

He started with the chest of drawers in the little living room.

The first interesting thing he found was photos. Not pictures of the ski slopes, as he might have expected. The beach. With palm trees. And the subjects were Omar Borghetti and Luisa Pec. On a lounge chair with a cocktail. Under a giant banana leaf. Her riding on his shoulders as he stood chest deep in cerulean water. The two of them, tanned, eating by candlelight and looking out at a breathtaking sunset. Again the two of them, in front of the glass pyramid of the Louvre. The two of them at a café in the Latin Quarter. Always and exclusively the two of them.

Clearly Omar Borghetti was obsessed. In addition to the passion that the man felt for Leone Miccichè's wife, the other thing that Rocco discovered, thanks to the beach photos, was Luisa Pec's body.

"Fuck!" the deputy police chief commented tersely.

Perfect.

Did it make sense to die for a woman like that? Maybe it did, he thought, answering his own question. It made sense to kill, too. Luisa Pec had torn out Omar's heart, shredded it, and dropped it into her pocket, and now he was hiding like a bear in its den, licking his wounds and remembering the skin, the buttocks, and the eyes of Luisa.

Love.

Love and Rocco had run into each other more than once along the way. There was a time when he would fall in love at the drop of a hat. His heart and his thoughts chased after his classmates in high school and at university, and then after the women he worked with. Mariadele, Alessandra, Lorenza, Myriam, and Finola. All it took was a lingering glance, a certain hairdo, an up-from-under look and Rocco Schiavone's heart started racing, surging in excitement, leaping into the air, only to collapse in misery on the ground. Then one day Marina showed up, and he married her. And there was a click, like the sound of a window lock snapping shut. At age thirty-five. Marina had pushed a button, and Rocco's heart from then on leaped up only at the sound of A.S. Roma fans roaring in the stadium on a Sunday. He was with his wife, he loved her, and there was no room for any other woman. That was it. Over. Done with. And it didn't bother him in the slightest. Sure, he looked at other women, but in the way you might admire a nice painting, or a landscape so beautiful it leaves you breathless. Marina was his port in the storm. He'd tied up and he no longer felt the slightest inclination to go sailing on the sea.

In Omar's bathroom, there was a succession of hand creams and face creams, scented with calendula, with brands such as Nivea and Leocrema. The attention that Omar gave to skin care clashed with the contraption he used to shave: a single-blade straight razor, an antique, the kind you'd see in an old gangster movie, where the barber is shaving Al Capone or a pair of bandits are fighting it out in an East Harlem alleyway. Bone handle, and a very sharp blade.

But Omar Borghetti's clothing and knickknacks were of no interest to Deputy Police Chief Schiavone. He wanted to take a step further. Discover a detail, a foolish banality that would open a world to him.

And it turned up.

Between two fat file folders full of papers and documents—including pension plans, receipts for utility payments, the deed to the house that Omar had purchased in 2008 for 280,000 euros—he found the floor plans for a building on a sheet of copy paper. It was a xerox of a document from the local land registry. Up top, the scale of the plan, 1:100. And the name of the village where it was located: Cuneaz.

It was an enormous house. There was no mistaking it for anything but what it was: the floor plans of the hut that Luisa and Leone had renovated together.

Why do you have this? Rocco wondered, and answered his own question immediately, aloud. "The Sicilian beat you to the punch, with his timing and his cash, my friend," and Omar had used the money he'd borrowed to purchase the little house where the deputy police chief, like a common burglar, was now lurking and rummaging, sticking his nose into the owner's past and present.

"You were in there for more than half an hour," Italo Pierron said to the deputy police chief as he put the screwdriver back into the glove compartment.

"So?"

"I was just wondering if you found anything interesting."

"Plenty. I'm hungry. Let's find a decent place to eat, and we can talk over lunch."

Italo started the engine and put the car into first gear. "Did you close the window good and tight behind you?"

Rocco looked at him. "He'll never know we were even inside."

"*We* were?"

An ironic smile played across Rocco's face. "Okay, I was. Why? Don't you like working with me?"

"I love it. I just wish I could do more, though."

"If I'm going to let you do more, though, I'd have to trust you."

"Rocco, you already trust me."

The deputy police chief's smile broadened further. "You're a sly fox, Italo."

"Never as sly as you, Rocco. We're on a first-name basis, right?"

"You just called me Rocco. But at headquarters we're going to stick with rank and surname, or just 'sir,' okay?"

"Got it. So what are we going to do, subpoena this Omar Borghetti?"

"Well, he already knows he's been invited to come in for a little talk. Let's let him sweat for a while."

They found a place near Frachey, in a hotel by the promising name of Le Charmant Petit Hotel. The hotel's restaurant was inviting, and the smells that came from the kitchen seemed to fulfill the promises offered by the name. The place was covered with antique wood—walls, floors, and ceilings—and a fire was crackling in the fireplace. Enormous windows overlooked the forests and the snowy park. Rocco munched a breadstick as he and Italo listened to Carlo, a young man with a beard and a candid open face that had a Mediterranean, almost Arabic, beauty.

"For starters, we have a risotto al Barolo that's out of this world. Otherwise—"

"Halt!" Rocco said. "You had me at 'Barolo.' I'll have that."

"Me, too," said Italo.

"Wine?"

"I like Le Crete. Do you have any?"

"Certainly. Shall we decide on the entrées later?"

"Sure. Carlo, would you satisfy a curiosity of mine? Are you friends with Caciuoppolo?"

"Who?" asked the young man with a smile.

"He's a colleague of ours; he works on the slopes."

"Ah, yes, I know him. He's from Vomero. I'm from Caserta,

so we're practically neighbors. You're here because of the horrible discovery up at Crest, right?"

"Yeah," Rocco replied.

"Are you going to catch the son of a bitch who murdered Leone?"

"We're doing our best."

Italo broke into the conversation. "What are people saying in town?"

Carlo leaned forward, his knuckles on the tabletop. "Everybody has something to say. Some people suspect that Leone stepped on someone's toes down in Sicily. Others think he'd run up too many debts and couldn't make the payments."

Rocco liked the young man. He had a wide-awake, intelligent face. "What's your take on it, Carlo?" he asked him.

"I've got nothing. I didn't know him well enough. Or anything about his business. But the idea that it was someone from down south looks like bullshit to me. If they kill you for a vendetta or because you've broken the ground rules, they might arrange for the body to be found in the center of the city, or else they make sure it vanishes once and for all. Leaving it up there makes no sense."

"*Bravo*, Carlo. That's right."

"But someone hated him," added Italo.

"Look," Carlo said, taking a deep breath, "there's just one thing that Leone had that everyone here in Champoluc wished they had."

"The hut up in Cuneaz?" Rocco ventured.

"No. Luisa Pec. You've seen her, haven't you?"

"I'll say I have," Italo replied.

"If you'll excuse me, I'd better get into the kitchen, or I'll be serving you that risotto for dinner."

And he took his leave of the two policemen, vanishing behind the saloon doors.

Italo lowered his head and leaned forward toward the deputy police chief to make sure he wasn't overheard by the three couples seated at the tables around them. "Rocco, I can't really afford to eat in a place like this."

"Italo, don't worry, you're my guest. What the fuck, if I can't buy you lunch, then what were we even put on this planet to do?"

Italo shrugged his shoulders slightly. "That's right. And why were we put on this planet if at age twenty-seven I have to keep living at home with my father to save on rent and bills, and if I have to count my pennies before going out to the movies and to eat a pizza …"

"Sure." Rocco bit off half a breadstick. "You're talented, Italo. Your career prospects in the police force aren't exactly blindingly bright."

"I know that. And I'll tell you something more. My prospects in general aren't all that bright. But if I find something better, I'd be glad to leave the police."

Italo wasn't opening the door a crack, Rocco realized. He'd just thrown it wide-open. Rocco charged through without wasting any more time. "There's something we can do to improve our lives on this planet a little. You interested?"

"What is it?"

"It's something illegal."

Italo picked up a breadstick and bit into it. "How illegal?"

"Very, very illegal."

"Steal something?"

"From the thieves."

"I'm in!" he said, and took another bite of the breadstick. "So I'm the uniform you were talking about with your friend on the phone, right?"

"Exactly. Do you want to know the details?"

"Maybe we'll get to those later. Just tell me now: what would be involved? No shooting, right?"

"No. It's marijuana. A lot of it."

"We're going to bust someone?"

"Exactly, Italo. But not all the weed we confiscate is going to be turned over to the law."

"How much is in it for me?"

"Thirty-five hundred."

"Done deal!"

Just at that moment, an intense aroma announced the arrival of the two risottos al Barolo. Italo and Rocco turned toward the kitchen door. Carlo was walking toward them with an enormous steaming pewter platter and a smile on his lips. He set the risotto down on the table. He served the two men as plumes of aromatic steam rose from the rice. In a religious silence, the policemen looked down at the reddish grains and sniffed at the paradisiacal scents that wafted across the dining room. Carlo didn't say a word. He finished serving, made a slight and amused bow, and walked away from the table. Rocco picked up a fork. He put a mouthful of the risotto into his mouth. He closed his eyes. After Luisa Pec and the perennial glaciers, that risotto would be the third thing from Champoluc that the deputy police chief would carry with him for the rest of his life.

It wasn't until he was sipping a juniper berry grappa and chatting amiably with Carlo and Italo that Rocco suddenly remembered that Magistrate Baldi had summoned him to his office at three thirty.

The face of the magistrate waiting impatiently at his desk had appeared before him with all the violence of a sledge-hammer to the forehead.

Italo had driven recklessly, slicing across the opposite lane as he slalomed through the switchback curves and down-shifted like a madman. Rocco ordered him to slow down. Not because he was afraid of a crash but because of the very real risk that his portion of risotto al Barolo might wind up splat-tered on the floor mat, a horrible waste of a masterpiece for a summons from a judge.

They got there half an hour late.

But Baldi wasn't in his office.

Rocco sat at the magistrate's desk, looking out the window at the flat, gray sky. The picture in the silver frame was still there, off to one side on the desktop, facedown. He leaned forward. He turned it over and looked at it. It was a photo-graph of a woman in her early forties. Curly hair, a gleaming Colgate smile.

The judge's ex-wife wasn't bad-looking at all, at least judging from the framed head shot. Maybe not a woman you'd turn around to stare at in the street, but she wasn't bad. The breakup must have been recent. Because a photo turned facedown on the desk was only the first step on the path to a definitive divorce. A photo turned facedown meant that the judge still had hopes of repairing his marriage. Normally, the next step was to put the picture in the top drawer, a sign that things are getting worse, and then last of all, the photo in the trash—the end, the tombstone marking the burial plot. Rocco laid the photograph flat just as the door swung open. Baldi looked cool and cheerful, the lock of hair covering part of his forehead was finer and softer than the day before, and it bounced with every step. When the judge shook hands, his grip was dry, firm, and strong.

"I'm sorry I'm late, I was up at Champoluc."

"We have any news?" asked Baldi.

"Some. I'm running down the lead of the jealous ex-lover. A certain Omar Borghetti. I've summoned him to come in."

"I did find something, you know? Look here," said the judge, lifting his forefinger. He walked around the desk, opened a drawer, and pulled out a red folder. He sat down and opened the file. "What do we have here ... what do we have here," the magistrate repeated as he leafed through the pages, licking his finger as he went. "Ah, here we are. Luisa Pec and Leone Miccichè were married a year and a half ago. The ceremony was performed by a city clerk. Not in church. The ceremony was held in Cuneaz, where they own that sort of hotel up above the resort. Joint ownership of all property, et cetera, et cetera. Here." Baldi looked up at Rocco with his finger on the documents. "They'd asked the local office of Banca Intesa here in Aosta for a loan of several tens of thousands of euros. But the bank said no."

"So they had some project in mind, you think?"

"I'd say so. You see?" the judge pulled a sheet of paper out of the folder. "They'd offered a couple of buildings down in Sicily as collateral."

"Joint property of Leone Miccichè and his brother. But that doesn't prove anything."

"No. It doesn't prove anything. But they're tiles, Schiavone. They're all tiles in a mosaic, and if you put them together, they may give us a nice clear overall picture of the situation."

"Ah, yes, a nice clear overall picture of the situation. Speaking of tiles, by the way, look at this." Rocco pulled out the gloves he'd bought just a few hours earlier in Annarita's shop.

"Nice," said the judge.

"Right? They're identical to the gloves poor Leone had on. Can I smoke?"

"I'd say you can't."

"It's to prove a point."

"Then go right ahead."

Rocco put a cigarette in his mouth. He picked up the lighter. Then he put on the gloves. He tried to light the cigarette. He couldn't do it. The judge watched him. "What are you trying to show me?"

"Something very simple. Before Leone Miccichè was murdered, he smoked a cigarette. He went up to the middle of that shortcut, veering off the main piste, and he smoked a cigarette, and he probably had a conversation with his murderer. But he wasn't wearing gloves. That means, first of all"—and he lifted his thumb, still begloved—"that the cigarette wasn't one that his killer offered him, but that he must have pulled out of his own pack."

"He might already have been smoking it when he got there, no? Before heading up for a little chat with his killer."

"No, because if he'd already been smoking it, he would have had no reason to take off his gloves."

"Right."

"Second!"—and Rocco lifted his forefinger—"he probably lit it, too. But that still doesn't explain another thing."

"What would that be?"

"Why take off two gloves? Taking off one would be enough."

Baldi thought it over. "That's true. And did you come up with an idea?"

"No. For now I've got nothing. All I know is that the pack of Marlboros that Leone Miccichè had in his pocket was empty. Maybe he smoked the last one and didn't discard the pack on the ground because he didn't want to be a litterbug."

"Maybe so. Excellent, Dottor Schiavone. Excellent. Let's think this thing through."

Rocco took off the gloves and put them back in his pocket while the judge folded up the Leone Miccichè file and put it away. "But now, Schiavone, let me get some work done. I've got the financial police coming at me fast and furious. We've nailed a couple of tax evaders. Major players."

Rocco stood up from the chair.

"You know what? If it wasn't for all this tax evasion, we'd be one of the richest countries in Europe."

Rocco stopped to listen. He felt sure that he was about to be treated to one of the magistrate's jeremiads.

And in fact he was. "But no one recognizes the state as something that belongs to them. So many people in Italy think and reason as if it were still the nineteenth century, that the state is the enemy, an invader that battens off us and sucks us dry. And there's just one way, a very simple way, of eliminating tax evasion once and for all. And you know what that is?"

"Whether I do or not, you're about to tell me."

"Eliminate cash entirely. All payments, and I mean all of them, would have to be done with a credit card or a debit card. No one can pay in bills and coins anymore. And there, you're done! We'd have a way of documenting all payments and no one could ever again say that they weren't paid."

Rocco Schiavone thought it over. "That might be an idea. But there's still a *but*, Dottore."

"Tell me," the magistrate said encouragingly.

"What are we going to do about seigniorage?"

Baldi looked at him.

"Do you know how much it costs to print a hundred-euro bill? Thirty cents. And it's worth a hundred euros. The central banks pocket the difference. Now, you tell me whether you think the central bankers are likely to give up these immense and effortless earnings, just to combat tax evasion?"

"I hadn't thought of that. *Bravo*, good point. I'll give that some thought."

"What the fuck is all this junk on my desk?" shouted Rocco as he surveyed the envelopes and packages. It was Leone Miccichè's mail. He remembered that he'd ordered the Champoluc postmaster to forward it all to him. Zealous and terrified, the postmaster had complied. He sat down and started going through it. Bills. A letter from the bank. The monthly bills from Sky TV. A letter from the Italian Alpine Club. He opened it. Membership renewal. Nothing interesting. He tossed it all into the trash can.

He sat down at his desk, pulled the key out from under the framed photograph of Marina, and opened the top drawer. He needed to smoke a fatty, calm and untroubled, to relax his nerves and ward off exhaustion. He grabbed the first big joint, and already his thoughts were racing to Nora. Would he sleep with her tonight? He couldn't say. He didn't like to stay out all night. He liked his bed, his mattress and the way it recognized him every night and embraced him, along with the blankets. He lit the joint and took the first drag. Then Annarita came back into his mind, the woman from the ski shop. The woman who had rejected him with the force of an industrial spring. Sure, he'd mistaken the courtesy of an experienced saleswoman for a different kind of willingness. And sure, that was an unforgivable error. Perhaps, he thought to himself, it was because he was accustomed to the oafish rudeness of Roman shopkeepers. That kind of smile and that sort of courtesy have a very different meaning. In Rome. In Aosta and its surrounding province, on the other hand, it was nothing more than the simple courtesy due to a customer. Nothing more. He was on his second drag when someone knocked at the door.

"No!" shouted the deputy police chief. He took a third, deep drag, then crushed out the joint right on his desktop. A shower of sparks spilled to the floor like a fireworks display. He spat on the butt and dropped it into the trash. He stood up. The first thing he did was go over and throw open the windows. It was already dark outside. A blade of icy cold stabbed him in the chest.

"Jesus fucking Christ it's cold," he said, then waved his hands in the air as if he were trying to smack a fly and went over to the door of his office. He cracked it open. Officer Casella's face appeared.

"What do you want?"

"Farinelli from the forensics team is here. Shall I show him in?"

Rocco turned around and looked back into his office. He sniffed the air. The smell of weed was still too strong. He turned back around and looked at Casella.

"Does Farinelli have a cold?"

Casella made a face. "A cold? No, I don't think so, but why?"

"Well, then, show him into the passport room."

"Should I have him fill out the application form?" asked Casella.

"What application form?"

"For a passport."

"Casella, the only application form I wish you'd fill out is the one for being transferred to the Calabrian hinterland. Now get out of my sight!" he said, shoving him away and shutting the door.

Farinelli was toying with the plastic cup, still full of coffee. When Rocco Schiavone walked into the passport office, he didn't even look him in the face.

"How do you people manage to drink this filth? One of these days I'm going to have to take it in and have the laboratory analyze it."

"Don't do it," Rocco replied, sitting down across from his colleague. "There are certain things you'd be better off not knowing. You'll live longer."

"You can say that loud and clear, no?"

"Yes, I can say that loud and clear. Did you come here to dig into my past, or do you have something truly sensational to show me?"

Farinelli leaned over and picked up the leather bag. He opened it up. So slowly that he seemed like a Japanese Zen monk performing the traditional tea ceremony. Rocco propped his chin on his hand and sat there watching. Farinelli had a big nose, but it looked good on his broad, round face. He had a slight case of prognathism, and thanks to his jutting jaw, there seemed to always be a mocking smile playing on his lips. His quick, dark eyes were intelligent, but with that precise intelligence of an accountant who will split a hair four ways. He didn't remind Rocco of any particular animal. He'd been racking his memory for a resemblance for some time now. And he was searching in particular among the reptiles. Because only reptiles had eyes like that, dark and steady.

"How is your wife?" he asked him.

Farinelli stared at him. "Fine. Why?"

"No reason, just asking. Is she still pretty?"

"I'd prefer it if you didn't give my wife too much thought, frankly."

Finally, Farinelli pulled out some papers. "Well, then, two very important items. The first has to do with the handkerchief found in the corpse's mouth."

"Right."

"Soaked in blood. We examined it."

"Let me guess: the blood was Leone Miccichè's!"

Farinelli ran his tongue over his teeth. It looked as if he was tempted to spit in the deputy police chief's face. "Of course," he replied, "but that's not all. You see, we did a simple analysis and found that it belonged to type A negative. Which was Miccichè's blood group. But then, almost by accident, you know what we discovered?"

"That there's another blood group?"

"That's right. Group O. Got that? Group O negative 4.4, to be specific. And it was a man's blood. Which tells us one of two things: either the murderer cut himself, or maybe Leone bit him while he was stuffing the handkerchief into his mouth—if, that is, Miccichè was still alive when that was done—or else it's blood from an old wound. But I think that we have the killer's blood type."

"Excellent! Now all we have to do is take blood samples from a couple thousand people, analyze them all, find out which of them lacks an alibi, and bang! We've got the murderer."

"Was that a joke?"

"Forget about it, Farinelli. Excellent work all the same," he said and slapped him on the back. "That's wonderful news."

"Yes, but I have another piece of news that's even stranger."

"I'm all ears."

"You remember the tobacco that we found at the crime scene?"

"Yes, all crumbled, of course. Well?"

"It's not from a Marlboro."

Rocco suddenly clapped his hand to his mouth.

"What is it?" asked Farinelli.

"Do you know what kind of tobacco it is?"

"We'd have to do some very lengthy and labor-intensive analyses. But if it would be useful …"

"It would be useful as hell. As hell," said Rocco and, lost in thought, he stood up from his chair. "Tell me something, Luca, did you by any chance find the lighter up there?"

"No. We didn't find it. Why?"

"In that case I think I know why Leone took off both gloves. *Grazie*, Luca … great work." Then, as he strode out of the passport office, he shouted loudly: "Pierron!"

* * *

Italo braked to a halt at the foot of the cableway. Darkness had already fallen some time ago, and the skiers had left in their cars. Up high on the slopes, Rocco could see the headlights of the snowcats grooming the snow. The shops were still open, and the bright, cheery lights gave the whole town a Christmassy atmosphere, even if Christmas was long since over.

The temperature was well below freezing. Rocco made the futile effort of fastening the top button of his overcoat, but the chilly hand of winter cold still managed to worm its way under his clothing, sadistically caressing his skin.

"Where should we look for him?" asked Italo, clicking shut the BMW's electronic door locks.

Rocco said nothing. He headed straight over to Mario and Michael's bar, which was where the town's ski instructors met to drink and socialize. Outside was a stand that sold *vin brulé*, and a couple of instructors wearing red down jackets, their faces sunburned, their ski boots still on their feet, were joking and laughing, downing glasses of the mulled wine with several Brits.

"Deputy Police Chief Schiavone. I'm looking for Omar. Where is he?"

The cross-eyed ski instructor turned around, a glass of wine gripped in one hand. He was tipsy. "He's inside. Playing cards."

"*Grazie.*" Rocco went past the *vin brulé* stand and turned to Italo. "Have a glass. I'll be right back."

The bar's plate-glass windows were fogged up, a sign that the place was packed to the rafters. Rocco pulled open the double doors and walked in, and a wave of heat like a tropical rain forest washed over him, along with a strong smell of alcohol and coffee. There wasn't even standing room. The noise of the steam venting from the Faema espresso machine making punch, cappuccino, and tea, the loud voices, the laughter, and the clinking of glasses was deafening. The deputy police chief shot a look around the place, a full 360-degree observation. He glimpsed Amedeo Gunelli, the young man who had first found Leone, sitting at a small table with a couple of people. There was the chunky female ski instructor, along with her curly-haired younger lover and colleague. Then he glimpsed another patch of red. This was the regulation fleece worn by Omar Borghetti. He was sitting at a table with three other people, cards in hand, playing a round of Scopone Scientifico. He slapped a card down on the table and shouted *"Scopa!"* and his partner shouted in joy. Omar smiled. "Which makes twenty-one for us, no?" It was at that moment that he felt Rocco Schiavone's hand clamp down on his shoulder, as heavy as the scoop of a steam shovel.

Mario had given him two chairs and offered the use of the pantry, where they now sat, crammed in with the crates and cartons. They sat face-to-face, Rocco studying Omar. Omar studying the floor. The deputy police chief said nothing.

He waited. He let the seconds tick past without saying a word.

Omar Borghetti was a little older than forty, but his physique was that of a much younger man. His hair was full and short, flecked with gray. His face was tanned and lined with dozens of fine, light-colored wrinkles, especially around the eyes, where they seemed to highlight the aquamarine hue of the irises. *The man must clean up on the slopes*, thought Rocco. He imagined dozens of women and girls, young and old, exclaiming adoringly, "Teacher! Teacher! How'm I doing?" and carelessly falling into his virile, powerful arms so that he was forced to catch them.

The awkward silence made the skier uncomfortable, and he occasionally ran his hands over the skin of his freshly shaven face. Skin that was dotted with dozens of nicks and cuts, especially on the neck.

"Where have you been till now?" Rocco Schiavone asked suddenly. "I was looking for you. Did you know that?"

"No."

"I came all the way up to the ski school. You weren't there. Didn't your co-workers tell you?"

"Sure, but I just assumed it was about a fine I hadn't paid last month. You know, there's always time to take care of that kind of thing, no?" He put on a fetching little smile, as if to say, "You and I understand each other, right?"

"A fine?!" the deputy police chief roared, and Omar's little smile vanished like a receding wave on the beach sand. "Do you think for one second that a deputy police chief is going to waste his time chasing after a fucking fine?"

"Then why were you looking for me?"

"Because I've fallen head over heels in love with you," said Rocco. "You unsightly idiot, when the police come looking for you, you get right in touch, do I make myself clear?"

"Why don't you lower your voice?"

"Because we're not on the ski slopes here, Borghetti, and I could take you in right now if I wanted. In here, I'm a deputy police chief and you're less than shit, and you answer my questions, get it?"

"You're an animal. Address me with respect!"

Rocco leaped to his feet. "If you don't shut that toilet mouth of yours, I'm going to do something to you that'll give your dentist plenty of work to do."

"You're good at hiding behind your uniform."

"I'm not wearing a uniform, you piece of shit, I'm wearing a loden overcoat. And I'll wait for you whenever you want and wherever you want and I'll break you down into a steaming pile of chopped meat!"

"Ask me the questions you need to ask and then get the fuck out of my face!" Omar shouted.

The first thing Omar felt was a gust of air, then the impact of the hand slamming into his face and whipping his head around until he almost tumbled out of his chair. Omar's eyes bulged, as if in disbelief at what had just happened to him. Rocco was on his feet, both hands gripping the chair's back-rest, looming over him like an onrushing thunderstorm. "You don't understand who you're dealing with yet," Rocco said.

Omar put his hand up to touch his cheek. His right nostril was smeared with blood.

"Here," said the deputy police chief, suddenly shifting into the more respectful Italian formal and handing him a paper tissue. The ski instructor mopped blood from his mouth. "Okay, we started off on the wrong foot. I'll try to keep the tone of our conversation to one of mutual respect, Signor Borghetto."

Clearly bipolar, thought Omar. *This guy is completely insane.*

Rocco lit a cigarette. "Let's talk about us, okay?" He spouted a plume of smoke up into the air, then went back to looking at the ski instructor. "Why were you in the office, up at the pistes, on Thursday evening after closing time?"

"Thursday?"

"The night Leone Miccichè was killed. Why were you still up there?"

"Me? I wasn't up there. I never stay in the office after four thirty."

His chin was quivering, and his eyes were blinking. Rocco never took his eyes off him. "The office door was open. You're the only one who has a set of keys, besides whoever's turn it is to lock up. Who could have opened the door but you?"

"Whoever's turn it was to lock up."

"Wrong answer. It wasn't him. So?"

Omar Borghetti ran his hand over his face.

"If you weren't in the school, then can you tell me where you were?"

"It's a sensitive matter."

"Never as sensitive as a first-degree murder charge, trust me."

"Murder?" In spite of his handsome tan, Omar turned as pale as a piece of canvas. "What murder are you talking about? What—"

"To be exact, just a short time after you were done rummaging around in the office up there, somebody murdered Leone not fifty yards from there. You might not have known that, but now I hope that the situation is clear to you."

"No. Not me. I didn't know. That is, I knew that that night Leone … But I didn't know, not at that time of night. Oh my God, oh my God, oh my God," he said, covering his face with both hands.

Omar Borghetti finally understood.

Rocco took back the blood-soaked paper tissue. He looked at it with a smile and stuffed it into his pocket. "So now are you really not going to tell me what you were doing up there?"

"I want a lawyer," said Omar Borghetti, in a flat, toneless voice, as if someone else were dubbing him.

"You've watched too many TV shows, Borghetti. I'm just asking you—"

"You're just busting my balls, Commissario, so if you've got it in for me, you might as well say so. And whatever you have in mind, I want a lawyer!"

Once again, Rocco raised his voice. "I just asked you to help me keep this conversation on an acceptable level of civility. But you're starting to twist my balls counterclockwise, and let me promise you, that's not something I enjoy. All I'm doing here is asking you what you were doing up there the night of the murder!"

"And I'm telling you that I want a lawyer."

"Fine. Then here's what we'll do. I'll officially serve you with a notification that you're a person of interest in this case, and I can get that to you by tomorrow morning. Then you'll have to go in and see the judge, with your lawyer, and I have all the elements I need to keep you behind bars for a while. And let me assure you that, if by any chance you were to get off, I'll be delighted to spend three-quarters of my every working day making your life a living hell. I just got to Aosta, Borghetti, and I don't have a fucking thing to do in the office. You'll curse the day you refused to answer my questions in a civil manner. Take good care of yourself."

Just as Rocco turned to leave, Omar spoke. "I was at the Belle Cuneaz. With Luisa."

Rocco came back and stared at Omar. "Why?"

"I wanted to talk to her."

"You hated Leone Miccichè. He'd stolen Luisa from you, as well as your plan to renovate the hut above the slopes. Tell the truth."

"How do you know these things?"

But Rocco didn't answer.

Omar continued. "Luisa and I were—in fact, we still are—close friends."

"Still, the whole thing didn't sit well with you, did it? Then, when you found out that she was pregnant, you just saw red."

"Luisa loved Leone, and there was no room for me; I knew it then and I still know it, even now that Leone's gone. Luisa and I are like a brother and sister these days."

"So what did you want to talk to her about that night?"

"What did I want to talk to her about?"

"Eh, *bravo*. What did you want to talk to her about?"

Omar ran a hand over his face. "It's a sensitive subject."

"I'm a sensitive person."

Omar smirked sarcastically. Rocco responded with a smile. "I know that I might not seem that way, right? But have you ever read Pirandello? Everyone plays a role in this life, and then there's the mask, and blah blah blah?"

At last Omar spoke. "Luisa owes me money."

"How much?"

"Almost a hundred."

"A hundred thousand? Why on earth?"

"Last season was a disaster. Plus Leone had done some extra renovation work: he'd insisted on installing Jacuzzi tubs in every room and a hot tub outside. But they didn't have the money to cover it. So I helped her out. It was my life savings. I wanted that money back, you know, it's not like you can become a millionaire as a ski instructor."

"Or as a policeman, for that matter. Did you argue? Did you fight?"

"No. Very simply, she asked me to wait for a month at the very most, because this season was going great and she promised to pay me back in full."

"After that?"

"After that I left. I put on my skis and I went back down to town."

"What time was it?"

"I don't know. It was dark out. The snowcats were grooming the runs."

"Do you know how to ski in the dark?"

Omar flashed him his very brightest smile. "Mr. Deputy Police Chief, I took bronze at the Italian championships of 1982 and I was a member of the national team. I could ski backward along the edge of a crevasse blindfolded. I learned to ski before I learned to walk."

"Did you see anyone on your way back to town?"

"No. No one."

"Do you and Luisa see each other often?"

"Practically every day. Every so often she comes to see me. We talk, we have a cup of tea. Or else I go up to the hut. I told you, we're like brother and sister."

"And if I asked Luisa Pec to confirm this version of events, what would she tell me?"

"The same thing I just told you. The truth."

Rocco paced back and forth in the oversize broom closet. He looked at the painted Coke-brand mirrors, the ice cream deep freeze that was in storage until summer, a wine rack loaded with bottles of red, and the crates of gin. "So what do you think? Who could have been in the office at that time of day?"

"I have no idea."

"Is there anything in that office that could tempt anybody?"

"No, absolutely not. There's a big closet where we keep all sorts of things for any eventuality. Crap, really. Extra sweaters, goggles. Never cash or anything of any real value. Except maybe a twenty-year-old television set that as far as I know doesn't even work."

"What if I need to get back in touch with you?"

"Call the ski school. I'll check in with them every day to see if you were looking for me. I'll give you my home address, in any case."

"I'm not going to have to come looking for you, right?"

"No, you're not."

Rocco opened the pack of cigarettes and offered one to Omar Borghetti. "Do you smoke?"

The ski instructor shook his head brusquely. "No, *grazie,* I've never been a smoker."

Rocco took in that information. "Sorry about smacking you."

"No, *I'm* sorry. I behaved like an idiot."

Omar extended his hand, but Rocco wouldn't shake it. "If you don't mind," said the policeman, "I'll shake hands when this is all over."

"Are you saying that you still think that I—"

"When this is over," Rocco repeated, leaning hard on each individual word.

Italo was already on his second glass of *vin brulé* when Rocco left Mario and Michael's bar.

"This stuff goes down like honey. Did you find him?"

"All taken care of. Let's go home." Rocco gave him a look. "Are you okay to drive? You're not drunk or anything?"

"When it's as cold as this, it would take six glasses to get someone drunk."

"As long as you understand I don't want to wind up wrapped around a tree."

"It's all under control."

They started walking toward the car. "Should I take you home, sir?"

"We're not at headquarters. You can drop the formalities."

"Ah, right, that's true, I'd forgotten. So—are you going home?"

"First to the laboratory. I have to give something to Fumagalli."

"What?"

"A piece of tissue."

They got in the car. Six seconds later, the BMW, with Italo at the wheel, took off for Aosta, splattering mud and snow in all directions.

Scalding hot, I scrape away the skin. I want to hear it scream with the heat. I like to train the spray on the top of my head and shut my eyes. Only there's always something behind the eyelids that makes me open them again. There's some kind of photo album behind my eyelids. And they're all photographs that I never want to look at again. Still, there they are. Someone pasted them in. So I open my eyes again. The bathroom has turned into a steam room. I can barely even see my feet. The toenails have turned purple. I step out of the shower. There's steam billowing everywhere. Milky white, as if a cloud had floated into the bathroom. Nice. Warm.

"What are you doing?" It's Marina's voice. I can't see her. She's hidden in the steam.

"I have to go out, my love. Sebastiano's expecting me. In fact, I'm running late."

"Are you two going to do something stupid?"

I feel like laughing. The stupid things we do, as my wife calls them, though she doesn't know it yet, are going to make it possible for us to live in Provence someday. "Yes. We're going to do something stupid."

"Be careful. Don't get yourself in a jam."

"All right, my love. Where are you? I can't see you."

"Over here, by the door."

I wipe the fog off the mirror with my hand. My face appears. My whiskers have grown out. And just look at those bags under my eyes. "I look like a raccoon, don't I?"

Marina laughs. She laughs silently. You notice it only because little regular jets of air come out of her nose. Tchk-tchk-tchk-tchk … Like a sprinkler watering the grass. "Do you want to know the word of the day?"

"Sure. What is it?"

"Jactitation. When someone performs senseless actions because of a state of anxiety."

I start to apply shaving cream to my face. Jactitation. "Now who is it that's performing senseless actions because of a state of anxiety?" I ask her.

"That's something you ought to be able to figure out for yourself, Rocco."

"Me? What sort of actions are you talking about?"

"Sooner or later, we ought to address the issue, don't you think?"

I know. I just want to close my eyes. But then the photo album of horror could come back and see me, pay me a visit behind my eyelids. I open my eyes again. The steam in the *bathroom is gone now. All that's left on the mirror is the outline of a handprint. That must have been mine.*

But he didn't remember drawing a heart there. Rocco leaned his forehead against it. Then he went back to smearing shaving cream on his face.

Sebastiano Cecchetti was at the same table as the night before. When he saw Rocco come into the restaurant, he raised his hand and waved. There was a streak of sweat along his hairline, and a few drops of perspiration right under his nose. And it wasn't the temperature in the restaurant that was making him perspire. Seba was tense and nervous. You only had to look him in the eye to get that.

"What's up, Seba?"

"I'm waiting on a phone call. The truck might be coming early. Tomorrow at lunchtime."

"On a Sunday?"

"On a Sunday."

"Tomorrow A.S. Roma is playing Udinese. That's not a game I want to miss."

"Rocco, it looks to me like you're going to miss it." Sebastiano shot a glance at his cell phone. He was making sure he had enough bars. "Have you talked to the uniform?"

"All set. He's with us. He's just waiting for me to call him. I'd told him tomorrow night, but there's no problem."

Sebastiano rubbed his belly. "My stomach's tied in knots. I don't know. I smell something fishy ... I'm afraid something's gotten screwed up."

"Right. So what should we do?"

"I'm not going to have anything except maybe some cheese."

Rocco shook his head. "I mean tomorrow. Are we going ahead with this?"

"I'll tell you as soon as I get the phone call."

"*Ciao*, Rocco!"

He hadn't even heard her creep up behind him. She just appeared from around the pillar. Nora munching on a breadstick, languidly leaning against the wall. Her hair in a ponytail, revealing her long neck and the delicate hollow of her throat, adorned with a pearl necklace.

"*Ciao*, Nora."

Sebastiano turned to look at the woman.

"You dropped off the face of the earth," she said. "Have you been busy?"

"Busy as hell. This is my friend Sebastiano. He's up from Rome."

Sebastiano stood up and bowed elegantly, planting a kiss on her hand. "Such a pleasure."

"Are you alone?" Rocco asked her.

Nora pointed to a table where a well-dressed man and woman in their early fifties were sitting and laughing, their gleaming teeth on display, shining even brighter than the glasses and silverware on the table.

"Who are they?" asked Rocco.

Nora chewed on a bit of breadstick. "Friends. Jealous?"

"No," Rocco replied as Sebastiano swept her with a gaze that ranged from head to foot, as relentless as a scanner at the airport. Nora stood there against the wall in her charcoal gray skirt suit. She felt Sebastiano's eyes on her, and it seemed to give her a subtle thrill of pleasure.

"Tomorrow's Sunday. What do you want to do? Should we get together?"

"Look, Nora, this isn't a good time. If you want, I'll call you later."

"Later on is too late."

"Then let's talk tomorrow and I'll tell you what we can do."

Nora winked at Rocco, flashed Sebastiano a smile, and headed back to her table. Sebastiano kept both eyes on her until she sat down.

"Nice piece of ass. Who is she?"

"A girl."

"You treat her like shit."

"You think? I treat her the way we treat each other in bed. Nothing more and nothing less."

"The two of you look good together."

"You think so?" Rocco asked.

"I do. You going to see her tonight?"

"Couldn't say."

"Take her home, no?"

"The thought never crossed my mind, Seba. I don't take any women home."

Sebastiano poured himself a glass of water. "Someday you're going to have to get over this thing, Rocco."

Rocco said nothing. He looked at the tablecloth, flicking away imaginary bread crumbs.

"You can't keep this up. It's been four years. When are you going to …"

Rocco looked up at his friend. "Sebastiano, you know I love you. But stop talking about this one thing, please. Stop giving me advice about things I already know. I can't take it. Period."

"Rocco, Marina is—"

"That's enough, Seba! Would you please stop," shouted Rocco, his eyes red and glistening, his mouth twisted into a shout that was choked into silence by the despair paralyzing his limbs and constricting his throat, to the point that he practically couldn't breathe.

Sebastiano patted the hand that was lying on the table. "Sorry, Rocco. Forgive me."

Rocco blinked a couple of times. He brushed away a tear, sniffed, and then smiled. "It's nothing, Seba. I love you, man."

The clouds had moved on, and the birdies were once again tweeting happily. Sebastiano regained his smile and pointed at Nora at the other table. "I wouldn't kick her out of bed."

"Wasn't the Ukrainian girl enough for you?"

"You're right. She sucked me inside out."

They both burst out laughing, and at that exact moment, Sebastiano's cell phone vibrated. In one fast move, the big man's paw shot out and grabbed the BlackBerry. He held it to his ear without saying a word. He sat there listening, paying close attention to what the person on the other end of the line was saying. Rocco couldn't hear; Sebastiano betrayed no emotion. Then the big man lowered his head, accompanying the act with a couple of grunts: "Mmm. Mmmm." Then he started squeezing a piece of bread into a white ball. More grunts. Finally he said a word with a clear meaning all its own—"Fuck!"—and hung up.

He looked Rocco in the eye. "It's not for lunchtime tomorrow."

"That's a relief."

"It's for tonight, Rocco!"

SATURDAY NIGHT

Exactly half an hour after Rocco's phone call, Italo Pierron appeared on Corso Ivrea, in uniform, pressed and neatly shaved. He slid behind the wheel of the deputy police chief's Volvo. Rocco pulled out the flasher and placed it on the car's roof. As Italo was gunning it toward the highway, Rocco made the introductions.

"Seba, meet Italo. Italo, meet Sebastiano."

"It's a pleasure," said Italo. Seba, on the other hand, said nothing. He was looking out the window at the lights of the other cars and the dark, looming shapes of the mountains.

For half an hour, no one spoke.

Then Sebastiano started up. "All right, then, here's the plan. The truck is easy to spot. It's orange, and on the side of the cargo body is painted the name Kooning N.V. Is that clear?"

"Do we know what route it's going to take?" asked Rocco.

"The truck will leave the highway after coming through the tunnel at about eleven, and then it'll take State Road 26. It's scheduled to make a stop at Morgex, but we need to pull it over before there."

"At Chenoz?" suggested Italo, taking a guess.

"Bravo!" said Sebastiano, in astonishment.

"He's a native," Rocco put in. "Once they've stopped, we show our badges, we make them open up the truck—and what about you, Seba?"

"You'll drop me off before Morgex, at Chez Borgne. I have a van there. I'll catch up with you where you pull the truck over, we'll load the van, and then we'll get going."

"Aren't we supposed to take them in to police headquarters?" asked Italo.

Rocco replied, "That depends. If they accept our proposal, we'll let them go after lightening their load. But if they decide to give us a hard time, then yes, we'll have to take them in to headquarters."

"And our share?" asked Italo, who seemed to be as comfortable as if he'd been pulling off heists his whole life.

"We'll take it after we confiscate the drugs," said Rocco.

A powerful, insistent wind twisted the tops of the trees, which bent over almost double, as if they were trying to retrieve the pinecones they'd just lost. The shredded heaps of snow lining the street were dirty black. Italo was stationed around a curve in the middle of the road with the police traffic paddle in one hand, stamping his feet to ward off the chill. Rocco, on the other hand, was smoking a cigarette, stretched out against the car roof, illuminated intermittently by the blue police flasher. The high clouds went racing overhead and every so often revealed a glimpse of starry night sky. A single streetlamp two hundred yards away colored the snow and the road with a sickly yellow light. The few cars that went by slowed suddenly the instant the driver glimpsed the police officer by the road. But each time, Italo waved them on with the traffic paddle and they vanished into the night. It was 11:30 p.m. It wouldn't be long now.

"What else have you found out about me?" Rocco asked in the silence of the night, broken only by the rustling of the trees. Italo turned to look at him. The deputy police chief, his eyes focused on the road, spewed the white smoke from his cigarette together with the condensation of his breath.

"That you're suspected of a couple of deaths and something that has to do with a politician."

Rocco took another drag on his cigarette. "Ah. And what do you think happened?"

"Me? No idea. Or rather, I've got a few thoughts about the two deaths. Did they have names?"

"Sure, they did."

"But was it you?"

Rocco flicked the cigarette away. "You want to know something? Revenge is good for nothing. Or really, it's good only for making you think you've taken care of everything, that you've reassembled the mosaic. But the truth is, all you've done is vent your frustration. Understandable, but still, it's about frustration. But here's the problem: until your vendetta is done, you're blind to these things. It's pointless to eliminate someone who's hurt you. You just perpetuate the same mistake. And I'm going to die with that mistake."

"Is that why they sent you here?"

Rocco smiled. "No. That's an old story. From four years ago. No, I'm here for another reason. You don't know anything about it because it was kept very quiet."

"You feel like telling me about it?"

"A thirty-year-old asshole who was raping young girls. I caught him, and instead of handing him over the way I should have, I broke him down and rebuilt him, so to speak. Now he walks with a crutch and can't see out of one eye. Is that enough?"

"Jesus … And they reported you?"

"No. This guy's the son of someone powerful enough to fix me good. And he fixed me good."

"How many young girls did he rape?"

"Seven. One of them killed herself six months ago. You know where I went wrong? I went to talk to them, to the girls' parents—I saw them and I got a clear picture of just how much damage he'd done. Never let yourself get sucked in emotionally, Italo. It's a mistake. A big mistake. You lose objectivity and self-control."

"And where's the guy now?"

"I told you: out on the street. Though hobbling around on a crutch. And sooner or later he'll do it again. Nice, no?"

Italo shook his head. "And that's why they transferred you from Rome?"

"Would you believe it? For that. And it's one of the truly just things I've done in my life."

"I'd have killed him."

"Don't say that, Italo. Have you ever killed anyone?"

"No, I haven't."

"Don't do it. Because then you get used to it." Rocco looked at the sky. Then he smiled faintly. "You can see the stars. It'll be a sunny day tomorrow."

Italo looked up. "Not necessarily. In ten minutes the sky could cloud over."

A dog barked in the distance. A sheep bleated in response. Then there was a distant roar. A continuous subterranean rumble. It could have been a river overflowing its banks or an avalanche tearing downhill toward them.

But it was the sound of horsepower under the hood of a truck. Rocco stepped away from the Volvo. "Go on, Italo, it's time."

Italo spat on the ground, stiffened, and grabbed the traffic paddle in one hand.

"Click off the safety," the deputy police chief suggested.

Italo undid the automatic holster lock and gave his pistol a tug. "Are you packing?"

Rocco nodded. He walked toward the road. The noise grew louder. The truck was coming closer. It wouldn't be long before the behemoth's headlights came around the curve, illuminating the asphalt and the woods lining the road. Italo gulped. Rocco tossed his cigarette onto the muddy snow.

"Let me do the talking. Just follow me."

The young policeman nodded edgily.

"Keep cool, Italo."

The noise came closer and closer. Rocco sniffed, and suddenly, as if by enchantment, the wind stopped slapping people and things. Then, from around the curve, eight blinding headlamps appeared, along with the screaming roar of many hundreds of horses of internal combustion engine. The truck, an enormous, smoking metal dragon, seemed bent on devouring the valley and all its inhabitants. Italo promptly lifted the traffic paddle. Rocco broke away from his car. The behemoth's engine jerked, the sound of downshifting came through the air, and the vehicle lost speed as it gradually approached the two policemen. It was a truck without a trailer. On the side, clear and unmistakable, was written KOONING N.V.

"This is it," shouted Rocco.

The behemoth was slowing down. A blinker started to flash on the right side of the vehicle as it slowly rolled past the policemen. The interior of the cab was dark. As it went past him, Rocco managed only to glimpse a couple of little flashes of light on the dashboard. Puffing and rattling, the truck came to a halt fifty or sixty feet past the two policemen. The monster stood there, its brake lights glowing, exhaust pouring from the rear pipes. Waiting. The driver's-side door remained shut.

"Let's go!" said Rocco. And he started toward the truck. Italo set the traffic paddle on the Volvo's roof, checked to make sure that the pistol was where it was supposed to be, then followed the deputy police chief.

Rocco had reached the truck. The chrome glittered in the light of the one distant streetlamp that illuminated the intersection. The engine puttered in neutral, rhythmically tapping at the night. The deputy police chief knocked three times and then heard the sound of the window being lowered. The driver's face emerged. Blond, with a flattened nose, light-colored eyes, covered with pimples. Not much older than twenty. He looked down at the deputy police chief and smiled. He was missing at least three teeth.

"*Ja?*" he said.

Ja, thought Rocco. "Open up, idiot!" he shouted.

The man gesticulated to show that he didn't understand the language.

"*Open and come down!*" shouted Italo, who had just come up, in English, with a timbre and tone of voice that was very convincingly authoritative.

The door swung open, and the driver hesitantly set foot on the first step of the ladder. "*Am I to come down?*"

"*Yes! Now!*" Italo replied.

The man obeyed. He climbed down the steps and leaped to the pavement. Rocco signaled to him to come toward him. The driver obeyed calmly, still with a smile on his lips. Then Italo climbed up onto the truck. He leaned into the cab: "*You!*" he shouted in English. "*Come down. Documents!*"

Rocco couldn't see whom he was talking to. But clearly there had to be two drivers. Officer Pierron pulled back from the cab and climbed back down the steps. After a short interval, a second man came out of the cab, with the look of someone who'd just woken up. He was big and black, with Rasta dreadlocks. He had a plastic bag in one hand.

The two truck drivers stood side by side, dressed only in sweaters, apparently indifferent to the cold, steady and untrembling. They just stood there as if it were springtime and the cherry trees were already blossoming. They were both a good four or five inches taller than Rocco, and their biceps bulged almost indecently.

"Biggish, eh?" Italo said, then addressed them in English. "Stay quiet and calm down, okay?"

"Okay," the two truck drivers replied in chorus while Rocco opened the folder with the documents. He feigned interest, but he really didn't give a damn about the customs stamps and notations.

He was hardly surprised to find two banknotes concealed in the registration. Two hundred-euro bills. He smiled as he looked at the two truck drivers. They smiled back at him, winking cunningly. Rocco took out the two green banknotes and showed them to Italo, asking in Italian, "Look what I found in the bills of lading. Is this yours?" Rocco held out the money, but neither driver gave any sign of being about to take the money back. "Is this for me? What is it? A tip? Translate for me, Italo!"

Italo said in English, "It's a tip?"

The black driver smiled and nodded.

"Ah, *grazie*, *grazie*, thanks very much. You understand, Italo? This is an attempted bribe. According to these two pieces of shit, you and I are worth two hundred euros. Doesn't seem like quite enough, does it?"

"Not really," Italo replied, poised with one hand ready to draw his gun.

Rocco slowly crumpled up the banknotes and slipped them into the young blond man's jeans pocket. "You can understand me, right?" he said, and the man's eyes opened wide in fear. "You can take this money and stick it up your ass." Then he reached into his inside jacket pocket and pulled out some folded sheets of paper, slapping them right under the blond fellow's nose. "Italo, tell him that this is a search warrant!"

Actually, they were the expense accounts for their activities at Champoluc.

"I don't know how to say that in English."

"*Perquisizione!*" shouted Rocco, using the Italian word for "search." "Understand?"

The truck driver turned pale. "Perquisition?" he asked.

"*Bravo*. That's right. Open up," Rocco said, pointing to the back of the truck.

"But ... *Polizia italianna* good! *Forza l'Italia!* Cannavaro!"

"What the fuck is this mental defective trying to say?" Then the deputy police chief leaned forward until his face was an inch from the fair-haired young man's nose. "Open up immediately or I'll beat you down!"

The truck driver said: "I have to get the keys ... May I?"

Italo translated for Rocco.

"Tell him I'll get the keys."

Rocco stepped up onto the first step and hauled himself into the cab.

The dashboard was a sea of lights big and small, of all colors. Stuck to the windshield was a GPS, and it was working. Rocco turned the key and switched off the engine. He pulled out the set of keys. Then he showed them to the driver. "Are these the right ones? *This?*"

The driver nodded.

As Rocco and the blond driver headed toward the rear of the truck, the other driver, the black man, stuck close to the truck, with a slightly frightened expression on his face. Italo looked at him, his hand on the holster that held his pistol. The man noticed and smiled. One of his eyelids was twitching, and from time to time he licked his lips.

"This guy is shitting himself!" Italo shouted.

"Bring him here!" Rocco replied. "And pull out your gun. Things are getting intense here."

Italo drew his pistol and looked at the young Rasta, whose eyes got big at the sight of the weapon. "C'mon, let's go ..." And the two men moved off together.

They were all clustered around the truck's rear doors. The driver was inserting a key from the ring into the container's double door lock. The guy was taking entirely too much time, as far as Rocco was concerned. So he grabbed the keys out of the driver's hands and opened the lock himself. The tumblers clicked and the handles turned freely. Italo, pistol in hand, never took his eyes off the two truck drivers. The container's two large doors swung open. Inside the truck, instead of boxes or crates, was another container.

"What the fuck? A container inside a container?" said Rocco. "Let's climb in and open this one too."

The noise of an approaching vehicle made Italo turn around. It was a dark blue Fiat Ducato delivery van, slowing to a halt right next to the truck.

"What now?" asked Italo.

"Relax," the deputy chief replied just as Sebastiano opened the driver's-side door and got out of the van. Italo smiled. "I'd forgotten about him." And he snapped a sharp military salute. Sebastiano, fully immersed in the role of a cop, saluted back. The two truck drivers silently observed the new arrival. Sebastiano glared menacingly back at them. He stood six foot four, making him the same height as the two young men. Then he spat on the ground and sized up the truck's contents.

"Well, well, well. What have we here?"

"A container inside a container," Rocco replied as he gestured for the young blond man to follow him. They climbed in.

The smaller container was red and had a lock on the two rear doors. The deputy police chief looked at the set of keys. He held them out to the pimply truck driver. "Which one?"

He took the key ring in hand and started sorting through them in search of the right one. Then it all happened in an instant. The pimply blond driver hurled the keys at Rocco's face, and Rocco, caught off guard, stumbled and fell backwards, just far enough to allow the driver to leap out of the truck and take to his heels. The black man, quick as a bolt of lightning, unleashed a straight-armed punch at Italo, who slammed to the ground; his pistol went spinning away from him. Sebastiano was just in time to turn around and see them both running away down the road. Rocco leaped off the truck and went over to Italo, who was holding a hand to his lip and grimacing with pain. He picked up his pistol and took off after the two fugitives. Sebastiano, by contrast, shrugged and gave up the chase even before starting.

The bastards were running hard. At the crossroads for Chenoz, the two went in opposite directions. Rocco decided to follow the white driver. Too many cigarettes and too much time spent without exercise were already leaving him out of breath. The young blond man was pulling away. The deputy police chief's knee was screaming in pain. He could have shot him, knocked him down, and taken him in. But then his professional instincts vanished all at once.

What am I doing? he asked himself. *Fuck this.* And he slowed to a halt. "Go on, handsome, go ahead! Run all the way back to Rotterdam, you asshole!" he shouted after him.

Bent over double and heaving from the exertion, he spit a gob of saliva onto the asphalt. Then he pulled himself erect with both hands flat on his lumbar muscles and tried to stretch, an exercise as pointless as it was painful. He felt his spine pop a couple of times. At last he turned around and made his way back to the truck.

Italo had a split lip. Sebastiano had put a little snow on it. Nothing serious. Rocco picked up the truck keys from the pavement. "Better this way, if you ask me. It gives us more time to work, no?" Sebastiano nodded. Italo smiled. "But

they made complete fools of us," he said, "and I don't like
that."

"No, we made fools of them," Sebastiano replied. "Come
on, Rocco, let's go—open up."

Rocco climbed back onto the truck and went over to the
lock on the interior container. He tried the first key. Then the
second. Finally, the third key turned in the lock. The doors
swung open with a metallic screech.

Eyes.

Dozens and dozens of eyes looking at them. Rocco stepped
back and almost fell out of the truck.

The container was full of people.

"Holy shit!" said Rocco in a faint voice, little more than a
whisper. From the darkness of the container inside the truck
emerged eyes, teeth, and faces. "Who are they?"

Sebastiano shook his head. Italo cautiously came forward,
one hand on his aching lip. "Indians?" he asked in an under-
tone as Rocco got down off the truck. The truly weird thing
was the absolute silence that reigned inside that surreal
cubbyhole. None of the inhabitants of the metal cavern emitted so much as a peep.

"Let's get them out of there. *Out!*" he started shouting in
English. *"Out of here!"* And together with Italo and
Sebastiano, he started gesticulating to get the people to leave
the truck.

Slowly the dark mass produced a tangle of arms, legs, and
heads. And teeth. These human beings were smiling, and
whispering something in a distant language that sounded like
a prayer. Italo started lining them up along the side of the

road. "One, two, three ..." And women started climbing out of the truck, some with children in their arms, and there were young men, and boys and girls of all ages.

Italo went on counting: "Fifty-six, fifty-seven, fifty-eight ..." They practically overflowed the roadside by now. "And fifty-nine ... Rocco, what are we going to do?"

Rocco stood staring at the truck as it went on vomiting out people. A cornucopia of human misery.

Italo stopped when he got to eighty-seven. They were all out. And there they stood, eyes wide with fear. Terrifyingly skinny, shivering with the cold. One of them extended a hand gripping a passport. Sebastiano leaned toward him and took the document. "Acoop Vihintanage ... They're from Sri Lanka."

The man's head wobbled from side to side. "Ah!" he said. Then he threw his arms around a man to his right and a woman on his left. *"Amma ... akka!"*

"I don't know what you're saying," said Sebastiano.

"Brother ... sister ... mine."

"He says that these are his brother and sister," Italo translated.

"Well, who the fuck cares," said Sebastiano, handing back the passport. Then he went over to Rocco. "What now?"

"What do I know? Let's try to understand where they were going. Italo? These people speak English—find out more or less where they were heading."

"Right away." Italo went over to the man who had handed over his passport. Rocco climbed back into the rear of the truck.

"What are you doing?" Sebastiano called.

"I want to take a look around. Figure out what's inside."

"Here," said his friend, tossing him a pocket flashlight. Rocco switched it on and walked into the truck.

A stench of sweat and massed humanity assaulted him with the ferocity of a starving wild animal. He was forced to run back out, coughing. "Holy shit ... There must be an outbreak of cholera in there!"

"Who knows how long they've been locked up in that container. Put a handkerchief over your mouth." Now Sebastiano tossed him a white handkerchief.

"Is it clean, at least?" Rocco said, examining it.

"Even if it isn't, it couldn't be worse than what's inside the container; so don't worry," Sebastiano replied. Rocco covered his mouth and nose, switched the flashlight on a second time, and went in.

He could barely fit inside without bumping his head against the ceiling. Millions of grains of fine dust danced in the shaft of light that cut through the darkness. There were rags on the floor. Patchwork bags. A wooden rocking horse and a tin car. Then the flashlight lit up what looked like a switch. Rocco flipped it, and a fluorescent light went on on the container's ceiling. Now he could see the scene in all its squalor. Heaped up on the floor were the few possessions of those people, wrapped in plastic trash bags or bundles of torn and filthy rags. Rocco walked the length of the container. His footsteps echoed metallically in the small space. He reached the end of the container. There was nothing else. Still, something didn't add up. He walked back, and this time he counted ten paces, stepping on papers, rags, and apple cores as he went. Then he jumped down out of the truck.

"What's going on?" asked Sebastiano, noticing Rocco's furrowed brow.

Rocco said nothing. He retraced the same ten paces outside the truck. He stopped. It was another three paces to the end of the truck's container.

"Seba?"

His friend walked over to him. "What is it?"

"The container is ten paces long. Which means it runs to here, you see? It's at least three yards from here to the end of the truck."

"What are you saying?"

"That there must be something in there, behind the container."

"What are we supposed to do about it? We can't hope to haul it out of there—you'd need a crane."

"Right, or else ..." And he felt the metal shell of the truck. He banged on it. Then he grabbed a rock and slammed it against the exterior of the truck. Not a scratch. "This sucker is tough."

"Do you want to try to punch a hole in the container?" Sebastiano suggested.

"With what?"

"We'll hammer it with a tire iron." Sebastiano turned around and headed toward the dark blue van. He opened the rear doors while the silent army of Sri Lankans watched the two men busy themselves around the truck. Italo was still talking with the man who'd presented his passport and with his brother. Sebastiano climbed into the truck, brandishing a cross-shaped tire iron. He walked back to the far end of the container and started banging away. The metal was barely dented, and aside from scratching the paint and making a hellish amount of noise, Sebastiano obtained no appreciable results. He threw the tire iron to the floor and came back. Outside the truck, Rocco was waiting for him. "Well?"

"Nothing. What we need here is a drill, a milling cutter, something like that."

Rocco looked around. Countryside with ditch on the right, countryside with trees on the left. He walked into the middle of the road. He walked toward the curve. Just then, Italo walked over to Sebastiano. "So they were heading for Turin. That's where they had an appointment with someone, I don't know, who was going to get them a place to stay and some paying work."

"What the hell do I care? I mean, I'm not a cop, Italo!" Sebastiano replied.

"I was just telling you what I found out," the officer replied. "I sweated my ass off to get that much information out of them." At least his lip wasn't swelling up. "What is he looking for?" the officer asked, motioning to the deputy police chief in the middle of the road.

"Who knows."

"What are we going to do with these people?" asked Italo. "We can't just leave them in the middle of the road here. They're going to freeze before long."

"Let's get them back aboard the truck. At least that'll keep them warm. I can't think of anything else," said the big man, throwing his arms wide. "You tell me, of all the things to have happened!"

Italo moved toward the column of Sri Lankans just as Rocco was coming back. Rocco saw him leading the group of huddled refugees toward the truck. "What are you doing?"

"Sebastiano says to put them back in the truck. Otherwise they'll freeze to death."

"No. I have a better idea. Sebastiano, you stay here and keep an eye out!" he shouted at his friend, who responded with an affirmative thumbs-up.

"You have your gun?"

Sebastiano pulled out a Beretta that he'd tucked under his belt behind his back and displayed it to Rocco.

"Excellent!" he shouted and headed off.

"So where are we going?"

"Get the people and tell them to follow us."

Italo nodded, went over to the man with the passport, and spoke to him in English. "Okay, you. Follow us. Follow!"

Marco Traversa and his wife, Carla, were returning home. They'd just spent a horrifying evening at dinner with old friends from high school. One of those reunions that Marco usually did his best to avoid. He knew that it's best after thirty years not to see old friends. They are never enjoyable evenings. They're hours and hours spent telling one another about health problems and troubles with your children or carefully calculating who's covered the most ground since school or kept the fullest head of hair. Marco worked in a bank. The Audi he drove was secondhand, and Carla worked from home, doing translations for a small Val d'Aosta publishing house. No children, no world travel, a humdrum existence. He didn't have a lot of stories to tell his former classmates. And he'd never much liked the role of the listener. Especially if that meant sitting and hearing Giuliano's stories about his sailboat or Elda talking about the pit bull puppies she raised in Champorcher. Luckily, Signor and Signora Traversa had been able to get away early with the excuse of a predawn appointment the following day and had left the newly renovated villa owned by the Miglios, with a good-night to the other fifteen members of their class, the old Terza B of the Liceo Classico XXVI Febbraio. The only thought that went through Marco's head as he took the curves on the road to the highway was the Breathalyzer test. If the highway patrol stopped him, he'd be in trouble. It wasn't as if he'd had a lot to drink, but everyone knew that two glasses were enough to get your license revoked, your credit card demagnetized, and a sentence of forced labor in Cividale del Friuli, breaking karst rock with a pick. He was driving slowly, just 45 miles per hour, even though Carla was urging him to accelerate, if nowhere else, at least on the straightaways, where, if the police are out, you can see them from miles away.

"After this curve I'll speed up, I promise," he told her with a smile. He took it at 40 miles an hour. Then, right in front of him, lit up by his car's halogen headlights, he saw a man in a loden overcoat, arms spread wide. Marco slammed on the brakes. "Shit!"

"What is it?" asked Carla.

"No idea. Let's hope nothing serious."

A second man wearing a police uniform went by in front of the windshield.

"Jesus fucking Christ, the highway police!" said Marco Traversa, gripping the steering wheel so hard that his knuckles whitened. He could just see his driver's license being shredded before his eyes and dropped on the asphalt. But to his surprise, the policeman ignored his Audi entirely. Instead he continued across the road.

"Where are they going?"

"Carla, what do I know?"

After the uniformed policeman, a dark-skinned man appeared. Skinny, short, slightly hunched over. Then another, and another, and another.

"Who ... who are they?" asked Carla in a faint voice. Marco stroked his chin. "No idea. I really have no idea."

Men, children, and women in saris with their heads covered continued crossing the road. As they went by the car, they smiled and greeted the couple inside with a slight nod of the head. Marco smiled back like an idiot, waving with one hand like a child. He and his wife watched that biblical diaspora, a desperate flock, black in the darkness of the night, dressed in rags and scarves.

"Are they Indians?" asked Carla.

"Huh ..." said Marco, "maybe so."

"But where are they going?"

"Come on, Carla. How am I supposed to know?"

They just kept coming. The stream of people never seemed to end. Then, as suddenly as they'd appeared, they vanished, swallowed up by the dark countryside. Marco waited, motor chugging, headlights illuminating the empty lane ahead. "What do you think? Should I go?"

"Go on, my love, you can go," said Carla as she caressed the hand with which he was gripping the stick shift. Marco Traversa put the car in first gear and slowly pulled out. He looked to the left, but there was no sign of that interminable single-file line of people.

When Emilio Marrix opened his front door, he saw a man wearing a loden overcoat, a police officer, and, half-hidden in the shadows of the larch trees, a group of men and women.

"Who ... who are you?" asked Emilio, and his cheeks, already flame red, turned redder still.

The man wearing the overcoat pulled out a badge. "Deputy Police Chief Schiavone, mobile squad of Aosta. This is Officer Pierron."

"My pleasure. Emilio Marrix, retired mailman," he replied with a smile, brushing back his full head of white hair.

"May we?"

Emilio nodded his head yes and stepped aside. Rocco walked in, followed by Italo. Then, one at a time, the Sri Lankans entered the house. Emilio smiled, having no idea what to do, and they responded by pressing their hands together over their hearts and bowing their heads ever so slightly.

"What can I do for you?" asked Emilio.

Rocco looked around at the interior of the house. A lovely little detached villa, neat as a pin, with the television on. In front of the television, on a velvet sofa, was a woman, fast asleep. A cat was curled up on the marble apron of a fireplace where a crackling fire burned. The wood-lined walls were dotted with landscape paintings. In one corner stood an easel and a half-finished canvas. Tubes of paint sat on a low, wheeled table.

"Are you the painter of the house?" Rocco asked.

"No, my wife," Emilio replied. "Ginevra!" he called.

Ginevra jerked awake. The minute she saw her living room as crowded as a commuter bus at rush hour, her eyes opened wide. "What … what's happening?"

"This gentleman is the deputy police chief of Aosta," her husband immediately reassured her.

The woman got up from the sofa. Her chin was quivering. She looked at the mass of people as she straightened her white hair with a simple gesture, then her hand adjusted her flower-print dress, and finally she pulled up the zipper of her green pile sweater.

"*Buona sera,*" she said in a faint, small voice.

"Don't be afraid," said Rocco. "Let me explain. We've pulled over a truck that was transporting a full load of these immigrants."

"Sure, but we don't have room here. All we have is an extra guest bedroom," Emilio objected.

The Sri Lankans had lined up along the interior walls. They stood more than three deep and left just enough space for Ginevra and her husband to talk to the policemen. The cat swished its tail. Then it started performing its ablutions, licking its forepaw.

"I'm not asking you to let them sleep here," said Rocco. "I'm just wondering if you could let these people stay inside, out of the cold, while my colleague and I finish up with the truck."

"They must be hungry," said Ginevra.

"Don't worry," said Rocco. "It won't be long. Emilio, can I ask you something?"

The master of the house flashed him a smile. "At this point, one thing more hardly makes a difference, does it?"

"Do you have a rotary cutter?"

"One of those power tools for cutting metal?"

"That's right."

"Yes, but it's battery-powered."

"All the better. Can I borrow it?"

"Certainly. Come with me. Excuse me …" Emilio was doing his best to push through the throng of Sri Lankans filling the few dozen square feet of his living room. "Excuse me, pardon me. Can I get through?" and he crossed the room, followed by Italo and Rocco. They managed to make their way through the mass of humanity and reached the front door. "Here we are, pardon me. May I?" he said to two women, who stepped aside, and managed to open his heavy security door. At last the three men were able to leave the house.

Ginevra was standing in the middle of her living room, looking at all the men and women with downcast eyes. They seemed to be ashamed.

"Does anyone here speak Italian?"

No answer. Not even a fly buzzed. Even the littlest ones remained silent: not a whimper. Ginevra looked a woman in the eye. She could have been thirty or she could have been fifty. She tried Italian and then French: *"Lei ... venga con me. Venez avec moi, okay?"* and waved for her to follow. *"Tout le monde,"* she said, addressing the whole room. *"Asseyez! Asseyez, s'il vous plaît."* And with her hands, she mimed instructions for everyone to sit down. Men and women started looking around for a place to sit. Some sat on the sofas, others on chairs, many on the floor. In the meantime, Ginevra and the woman went into the kitchen. The mistress of the house began to open cabinets and drawers. She pulled out everything edible that she could find and put it on the table. She spoke slowly and clearly. "Let's make a delicious bowl of pasta and whatever we have we'll share, all right? For the children I have milk. I milked the cow today. *Lait, compris? Pour les enfants!"* And she smiled at the woman, who thanked her, bowing her head. "I'm sorry there's so little to eat. Darn it, if I'd known you were coming I would have done some shopping." Then Ginevra started getting out pans and pots.

Sebastiano lay huddled among the crates, listening for any noises. The two truck drivers could come back at any moment, and there he was, half-hidden in the shadows, a bullet chambered, ready for them. Every rustling branch, every gust of breeze and snapping of a twig jolted his nerves into high alert. Shadows emerged from around the curve. He cocked the pistol. Then he eased the hammer back down with a smile. It was Rocco and Italo, accompanied by a man who looked to be in his early seventies, carrying a power tool of some kind.

"This is Emilio. He's going to help us," said Rocco. Emilio smiled at Sebastiano, and the two men shook hands. "He brought a rotary tool," Rocco added.

Emilio showed it to Sebastiano. "If a person isn't experienced with these things, it's best for them not to try to use one. That's why I came along."

Sebastiano glared at Rocco. But Rocco just shrugged. Then he climbed up into the truck and reached down to help Emilio up, but the old man clambered up unaided, in a surprising display of agility. The minute Emilio saw the container, he started shaking his head. "They were in here? That's out of this world!"

"Right? But it's actually very much part of this world, Signor Emilio. Come down here to the far end, if you would!"

Emilio went over to the deputy police chief, who was rapping his knuckles against the far wall of the container. "My dear Emilio, we have reason to suspect that there's something behind here."

"But the ones who were driving the truck, where are they, Dottore?"

"They ran away. All right, then, shall we punch a hole through here?"

"Certainly, certainly." Emilio grabbed the rotary cutter. "All right, then, stay back." He turned it on. The noise was deafening, and it was only amplified by the enclosed space. When the blade actually cut into the metal, it became intolerable. A shrill noise halfway between chalk on a blackboard and a dentist's drill. Outside the truck, Italo covered his ears. Sebastiano was keeping an eye on the road. But Rocco simply twisted up two pieces of paper and stuffed them in his ears.

Emilio took less than five minutes to open a space through which a ten-year-old child could easily pass. He turned off the saw and wiped his lips on his sleeve. "There you go."

Rocco went over to the cut while Italo and Sebastiano climbed up into the truck to take a look. The deputy police chief braced himself against the metal wall, then he delivered a kick to the middle of the cut sheet metal. It started to break loose. He kicked it again, and then a third time. Sebastiano and Italo stood there, eyes bulging, in a state of feverish anticipation. Emilio had taken a seat on one of the side benches and was politely awaiting further instructions.

On the fifth kick, the sheet metal finally yielded, falling into the secret compartment. Rocco picked up the flashlight and wiggled his way in. Sebastiano and Italo stepped closer to the opening.

Crates. Wooden crates. Square ones and rectangular ones, stacked up. In the narrow space, Rocco could barely manage to turn around. He shone his flashlight on the stacked crates while Sebastiano peered into the newly opened gap and did his best to read the words on the wooden crates.

"See if you find one marked CHANT NUMBER 4. That is our crate!"

"No such luck," Rocco replied. His voice echoed against the metal. "Just numbers."

"What's in them?"

"Couldn't say. Let's pull a few out and take a look."

The crates were heavy, and Emilio was helpful as ever. After an hour's hard work, sweaty and exhausted, the men sat down on the crates that they'd unloaded onto the roadside. A wooden pyramid. Each case had a padlock. And a mysterious code written on the side. The sky had cleared, and the chilly stars were blinking down from on high. It was one in the morning, and there were no more cars going past on the road. Emilio came back with a nice hot thermos. "Here. My wife made some coffee. She gave those poor wretches some food. Now they're all asleep."

They poured out the coffee. It was good and, most important, it was hot. Rocco and Italo each lit a cigarette. "Now what do we do, Rocco?"

"Let's open them up and see what's inside."

With a sure cut from the rotary blade, Emilio sawed the padlock off the first crate. Rocco opened it. It was filled with straw. Under the straw were rectangles of a plasticky-looking material.

"Holy shit!" shouted the deputy police chief.

"What is it?" asked Sebastiano.

"Plastic."

Sebastiano and Italo exchanged a glance. Emilio was baffled. "Plastic?"

"Plastic explosives," Italo corrected him.

Emilio's eyes opened wide in fright.

"Let's open another. Come on, Emilio."

"At your orders!"

In the second crate they found automatic assault rifles. More plastic explosives. Then detonators. Still more plastic explosives. A disassembled shoulder-mounted rocket launcher. Ammunition.

Seated on the opened crates, the four men looked at one another in bewilderment. "Sebastia', I'm starting to have some doubts," said Rocco. "You don't think that 'Chant number 4' stands for C-4, do you? Plastic explosive? Look how much of it there is!"

Sebastiano nodded. "Maybe so. What the hell was I thinking? I should never have trusted Ernst," his friend replied.

"Let's call the police!" Emilio suggested.

Rocco slapped him on the shoulder. "We *are* the police, Emilio." Sebastiano and Italo exchanged a baffled glance. "All right," the deputy police chief continued, "now why don't you take your rotary tool and head on home. Get yourself some rest, because you've probably caught a chill. Thanks for all the help you've given us. Without you, we couldn't have done a thing." The retired postal worker smiled and nodded. "Ah, don't mention it, it was nothing. In fact, I really enjoyed it, you know?"

"All right, go take care of Ginevra. Then we'll catch up with you and decide what to do with the Sri Lankans."

"All right. I'm heading back then. I'll wait for you inside. It's been a pleasure to help you. A real adventure, a real adventure …" And Emilio headed home with his saw and a light step.

"The thing to do here is call Interpol, if you ask me!" said Sebastiano. "No, seriously, do you realize what we have here? This is a military-grade arsenal!"

"Yes, we're going to have to impound the truck. No two fucking ways about it," Rocco said and flicked away the dead cigarette butt that he still had clamped between his lips.

"Chant number 4!" shouted Italo.

"What?" called Sebastiano and Rocco in unison.

Italo was squatting on the ground, peering at the side of a crate. "Right here—it says CHANT NUMBER 4!"

The two men went over. It was true. On one of the crates, someone had written CHANT NUMBER 4 with a marker. Sebastiano and Rocco looked at each other. Rocco grabbed an automatic rifle from the closest crate and, with two sharp cracks of the rifle butt, broke open the lock. They opened the crate. Inside were eight stone Buddha heads. Sebastiano grabbed one. He smashed it on the road. Among the fragments were three cellophane packets full of marijuana. The smiles returned to Rocco's and Sebastiano's lips. And to Italo's as well. This was what they had come for.

"Come on!" shouted Sebastiano, picking up the packets they'd just found and three more of the Buddha heads. "Let's get moving!" He trotted over to the van. "Good work, Ernst, *bravo*! It was true!" he kept shouting at the top of his lungs.

Italo and Rocco finished loading the sculptures. Then Sebastiano turned to look at his friend. "I'm going. No question, I'm leaving you in a sea of shit."

"Don't worry. In any case, you know my account number, right?"

"Three days tops and you'll have your money."

"Him too!" said Rocco, pointing at Italo.

"We can take care of him right here and now!" Sebastiano stuffed his hand into his pocket. He pulled out a wad of green one-hundred-euro banknotes. "Thirty-five hundred. Here, go ahead and count it."

"I trust you," said the officer as he pocketed the money.

Sebastiano slapped him on the back, got behind the wheel of the van, and put it into reverse. "*Ciao*, Italo. You're a good kid. See you soon, Rocco!"

"See you round, my friend. Don't forget about me. Stay in touch."

"Say hi to the Ukrainian chick if you see her."

"I'll be sure to."

The van vanished into the night, engine roaring as Sebastiano accelerated. Italo and the deputy police chief stood there watching until the taillights were swallowed up by the darkness.

"Okay. Now what about the Sri Lankans?"

Rocco pointed to the truck, with its lights still on. "Do you know how to drive this thing?"

"I even know how to drive a semi-trailer. Why?"

"It's a ninety-minute drive from here to Turin." Rocco looked at his watch. "It's one forty a.m. right now. Say we load up, you take off, and you're in Turin by three thirty. You drop off the Sri Lankans, and by five thirty you're back here."

"And then?"

"And then at six a.m. I'll call headquarters. And then all hell breaks loose. Does it strike you as a good idea?"

"Give me that thermos full of espresso, otherwise I'll be asleep by the time I reach Verrès."

Rocco handed Italo the thermos, then walked toward the truck's cab. He sat down behind the wheel. Fastened to the windshield, in plain view, was the GPS. Rocco smiled and shouted to Italo: "The address in Turin is right here. You're in luck, my friend. You won't even have to leave the highway. It's at a service area. Happy?"

"For thirty-five hundred euros, I'll take this truck all the way to Catania!"

Rocco climbed out of the back. "By the way. Give me five hundred euros. I'll repay you tomorrow."

"What for?"

"We parked eighty-seven Sri Lankans in his house. Don't you think we ought to give him a little something for his troubles?"

Italo nodded and pulled out the wad of cash.

"All right, I'm going to get those poor wretches. You stay here. Stand guard—pistol in hand. Those two piece-of-shit truck drivers could show up again. This load is too important. Keep your eyes open, take it from me."

The sky was starting to lighten. Sitting on a wooden crate with a semiautomatic AK-47 in his lap and what seemed like the thousandth cigarette in his mouth, Rocco Schiavone was waiting. He was thinking about Ginevra and Emilio, who had accepted everything that had happened without a word. They'd even objected when he offered them the five hundred euros, but in the end Rocco had won out. They promised not to say anything about the Sri Lankans, and in fact they supported the deputy police chief's decision not to report their presence to the authorities. Forgetting the minor detail that in this case, the authorities were none other than Rocco Schiavone himself.

The cars that went by slowed down to stare at that strange pile of wooden crates abandoned on the roadside and the man dressed in a flower-pattern down jacket sitting with an assault rifle in his lap, like an old Apache lying in ambush. It was five in the morning on a freezing-cold Sunday, and the temperature was like that of the freezer aisle at a supermarket. If it hadn't been for the coffees, the grappas, the prosciutto, and the chocolate that Ginevra had brought him continuously until four in the morning, along with the flower-pattern down jacket, Rocco would have wound up like an amateur mountain climber recklessly challenging Everest. His nose was red, and he could no longer feel his ears. Otherwise, aside from the pain in his knees, he was doing fine. He'd followed Emilio's advice and had kept his legs inside the straw-filled plastic-explosives case.

Finally he saw in the distance the truck's headlights approaching. Italo was back half an hour early. The deputy police chief stood up, flicked the cigarette far away from the crates, folded up the down jacket, and walked over to the road. The truck slowed to a halt, screeching like a locomotive, then the brakes ground down and it finally rolled to a stop next to the deputy police chief. Italo's face, tired but smiling, appeared at the window. "All taken care of, boss. I'm going to park this thing!"

Rocco smiled. "Go ahead, Italo, go ahead!" Then he grabbed his cell phone, thrilled at the idea of yanking the chief of police, the judge, journalists, and everyone else out of bed.

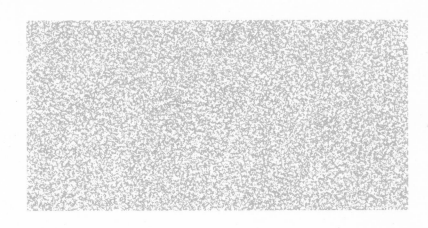

SUNDAY

The whole thing had a national impact. The police chief was beside himself with pleasure and kept holding press conferences one after another, even though it was a Sunday. The magistrate hailed the intelligence and enterprise of a deputy police chief and an obscure officer with a brilliant future ahead of him, and unbridled speculation began on whom that arsenal might have been intended for. Italo and Rocco had agreed on a story, and they stuck to it. A tip from an informant on the border who was friends with the deputy police chief, the escape of the two truck drivers, and the chance discovery of the explosives.

"Certainly, that container, so big and completely empty …: it's just strange," the police chief said, and the judge echoed that sentiment. And Rocco had spread his arms wide and smiled. "Evidently, someone unloaded some of the cargo before the border, or who knows what else."

Not a word about the Sri Lankans, and those men and

women faded back into indistinct shadows in the everyday lives of Italian citizens.

"Did you know that inside the driver's cab we even found a baggie of marijuana?" Chief of Police Corsi went on.

Rocco had smiled and shrugged helplessly once again. "What can you do about them? Those people are godless heathens."

"Yeah. Driving a behemoth like that while they were high as Jimi Hendrix. It's pure insanity."

"You know who Jimi Hendrix is?"

The police chief fell silent for a moment. "*Caro* Dottor Schiavone, when you were still in fifth grade, yours truly was dancing to the notes of 'Hey Joe,' 'Little Wing,' and 'Killing Floor' outside the architecture building."

"I can't believe it! You were a sixties radical?"

"I was nineteen years old and I was in love."

"Did you battle the police in the streets with the rest of them?"

"No. I turned and ran. Now I think that the two of us have more important things to do, don't you agree?"

The rest of that Sunday Rocco just spent sleeping. And he missed Roma–Udinese. But it wasn't such a big loss. The Rome team took a heavy beating.

MONDAY

Rocco didn't like hospitals, and he especially didn't like morgues. But Alberto Fumagalli worked in one, and Rocco knew that if you want things done right and fast, the best thing is to have them done by someone who's very busy. When the door to the morgue swung open and Alberto emerged with his usual apron spotted with rust-brown stains—or maybe it wasn't rust after all—Rocco got to his feet and walked toward him.

"I just got a phone call from the lab. The tests on the blood from the piece of tissue you brought in are ready."

"This afternoon is Leone's funeral."

"Yes, I know. I sent all the autopsy results to Magistrate Baldi. I worked all weekend. On the internal organs and so on and so forth."

"Did you figure out anything fundamental?"

"Yes. Leone Miccichè was in excellent health."

"Nothing else?"

"I'd bet my left testicle—in fact I'd bet them both—that Leone died between seven and nine that night."

Rocco stopped in the middle of the hallway. "Do you know what that means?"

"Yes. Practically speaking, Amedeo Gunelli killed him unintentionally. When he ran that Sherman tank of a snowcat over him, odds are that Leone was still alive. Half-frozen, buried under eight inches of snow, but still alive. Bad luck, eh?"

"You think so?"

They continued walking and left the hallway from the morgue to catch the elevator. "You look tired," said Alberto. "I heard you pulled off quite a coup last night."

"Yes. We impounded some firearms."

"That was a nice piece of luck, eh?"

"It's just a matter of having the right information."

Alberto looked at him with a blank gaze, the look he usually put on when he wanted to make sure no one could make a fool of him. "Who was in that container?"

Rocco scratched his head. "Eighty-seven Sri Lankan immigrants."

"Where did you take them?"

"To Turin. They had a contact there who had jobs for them."

Alberto Fumagalli nodded a couple of times. The elevator doors opened, and they walked out. "You're quite an asshole, Rocco."

"I know."

"Would you have done the same thing if they were Romanians?"

"First of all, I don't bring race into this. There's no such thing as race. And after all, Romanians are members of the European Community, so they hardly have to be smuggled across the border. They can enter freely."

"*Touché!*"

"Fuck off."

"I love you, Rocco."

"Enough with the faggoty talk, Alberto."

"No, I really mean it."

"If you knew me better, you wouldn't say such a thing."

"Now you're the one who's starting to talk like a cocksucker."

"How much farther is it to the lab?"

"Not far. Why?"

"Because carrying on a conversation with you is exhausting, and it puts me into a state of emotional apprehension."

"Rocco, you don't have the capacity for emotional apprehension." Then Alberto opened the lab door.

The technician handed the deputy police chief a sheet of paper. "The blood on the tissue that you gave us belongs to Group O negative 4.4."

"Why, that's the same blood group that we found on the bandanna that was stuffed in Leone's mouth!" Alberto exclaimed.

"Fuck," Rocco Schiavone murmured between clenched teeth.

"Is it bad news?" asked the medical examiner.

"It is for Omar Borghetti. The blood on the tissue is his. I took it off him with a slightly unorthodox method. See you around, Alberto. *Grazie!*"

"Then we've nailed him! I love you," he shrieked after him, then the medical examiner broke into solemn laughter while the lab door closed behind Rocco.

Beethoven's "Ode to Joy" alerted Rocco to the fact that his phone was ringing. He picked up without glancing at the display. "Schiavone here, who is it?"

"Italo speaking, Dottore. Forgive the intrusion."

Italo was addressing him formally, which meant that he was sitting next to someone else at police headquarters.

"What is it, Italo?"

"You need to come in to the office. Inspector Rispoli showed me something that I think you'll be very interested in."

"Can you give me some idea?"

"No. Because it's a sealed envelope. And I have a feeling that you ought to read it."

The letterhead stationery read, LAB 2000—LABORATORY FOR CLINICAL ANALYSES. The envelope was addressed to Leone Miccichè.

"The postmaster brought it straight here just a couple of hours ago. I took the liberty," said Inspector Rispoli.

"You did the right thing."

Rocco opened the envelope. They were charts with medical tests. Spermiogram, scrotal ultrasound, TSH test, semen culture. Rocco tried to read it and understand some of it. "Azoospermia. What's that?"

"What does it say, Dottore?"

"No idea. It looks like these are medical tests that Leone had done ... let's see when"—he turned over the sheet, and the date stood out—"not even fifteen days ago."

"What kind of tests?"

"Well, just guessing, but I'd say fertility tests."

Rocco handed the sheets of paper to Italo. "Here, call Fumagalli. Get him to tell you what this stuff is. And have him call me on the cell phone—I'm going to see the judge."

He got up from the chair and slapped Inspector Rispoli on the back. "Good work, Caterina. If you ask me, this is something very important!"

Caterina blushed.

"Do you want an arrest warrant?" Magistrate Baldi asked Deputy Police Chief Rocco Schiavone.

"Not yet. You see, there's still something that doesn't add up. The blood on the red bandanna found stuffed down the corpse's throat belongs to Omar Borghetti with a ninety-five percent probability, which ought to pin the murder on him, but still ..."

The judge leaned toward the deputy police chief. "But still what?"

"You see, as I explained to you yesterday, Leone Miccichè smoked a cigarette up there in the middle of the shortcut. He took off his gloves, probably to light the cigarette. We never found the cigarette butt. Still, traces of tobacco were found on the scene of the crime."

"What does that matter?"

"Omar Borghetti doesn't smoke."

"So, who cares? That just means that the tobacco came from Leone's cigarette, no?"

"No. Leone smoked Marlboro Lights. Always did. The tobacco is a different kind."

The judge sprawled back in his chair, emitting a loud sigh. "So that means that whoever was with him does smoke, and doesn't smoke Marlboros?"

"Right. And I've come to the conclusion that the killer offered Leone a cigarette. And that he smoked it. First because, otherwise, we'd have found traces of Marlboros along with the traces of this other type of tobacco. Second because his wife told us that he'd smoked the last of his cigarettes. Okay, I'm a smoker, so I know that when I have three left in the pack, I say that I'm out of cigarettes and I go out to buy more, but still the pack found on the corpse was empty. The odds are very good that he didn't have any."

"But the cigarette butt? Why wasn't that found? The filter, something …?"

"Because the son of a bitch who murdered him collected them all. They're evidence, no?"

The judge started toying with his pen. He chewed on it a little while looking Rocco in the eye. "But you have an idea, don't you?"

"Me? Sure. But I'm missing just one detail, and then the whole thing starts to take on a whole new light. You see?

Omar Borghetti would have a motive. Jealousy—he finds out that now Luisa Pec is pregnant and he takes it out on the new boyfriend. But why wait three years? Why wait for them to get married? Do you see that it doesn't add up?"

"Yeah, it doesn't."

"So there has to be a different motive."

"Money?"

"Not only. Luisa and Leone owed Omar a hundred thousand euros. Business was so-so. Leone was desperately trying to sell his properties down in Sicily to try to make ends meet. And he'd almost persuaded his brother to do it. A brother who, just between you and me, wasn't exactly crazy about Leone."

Baldi stood up brusquely. "And if it wasn't about money?"

"Ode to Joy" rang in the pocket of Rocco's coat. "Do you mind? I'm expecting a very important phone call."

"Go right ahead."

"Schiavone here, who is it?"

"*Ciao*, Rocco. It's me again, your favorite medical examiner!"

"Did you read the test results?"

"Well, you hardly need a college degree to understand them."

"Well, what do they say?"

"One very simple thing: Leone Miccichè was infertile. He couldn't have children. In fact, his semen test showed findings of azoospermia."

"Azoospermia? What's that?"

"Not a single spermatozoon in one milliliter of semen. Just consider that the minimum expected count would be twenty million.

"And there's more: this wasn't his first fertility test. Let's just say that these tests are the mother of all sperm tests, and I'm putting it that way so even a poor rube like you can understand it."

"Explain."

Alberto Fumagalli sighed in exasperation. "All right, before getting such a complete and accurate analysis, Leone must have been to a doctor who sent him in for it, and who must have already had his own well-founded suspicions. In other words, he'd almost certainly been to see a doctor. Then he went to the clinic and got these tests done."

"How can I find out the name of the doctor who ordered the tests?"

"Easy. Call the lab. They ought to have a record of the physician's referral. Which would include last name and even address."

"Thanks, Alberto—I owe you dinner!"

"Don't be silly. I didn't do anything special. Bye," and he hung up.

"Did I just hear what I think I did?" asked Baldi.

"I'd say so."

"Then who got Luisa Pec pregnant?"

"The son of a bitch who murdered Leone. Poor Leone must have figured out what was going on, he went to have his sperm tested, and the other guy found out about the testing. Does that make sense?"

"I'd say so. But what about the blood on the handkerchief? It belonged to Omar Borghetti, no?"

"I have an idea about that too. You take care of yourself. I hope to be back inside twenty-four hours with our little friend in handcuffs."

Rocco stood up. He slipped his cell phone back into his pocket. The judge called him back. "You're good. But that's something I already knew. Still, there's just one thing I'd like you to explain to me."

"What's that?"

"You see, the half-empty truck, with all the weapons."

Rocco put on his best innocent face. "Yes?"

"There's something there that doesn't quite work."

"Tell me about it, Dottore."

"The GPS. It kept a record of all the addresses. One of them was just outside Turin, on the highway, in a parking area."

Rocco gulped without realizing it.

"The other one, though, was … was …" And he started looking for a sheet of paper in the pile on his desk. "Here it is. Alekse Šantića, though who knows if that's the right way to pronounce the name. It's a street in the small town of Bečići, in Montenegro."

"Mmm."

"Bečići is close to a nice city called Budva."

"Mmm."

"Stop ruminating. Interpol was alerted early this morning. There's a good chance that the weapons were being sent there. Budva is a port city, did you know that?"

"I do now."

"But it's just that—and work with me here—if the weapons were almost certainly being sent down there, then why did we find the address of a parking area just outside Turin?"

Rocco started to feel a cold sweat dripping down his spine.

"So you know what I decided to do?"

"Please tell me."

"I asked the highway authority for their video feed of the A5, the Aosta–Turin highway. To see if that truck went that way. And as long as I was at it, I asked for the pictures from the service areas, too. And you won't believe what they told me."

He's got you! Rocco said to himself. *Caught in a trap, like a mouse in a cellar.*

"There were no pictures," the judge went on.

"What?"

"Just think, there was a breakdown of the A5's entire computer system. They fixed it, but there are no pictures left from last night. That's a shame, isn't it?" He looked at Rocco with a sinister smile, a smile that the deputy police chief had seen before only on the mouths of Mafia big shots and a few very ambitious politicians. The smile of someone who knows. But prefers not to say.

The deputy police chief cleared his throat. "That's a pity. If something can go wrong, it always will, eh?"

The judge looked at Rocco. "That's right, it's a pity. Or else a tremendous piece of luck. Am I right, Deputy Police Chief? Bring me the guy who murdered Leone Miccichè, Dottor

Schiavone. And I'll forget all about what happened with this container in Turin. Consider it advice from a friend."

Rocco nodded twice. He thanked Magistrate Baldi with a glance, then slipped through the door and left the office.

At 10:10, Italo and Rocco were already heading for Champoluc.

"Does your lip hurt?"

"No. The cold practically anesthetized it."

"My ears are starting to pop." Rocco held his nose and blew hard.

"Doing that can give you sinusitis."

"Lots of things are bad for you, Italo. One more or less ..."

Italo downshifted. "Should we be worried?"

"About what?"

"What do you mean, 'about what'? About the Sri Lankans."

"No, don't sweat it. Everything's okay. In fact, don't let me forget that I owe you five hundred euros."

"They don't suspect anything?"

Rocco drummed his knuckles on the glass. "Magistrate Baldi knows."

Italo went pale. "Knows what? About the grass?"

"No, he doesn't know about the grass. He knows about the Sri Lankans."

"Oh, shit!"

"Right. He dreamed up some bullshit about a software glitch with the highway authority. He saw the pictures, no doubt about it!"

Italo ran his hand over his mouth. "What's he going to do?"

"I don't know. I can't tell whether he's keeping this thing so that he has a hold on me or if he's just letting it slide. Baldi's not exactly normal."

"While you totally are, right?"

The deputy police chief burst out in a robust and croupy belly laugh. It was the first time Italo had heard him laugh like this, so freely. Suddenly he found himself laughing, too.

And they laughed. Together. All the way to the frozen fountain at the village gate. They stopped only when they saw two men putting up purple-and-black bunting over the portal of the church. They'd forgotten that Leone Miccichè's funeral was today.

"Are we going to get there in time?" asked Italo.

"Of course we'll get there in time. This won't take long at all. Take a right at the next intersection. There—it's upstairs from the grocery store."

On the third floor of a small building made of stone and wood was the office of Dr. Alfonso Lorisaz. Rocco climbed the stairs. He pushed open the door with the brass plaque that read, ALFONSO LORISAZ—SPECIALIST IN THE GENITOURINARY SYSTEM. He went in. The waiting room was full of people. When the policeman made his entrance, every head swiveled in his direction. A nurse who looked about sixty was sitting at a desk, printing out prescriptions.

"Yes?" she asked Rocco, keeping her eyes glued to the computer monitor in front of her.

"Schiavone. I need to talk to the doctor."

"Do you have an appointment?"

Rocco reached out and held his police badge in front of the monitor. That was when the woman finally raised her eyes.

"Do I have your attention now?"

"Yes."

"I'm Deputy Police Chief Schiavone, and I don't have an appointment. But I'm also quite confident that you're going to find a way to keep me from having to wait in line, *n'est-ce pas?*"

The nurse leaped to her feet and went to knock on the doctor's door. She went in. When she came out a few seconds later, her cheeks were bright red. "The doctor's finished with his patient. He'll see you now."

"Excellent!"

It was almost embarrassingly easy to classify Alfonso Lorisaz in the deputy police chief's mental bestiary. He was clearly a rodent from the suborder Sciuromorpha, and specifically a *Castor fiber*, the Eurasian beaver. His buck teeth and his eyes concealed behind a pair of tiny, round gold-framed spectacles, his small, apparently webbed hands, his bald head and the tuft of chest hairs bristling out at the shirt collar. He looked as if he'd just finished building a dam and was now sniffing the air nervously in search of impending danger. He leaped to his feet the instant Rocco walked into his office. He couldn't have been taller than five foot seven.

"What can I do for you?" Alfonso squeaked.

"I got your name from LAB 2000, which is down in Aosta, for a test referral that you authorized for Leone Miccichè. You know him, don't you?"

"Certainly I know him. I knew him, I should say. Poor man. He was a likable guy, you know? I remember—"

"Stop. The deputy police chief isn't here to find out about your interpersonal relationships. Tell me one thing: you do remember why he had come in to see you, right?"

"Of course. And I examined him. I did a preliminary analysis of Leone and I identified his problem. Then I prescribed some tests. My diagnosis—"

"Stop. The deputy police chief isn't interested in your diagnosis. In any case, if you care to know, Leone was found to be sterile."

"That's what I assumed. Do you happen to remember his sperm count? Just out of curiosity."

"Azoospermia. Not a single spermatozoon in one milliliter of semen. Happy now?"

"I'm not happy. I was just certain."

"Listen to me, now, Dr. Lorisaz, did you talk to anyone about this case?"

"This case … You mean Leone?"

"Right."

"No, not that I remember. But you know, this is a small town."

"What are you trying to say?"

"Word gets around. You know why I say that? We're all sort of related. It's not like in the city. Here everybody knows everybody else's business."

"If you had kept this information to yourself, how could anyone else have found out about it?"

"You're certainly right, but …"

"But you didn't keep the information to yourself."

"No, no, I certainly did, and how. I said nothing to anyone, of course; such a sensitive subject."

"Well?"

"Well, what can I say? We did the first semen culture here, in a little lab that I have on the ground floor. Maybe the nurse found out. Or someone else, who can say?"

Rocco looked the doctor hard in the eye, those little eyes protected behind lenses. "Why do I have the feeling that someone's hiding something?"

"It's a mistaken feeling, Mr. Deputy Police Chief. I didn't tell anyone anything."

"Listen, this is very important. There's a murder mixed up in it, and if you're concealing information, you could be committing a felony and facing jail time. It's required by law to assist in an investigation, in case you didn't know."

"Oh, Lord, now you're starting to worry me."

"Good. By all means, worry."

The doctor looked at the floor, as if hoping to find help in the cracks between the terra-cotta tiles. Rocco knew that he was actually thinking about the smartest and least painful way out of the corner he was in. He blinked his eyes and bit his lips with his two buck teeth.

"Do you remember anything?"

The doctor had clearly run through his own calculations, and now he replied, "Nothing that could interest you. I don't think I told anyone about it."

"I hope you just told me the truth. Are you married?"

"Me? Yes. Why?"

"Can I ask your wife's name?"

The doctor's eyes bulged. "Why?"

"Professional curiosity."

"Certainly. My wife is called Annarita."

"Annarita. I imagine she has a last name, no?"

"Same as me, Lorisaz."

"I mean her maiden name."

"Pec. Just like poor Leone's widow. Annarita and Luisa are third cousins."

Annarita Pec. The young woman at the ski shop. The one who had rejected him with courtesy, dignity, and firmness. "Oh, right, you're all more or less related here, aren't you?"

"It is true. But why are you asking me that?"

"Because, you see, maybe one night, when you got home, you were chatting with your wife and you inadvertently let Leone Miccichè's secret slip. Couldn't that be the case?"

Alfonso heaved a deep sigh, shrugging as he did so. "Oh, Lord, I couldn't say. I'm certain I'd remember. Anyway, even if I had, my wife knows how to keep private information private."

"In other words, we can safely rely on her discretion?"

"Certainly, Dottore," said the physician, smiling as if a weight had just been lifted from his shoulders. "My wife is a vault."

"Your metaphor is in extremely poor taste, Dr. Lorisaz. Have a good day."

Italo started up the BMW at the very instant Rocco was coming out the front door of the doctor's building. As soon as he shut the car door, Italo released the clutch. "Where are we going now?"

"To catch the cableway. The doctor spoke to his wife about Leone's tests."

Italo steered around an old man who was walking down the icy road with a pair of skis on his shoulder like Christ on Calvary. "Well, maybe his wife didn't tell anyone."

"The doctor's wife is Luisa's cousin. And do you really think she didn't tell her? Her or maybe Mario, her friend at the bar?"

"Maybe so. Yes, you're right, Rocco. But why would she do it?"

"It's a small town. Gossip? Rumors? Or else out of a healthy and widespread feminine virtue. It's called sadism. Ever heard of it?"

"I'll say."

The sun rode high above and had triumphed over the clouds. The skiers were so many colorful ants swarming over a massive spill of sugar. Rocco and Italo were walking toward the ski school offices. They strode briskly. Under the hot sunlight, Rocco's loden overcoat released plumes of water vapor from the shoulders, giving him the appearance of a smoking demon straight out of the book of Apocalypse. They ran into Luigi, the head snowcat operator, intently rolling himself a cigarette as always. "*Buon giorno*, Deputy Police Chief!"

"*Buon giorno*, Luigi. You going to offer me a cigarette?"

"Certainly." And he held out the newly hand-rolled cigarette.

"Mmm, I used to smoke these in high school."

"They're the only ones I can stand."

"What kind of tobacco do you use, Luigi?"

"Samson. It's the best." Luigi lit the deputy police chief's cigarette. "Did you come up for the funeral today, Dottore?"

"You going?"

"Of course I am. Everybody is."

"Then we'll see you later, down in the church."

"You want to head down with me?" Luigi said, pointing to his four-wheel-drive quad. "I'd let you drive. A steep descent is more fun."

"No, no, you go ahead. I'll see you there. This is a good smoke, though. It's a little strong, but this tobacco kicks it."

When Rocco Schiavone walked into the office, he saw the slightly overweight ski instructor sitting at the desk and another, older instructor busy doing a diagramless crossword puzzle. As soon as she saw Rocco and Italo come in, the woman stood up. "Deputy Police Chief!" she said.

"Deputy Police Chief: that's correct! You're finally starting to get it right." Rocco looked around, then he headed over to the group photograph of the ski instructors of the Val d'Ayas.

"Did you ever find Omar Borghetti?"

Rocco didn't answer; he was focused on that group photo. Italo gestured to the woman to be quiet. She nodded, a little frightened.

"When was this picture taken?"

"At the start of the season."

"Is there a cabinet here where people keep their personal possessions?"

"This right here," said the woman, pointing to a low bin with a lid and a keyhole.

Rocco went over to it. "Do you keep it locked?"

"No. There's nothing in it but junk. Especially Omar's things."

Rocco squatted down and pulled open the lid. He pulled out a pair of ski goggles, a wool cap, a pair of white Gore-Tex gloves, lip balm, suntan lotion, two spare T-shirts, and two neckerchiefs, one green and one blue. "The kid is good," he said aloud, and no one understood whom he was talking about. Italo had a suspicion, but he kept it to himself.

"Three down: series of senseless actions performed in a state of anxiety. First letter *j*, last letter *r*. Eleven letters," said the ski instructor, lost in that week's copy of the puzzle magazine, *La Settimana Enigmistica*.

Rocco looked at him. "Jactitation."

"Wow, that's right—it fits with seven across! *Grazie!*" the man exclaimed happily, and he wrote it in on his crossword puzzle just as Omar Borghetti's backlit silhouette appeared in the office door.

"Dottore!" he said, pulling off his gloves and bringing a gust of clean air into the wood-lined office. He too was wearing a red down jacket and black trousers, but there was a handsome yellow bandanna tied around his neck.

"Ah, Omar Borghetti," said Rocco. "With the light behind you, I hadn't recognized you. You're exactly who I'm looking for. Where is it?"

"Where's what?" asked Omar, tossing his ski gloves down on the table.

"The red bandanna. The one you're wearing in this picture." And he pointed at the group photograph hanging on the wall. "In the laundry?"

"No. It ought to be in there," he said and went over to the bin that Rocco had just explored.

"It's not there."

"What do you mean, it's not there? I have a red one, a blue one, a green one, and this yellow one." He tugged at the bandanna tied around his neck.

Rocco took the two bandannas, one green and the other blue, between thumb and forefinger and held them up as if they were two dead mice. "Here's the blue one and the green one. But the red one's missing."

The bandannas dangled inertly in front of Omar's face. "I don't understand."

"But I understand, Omar."

Omar looked around confusedly at his co-workers. "What does this mean? What does my red handkerchief have to do with this?"

"Oh, believe me, quite a lot!" Rocco looked at Italo. Italo understood instantly and continued, taking over from his boss. "The red handkerchief was found on Leone Miccichè's corpse."

Omar turned pale. The silence of the tundra fell over the office, and it seemed as if the temperature had just dropped twenty degrees. The older ski instructor looked up from his crossword puzzle while the young woman put her face in her hands.

"On the … corpse?" Omar Borghetti murmured. "But, excuse me, do you know how many red bandannas there are around here? Why would you assume that it was mine? Maybe mine's at home in the laundry, no?"

"No," Rocco replied tersely.

"Why not, Deputy Police Chief?"

"Believe me, Borghetti. That one is yours. And you know how I know that?"

Omar shook his head.

"Because there were bloodstains on that red handkerchief that you like to wear around your neck"—and here Rocco walked over close to Omar—"and the blood belongs to your blood group. O negative 4.4. Same as you. Not good, eh?"

Omar suddenly needed to sit down. "How … How?"

"Forget about how I know these things. But I've come to a conclusion. And at this point, I'm very sorry, but I'm going to have to tell you something you're not going to like very much." Rocco leaned on the armrests of his chair and tilted forward till their faces were about four inches apart, so that Omar could smell the tobacco and the espresso on his breath. But he wasn't looking in Omar's eyes. He was observing his neck. Very closely.

"What ... are you going to tell me?"

"You need to buy some new razors."

On the cable car that was taking him back down to town, Rocco was silent. Italo limited himself to looking up at the blue sky, against which the ridgelines of the peaks and the glaciers stood out. The deputy police chief had placed his elbows on his knees and sat, hunched over, his hands in front of his mouth, moving his fingers ever so slightly, as if he were playing the trumpet. Officer Pierron, on the other hand, had a hollow feeling in the pit of his stomach, and the sudden jerks and lurches of the cableway only made things worse. The creaking of the cabin and the wind rattling through the air vents accompanied the cable car on its rapid descent toward Champoluc. Already he could make out the snow-covered roofs of the houses and the skiers' parked cars, reflecting silvery shafts of sunlight back up into the air.

"What time is it?"

"Almost one," Italo replied.

"What time does it get dark?"

"At five. Why?"

"We should wait until five. There are some things that ought to be done without a lot of show, don't you think?"

No, Italo didn't think so. Largely because he didn't have the slightest idea what the deputy police chief was talking about—though a sneaking suspicion was starting to take shape in his mind, a little more substantial with each passing moment. The one false note was the strange gloom that was enveloping Rocco. If, as he sensed, they had come to the end of the case, he would have expected to see a smiling deputy chief. But not so. Rocco's face and posture told a very different story. His eyes were dull and melancholy; there was a film that doused their usual gleam. It even looked as if Rocco had a few new gray hairs. Actually, as Officer Pierron knew full well, he'd always had those gray hairs, but now he noticed them more. They stood out and seemed to have overpowered Rocco's chestnut brown hair.

It was as if in just a few minutes, ten years of youth had poured off of Rocco Schiavone.

"You wait for me here, at Mario and Michael's bar. Have a panino, drink a beer, kick back. I won't be long."

"Where are you going?" asked Italo.

All it took was one savage glare from Rocco and Italo answered his own question. "I need to learn to mind my own business."

Rocco smiled and left the officer outside the bar.

He walked a hundred yards or so along the sidewalk until he reached the ski shop. He went in. The bell rang, echoing off the wood-paneled walls and the ski outfits on display. Annarita popped out of a door behind the cash register.

"*Buon giorno*. What's wrong, aren't you happy with the boots?"

"No, the shoes are great. It's you I'm disappointed in."

The woman's cheeks turned bright red, highlighting even more her glistening hazel eyes.

"Me? What have I done wrong? If you're referring to our conversation the last time you were here—"

"That has nothing to do with it. I'm a good loser; I have a sense of sportsmanship. I just wanted to give you a piece of free advice."

She was studying him with a nervous gaze. She didn't understand where Rocco was heading with this line of conversation. He went on: "There are things that are best kept to yourself, you know. Private matters, personal or family secrets. It's not a good idea to flaunt them around as if they were the latest items from this year's fashions."

"I don't know what you're talking about."

"Your husband. He's a doctor."

"That's right. So what?"

"Whom did you tell that Leone Miccichè was sterile?"

The smile faded from Annarita's lips, and her eyes widened like two deep wells, the bottoms of which were lost to view. She almost staggered, and in fact she put down one hand on the display case that held wool caps. "What? Are you saying that … How …?"

"You want to know something, Annarita? If you'd kept your nose out of other people's business, and if you hadn't gone around spouting off about Leone's private matters and the tests he took, this afternoon we probably wouldn't be about to attend that poor wretch's funeral."

Annarita put both hands over her mouth. "What are you trying to say?"

"Just think about it. Try to remember whom you told these things to. Put two and two together. In no more than three hours, I expect you'll have figured out that what I'm telling you is the absolute truth. I hope that for the future you'll have learned your lesson." Rocco opened the door again and then stopped. Annarita stood there, stiff, gazing at him with blank eyes. "You want to know something? I like the people in these valleys. You're clean, honest, and sincere. The same goes for you. You all have just one defect: You don't know how to mind your own fucking business."

He stood on the sidewalk, watching an old man walking along in a pair of carved wooden clogs. The uncertain step and clubfooted gait made the man look like an old worm-eaten marionette. Shaking his head, the deputy police chief pulled out his cell phone.

"Dottor Baldi?"

"Yes. Do you have news for me?"

"Yes. Can I send Inspector Caterina Rispoli over to the courthouse?"

"Would you like to tell me what for?"

"Two arrest warrants."

Magistrate Baldi said nothing. The silence of a volcano just before the eruption.

"Dottore? Can you hear me?"

"I can hear you fine, Schiavone. Do you know what procedure demands?" Magistrate Baldi went on, with great restraint. Perhaps Baldi wasn't alone in his office. "You, Schiavone, are supposed to come see me in my office and explain how and why, after which it's up to me to decide whether or not I should sign these warrants."

"There's no time. I'm afraid that Leone Miccichè's murderers might disappear any second now."

"What makes you think that?"

"They're very intelligent."

"Why do you say 'murderers'?"

"Because there are two of them. One of them killed Leone, the other was an accomplice to murder."

"Fucking Christ, Schiavone!" At last the volcano erupted. "You're dangling on a fucking thread and you continue to do exactly as you please? There's a procedure to be respected, you know that? Do you want me to send you back to the ministry to make photocopies all day?"

"It'd be okay with me," said Schiavone under his breath. "As long as I get the same salary, I wouldn't mind a bit."

"You cut it out, with your bullshit sarcasm! And tell me whom we're supposed to lock up and why. And try to be convincing, because this is not the way I work."

"All right. Do you have five minutes?"

"Oh, you bet I do. But try to make the best of those five minutes, because if you foist off more bullshit, I'll find a way of converting my threats into reality. Have I made myself clear?"

"Crystal clear, like the ice of these mountains."

"All right, then. Tell me everything."

Italo was sitting at the counter of Mario and Michael's bar. In front of him sat an empty beer goblet and a wooden plate scattered with the crumbs of his panino. He didn't notice that the deputy police chief was sitting outside at one of the little round tables munching on a piece of chocolate until he caught a glimpse of the back of his head and his upturned loden collar. The officer left five euros on the bar and hurried out to join his boss. Rocco, wrapped in his overcoat, was slowly chewing on his Milka bar. He was staring at a fixed point on the road. It could have been the tire of the Land Rover; it could just as easily have been the pile of snow by the curb. A bearded man with a large black Labrador went by. The big dog had a red neckerchief instead of a collar and was following the man without a leash. It went by the deputy police chief and stopped to sniff at him. Without even looking at the dog, Rocco started scratching it under the chin. The dog wagged its tail, which pounded loudly against the legs of the table. The bearded man stopped in the middle of the street and turned to look back at his dog. "Billo!" he called. But the dog ignored him now that Rocco was staring into its round, glistening eyes and massaging its back, driving his fingers deep into the dog's coat. Billo lifted a paw and placed it in Rocco's lap. "Hey, you," said the deputy police chief, "what a nice elegant bandanna you have."

The dog's owner came over, smiling. "Excuse me, but if you pet my dog he's yours forever."

"It's no problem. I love dogs. How old is he?"

"Six. But he's still a puppy. Come on, Billo, let's go!"

Rocco gave Billo one last scratch behind the ears. The dog yelped happily and trotted off after its master.

"Arrivederci."

Rocco raised one hand in response to the farewell. Only then did Italo come over and sit down next to him, without a word.

"I had a dog once. In Rome. Her name was India. She wasn't any breed, or, actually, she was four or five, and all she lacked was the ability to speak. I know: everyone who owns a dog says the same thing, but it was true about her. One day she fell sick, and inside six weeks she was dead. Do you know how she died?"

"No."

"I was taking care of her. I was giving her IVs. I got up for a moment and walked away from her bed to get something to drink, and when I got back, she was gone. You understand? She waited for me to leave. Because death is a very private thing for animals. More private than giving birth. Not something to be shared with anyone else."

Italo thought about what the deputy police chief had just said, but he didn't know what he was referring to.

"In nature, no guilt attaches to death. Death is just old age, illness, or survival. Dogs know that. You can see it in their eyes. You ought to get yourself a dog, Italo. You'd learn a lot of things. For example, you'd learn that there's no such thing as justice in nature. That's a completely human concept. And like everything human, it's debatable and dubious." Rocco turned suddenly to look at Italo. "Give me a cigarette."

Italo pulled out his pack. "Still Chesterfields? I told you I like Camels." But the deputy police chief took one all the same.

"I know, Rocco, but I hate Camels."

Italo lit the cigarette for him, and Rocco took a deep drag. Then he looked up at the sky. It had suddenly turned gray. A vast, formless sheet of gray, like the lid on an old tin can.

"One minute the sun is out, the next minute it's gloomy and gray."

"That's often the way up here in the mountains."

"The weather up here seems to suffer from a bipolar disorder, don't you think? Doesn't it scare you?"

"I was born to it. What scares me is riding a subway underground."

"Shall we head down to the church?"

"Sure. Rocco?"

"Yes."

"Who did it?"

"Inspector Rispoli is heading up now with the warrants issued by the judge."

"Warrants?"

"That's right. There are two killers."

"Who are they?"

"You'll see in a second."

* * *

Half the town had gathered outside the church. The tourists walked past, rubbernecking curiously. Only a few of them knew what this was about. Those who had been there for the discovery of the corpse had finished their holidays and left, while those who had just arrived tried to get some information from the locals. The deputy police chief and Officer Pierron made their way through the crowd. The odor in the air was a blend of suntan lotion, the sickly sweet perfumes worn by the ladies, tobacco, and car exhaust. They climbed the steps. There was no way to get in—the church was tiny and unbelievably packed. It was a wall of humanity, and there seemed to be no way to get through it. They could hear the priest's amplified voice echoing off the vaulted cement ceiling.

"And this is why every time we find ourselves face-to-face with death, we sense that we are in a situation of extreme loneliness. But it's not really that way …"

"Could I get through?" Rocco was saying in a low voice. "Excuse me. Could I get through?"

"A Christian knows that in this moment of departure, he is not alone. It was the same for Jesus, you know that? He experienced death …"

Once he'd made his way through the wall of people, the nave opened out before Rocco's eyes. Everyone inside was seated. Leone's coffin sat at the foot of the altar. There was a wreath of flowers on one side and a bouquet carefully laid on the gleaming wooden coffin cover. The priest, a man in his early forties, clad in vestments, stood next to the coffin. Every head was directed at him. Rocco continued toward the pews in the front. A few people shot fleeting glances at the deputy police chief. There was the postmaster, who waved at him, as did the barman, Mario, as well as the beaver-physician sitting next to his wife, Annarita. Instead of greeting him, she kept her eyes downcast. There were the ski instructors sitting in a group, dressed in their work attire, and Omar Borghetti was among them. Amedeo Gunelli, the one who had found Leone dead in the snow, was sitting next to his boss, Luigi Bionaz, who, at least in church, for once wasn't rolling a cigarette.

"On the cross, Jesus is alone. He no longer has his disciples with him, the apostles whom he taught for three years. There is no crowd chanting hosanna in the highest. There is only his mother, Mary, and John at the foot of the cross. But Jesus knows, deep in his heart, that God the Almighty has not abandoned him. And this is the meaning of Psalm 22 ..."

At last, Rocco came to a halt. He had spotted Luisa Pec's profile. He also saw Leone's brother, Domenico, with his wife.

"And he teaches us that death is only the beginning, that it is only a drawing closer to our Father who is in heaven, where he will take us into his infinite arms for a new beginning, the true new life. Let us pray. Our Father who art in heaven ..."

All of the faithful joined with the priest in prayer. All except Luisa, who sat there, eyes downcast, looking at the floor of the church. Then she slowly raised her head and turned to look at Rocco, as if she'd sensed the deputy police chief's eyes on her.

They looked at each other. She was a *mater dolorosa* of a stunning, Renaissance loveliness, with her copper blond hair tumbling down over her shoulders.

Yep, Rocco thought, *you could die for a woman like that. And you could kill.*

"Words serve no purpose," the priest continued. "The whole valley, this whole city, gathers close around Luisa, around Leone's brother, Domenico, and his wife, around Leone's friends, Leone who was welcomed as a brother in these mountains, where he was not born but that now, without him, seem a little emptier; in short, we are all yearning, we all wish to know, we all need to know the truth. And I see that we have the police here among us today"—the faintest of smiles appeared on the priest's lips—"and we thank them, do we not? We thank them for the work that they will do to ensure that whoever committed this horrible murder may be apprehended and brought to justice."

Rocco didn't like the priest's tone of voice. It was clear that this shepherd of souls placed no trust in him or in the officers who were with him. Certainly, when he thought of Deruta and D'Intino, how could he blame this minister of God? Still, the irony that veined the priest's voice was starting to irritate him.

"We've seen them at work, no? The deputy police chief and his dauntless officers."

Now the priest was taking it too far. But Rocco stood motionless, listening with his arms folded across his chest, the eyes of the entire community focused on him.

"Perhaps now and again they employ methods that are somewhat unorthodox, our guardians of law and order ..."

Rocco shot a glance at the postmaster, who bowed his head. The little man had gone and spilled the beans to the priest about the slap in the face.

Piece of shit, Rocco thought to himself.

"But we also know that the path to the truth is paved at times with hardships and pitfalls."

He was tempted to break in and give the priest a piece of his mind, but he was playing on a hostile field. And after all, an open quarrel in the middle of a funeral sermon struck even him as out of line.

"And so we place our faith in them, certain that as soon as possible we shall have results. Am I right?"

This time he'd addressed him personally. The echo of the question amplified through the microphone was accompanied by the rustling of every head in the church turning to look at him. Rocco Schiavone smiled and cleared his throat. "You are right, Padre," he replied. "Much sooner than you might expect."

The priest bowed his head ever so slightly, looked out at his flock, and went on. "Luisa has asked to say a few words about our brother Leone," he said, stepping back from the microphone just as Luisa Pec was standing up from her seat. She walked to the lectern amid general silence. She had dark circles under her eyes. A black sweater and a pair of jeans were her mourning attire. Luisa took a deep breath and began.

"Leone isn't a Catholic."

A murmur ran through the church.

"Excuse me. He wasn't a Catholic. And this funeral was held at the devout insistence of the Miccichè family, with my support, because even though I have personally embraced another religion, I still feel strong ties to my original roots."

What the fuck? thought Rocco, but he said nothing. Even if he was an atheist, he still remembered that he was in a church.

"The words that Don Giorgio has given us here today were beautiful and heartfelt. And it's true, a funeral is helpful—it's a balm to the soul. A person might think that by sharing their sorrow with others they will suffer less. But that's not how it is. Grief, like everything, is subjective. It has various layers; everyone knows that and experiences grief differently." She cleared her throat. But it wasn't an emotional knot in her throat; very simply, some saliva had gone down the wrong way. "Leone was my husband. And I'm carrying his child. That is why …"

"Stop right there!" shouted Rocco, freezing the entire churchful of people to the spot. Padre Giorgio opened his eyes wide. Everyone turned their heads to stare at the deputy police chief. Luisa, too, stopped speaking and clutched at the microphone. "Just one thing, Luisa. Please stick to the truth, *grazie*." Then Rocco nodded his head as if to say, "You can go on," and sat waiting.

All heads now swiveled in Luisa Pec's direction. "But I *am* speaking the truth!"

"There's only one person here who knows the truth," said Rocco, and once again the congregation all turned to look at him. It was like watching the Wimbledon finals. "For those who believe—and we're talking about Truth with a capital T—we have Don Giorgio," and he pointed to the priest. "While for those who are less demanding, like me, those who believe only in what they can see and understand, in that case the repository of that truth, that truth with a lowercase *t*, I mean, well, in that case, they have me."

"Please, Mr. Deputy Police Chief, we're in the house of the Lord," Don Giorgio broke in.

"That's just the point, Padre. Here, of all places, and in the presence of Leone's coffin, lies are an abomination, and nothing but the truth should be spoken. You said so yourself only a little while ago. Leone was murdered. Everyone here knows it—we all know it. And God knows it better than any of us. I know it, too. The only difference is that, unlike the rest of you, I know who did it."

A buzz of excited conversation rushed through the pews lining the center aisle. Heads swiveled excitedly to get a better glimpse, to speak to a neighbor. Till that moment, the audience had been calm and relaxed, sober in its grief, like the surface of a calm lake. But suddenly, swept by shivers of curiosity, that smooth surface had been broken and small jets of spray and foaming waves sprang up. Officer Pierron, who now understood, backed up and left the church, hurrying outside. Omar Borghetti looked around, speaking in a low voice into the ear of his cross-eyed colleague, who was shaking his head. Annarita was clutching her husband's arm, eagerly gobbling up every detail with her eyes, ears, and nose, noting words, movements, and even smells. Amedeo Gunelli was staring at the deputy police chief, terrified that Rocco Schiavone might suddenly speak his name and place him at the center of attention.

"This is no place to hold a trial. This is a place of prayer," thundered the priest, and his voice rose all the way to the ceiling, where a triumphant Christ spread his arms to gather in the souls of the innocent.

"Certainly, Padre. Certainly. And in that case, by all means, pray. But don't say things that have nothing to do with the truth."

Now the audience was divided, unsure whether to stare at the widow, Rocco, or Padre Giorgio.

Luisa moved away from the pulpit and sat down again. Rocco leaned against the column and folded his arms across his chest. By rights, Padre Giorgio had the floor once again, and he slowly walked to the altar, followed by the altar boy, swinging the censer on a chain, wafting clouds of incense over poor Leone's coffin. But the audience continued to murmur. Suddenly out of that thicket of voices, one more powerful than all the rest made itself heard: "So who was it?"

"Yes, we want to know. Who was it?"

An elderly gentleman rose to his feet. "I'm an old man, and there's one thing I know for sure. Certainly the church is a place of prayer, that's true. But it's also a place of community. And the community wants to know. Who did this? I want to know—we all want to know!"

Padre Giorgio froze, caught off guard. He looked out at his congregation, and he looked at Rocco. The altar boy stood there, with the chain holding the censer dangling in his hand, the plume of incense smoke rising straight up toward the ceiling. "Please, Ignazio," said Padre Giorgio to the old man, "please! We're here to remember Leone, not to hold a trial."

But the elderly Ignazio wasn't giving up that easily. "Padre, the best way to honor Leone's memory is to throw whoever murdered him behind bars. Just a short while ago, you thanked the police for the work they've done. Well, here's a representative of the law who tells us that he knows who took Leone's life. If there's one thing that's sacred, it's life. God alone can take a life. And if that sinner is here in our midst, well, let me tell you from the bottom of my heart: he has no right to be here in the house of the Lord!"

"True!"

"Very true! *Bravo*, Ignazio!"

"Take the wine away from him!" called a voice from the choir.

At that point Rocco spoke up, doing his best to calm the audience with both hands. "Padre Giorgio is right: this is poor Leone's funeral. It's not the place to hold a trial. Please, Padre, go on with the service and please excuse me. And I beg all of you to forgive me for my inappropriate outburst." Then, just as he had entered, Rocco left the church, but this time without having to use his voice to clear his way, because the crowd parted before him like the Red Sea before Moses.

"Dottor Schiavone!" Padre Giorgio's voice echoed like the trumpet of the Last Judgment. "Do you know who did it?"

Rocco stopped. He turned to face the altar. The eyes of the audience were hundreds of pinpoints fixed on his face. He was about to answer the priest when a woman's voice caught everyone's attention. "Excuse me. Can I get through? Excuse me." Now the audience turned around to look back at the church doors. The Wimbledon finals were still under way. "Excuse me, let me through." And at last, among the faithful, standing by the doors, they saw the uniform and the tense face of Inspector Caterina Rispoli. The instant she realized that there were hundreds of people staring at her, she blushed. Her eyes sought those of Rocco, who was standing just a few yards away from her. "Everyone please forgive me. Dottore?"

The woman handed the deputy police chief an envelope. The priest stood there, waiting for an answer to his question. Rocco opened the envelope and read the contents amid general silence. Then he looked up toward the altar, at Padre Giorgio. "Yes, Padre, I know. And the guilty parties are right here, in the house of the Lord, where—as Ignazio said—they don't belong. Though, actually, as far as I'm concerned, they're perfectly welcome to be here, but I think that for the faithful, like Ignazio, it's grossly offensive. No?"

"Who are they?!" shouted an impatient voice, unable to remain silent a minute longer.

He could hear the breathing and the sighs; he could sense the tension in the eyes and nerves of that entire levelheaded, hardworking community raised to an extreme level. Amedeo Gunelli turned his head to look at his neighbors; the postmaster sat with both hands over his mouth. Signor and Signora Miccichè were now on their feet, glaring at the crowd in an accusatory manner. Annarita kept her eyes on the floor and shook her head slowly back and forth. Rocco retraced his footsteps, followed now by Inspector Rispoli. As he headed for the altar, he walked past Omar Borghetti. He stopped. The man turned pale. But Rocco held out his hand to shake Omar's. "I owe you an apology."

Omar smiled faintly. "No problem, Dottore. The slap in the face was to get a sample of my blood, wasn't it?"

Rocco nodded and went on walking as Omar heaved a sigh of relief and his cross-eyed co-worker slapped him several times on the back. The deputy police chief went past Signor and Signora Miccichè. He went past the priest as the eyes of the faithful clung to him like so many hungry bloodsuckers. Hundreds of eyes, eyes that were about to have their curiosity satisfied. Not even at the penalty shoot-out between Italy and France in the 2006 World Cup Final had Rocco sensed such tension. He stopped in front of Luisa Pec. He looked at her. Then, with a slow, one-handed gesture, he said, "Please come with me."

Luisa's eyes opened wide. The priest clutched at the microphone, and a chorus of shrill whistles broke the surreal silence. Domenico Miccichè turned pale. His wife collapsed into her pew. The faithful, as if complying with a specific command from a choreographer, all clapped their hands to their mouths. Luisa slowly stood up. She nodded twice, then slowly trailed after the policemen. Rocco shot an accusatory glare at Annarita, then walked around to the opposite side of the aisle. When he got to the middle, he stopped once again. Again, silence. The only sounds came in from the street: a bus horn and, in the distance, a child's joyful cry. Rocco looked at Amedeo Gunelli, whose jaw dropped in fright. Then the policeman swiveled his gaze over to Luigi Bionaz, the head snowcat operator. "Luigi Bionaz, would you please be so good as to come with me."

Luigi looked anxiously around at his neighbors. "Are you crazy or what?"

"Signor Bionaz, please don't force me to use methods that would be far worse than cursing in church."

"I ..."

But now there was a vacuum around Luigi. It was as if he were infected with the plague, and even Amedeo slid his ass down the bench, a good yard away from his former employer and benefactor. "None of this makes any sense. I wouldn't have ... Leone and I were friends!"

"Take a lesson from the widow," whispered Rocco. "You can come tell us about your motives at police headquarters. Move it!"

Luigi stood up. Everyone in the pew snapped to attention, standing up to allow him to file out. Slowly, and without the traditional excuse-me's, he made his way, walking sideways past his colleagues and townsfolk. But no one said a word, no one patted his arm in solidarity. Nothing. They simply stood and watched him walk toward the deputy police chief in the most absolute silence. "You'll hear from my lawyer," said Luigi.

"That's certainly your right."

At last Luigi emerged from the pew and started walking toward the exit, along with Luisa, Rocco, and Inspector Rispoli. A few steps before he reached the wooden double doors, Rocco stopped and turned to look back at the priest and the congregation. "I'm not in the habit of doing this kind of thing. But you asked me to." He nodded his head farewell to the audience and left the house of God without crossing himself.

* * *

Italo had managed to inch the car to within sixty feet or so of the front steps of the church. Behind him was the squad car, with Casella at the wheel; this was the car in which Inspector Rispoli had come up. The people outside had no idea what was happening. In particular, why the widow and Luigi were leaving the church before the coffin had. But news spread like an ebola outbreak, and when Rocco and Luisa climbed into the police BMW, and Luigi Bionaz and Rispoli got into the squad car driven by Casella, even the people who had been standing outside understood and began whispering, round-eyed and incredulous. Onlookers started snapping pictures with their phones, while others just stood scratching their heads. They clustered around the police cars like moths around a lamp at night. Rocco looked at them through the windshield. "Go, Italo. Let's get out of here."

Italo put the car in gear, and the cluster of men and women parted to let them through. To add a little drama to the scene, or perhaps just because regulations technically required it, Casella turned on the siren. Rocco picked up the radio handset and immediately called the squad car behind them. "Casella, either you turn off that siren or I'll shove it down your throat."

Not even a second later, the siren faded away, and at last Rocco could smoke a Camel in blessed peace.

"Couldn't you have waited until we got him to the graveyard?" asked Luisa.

"If it had been up to me, I wouldn't have even let you get into that church. But I got there too late," Rocco replied. "And now I'd appreciate a golden silence until we get down to Aosta," he said as he took a drag on his cigarette and spat the stream of smoke out the aperture atop the window he'd lowered half an inch.

The chief of police seemed giddy as he went on paying compliments to Rocco Schiavone, unable to stop. "Not even enough time to finish the funeral before you'd nailed them both!"

"Thanks, Chief," replied Rocco, trying to change the subject, but the chief insisted. The receiver was hot and sweaty. Rocco undid the top two buttons of his shirt. The chief had already called a press conference despite the late hour; he wanted to finally crow about his victory to "those guys" from the press; he wanted to annihilate them, to crush underfoot their chatter and their skepticism with undeniable results; he wanted to scoff at newsprint that was only good for lining birdcages the next day. And he wanted Rocco to take part. But that was the last thing Rocco wanted to do. Spotlights gave him worse acid than even the most indigestible meal.

He used every tactic at his disposal to worm out of that situation, until Corsi finally issued a peremptory command. "Schiavone! I expect you to be present at that press conference in exactly twenty minutes."

"Shitty line of work," snarled the deputy police chief as he jabbed as hard as he could on the red OFF button. And the usual unpleasant sensation of guilt descended over his senses, his weary, chilled-to-the-bone body. This was how it always was. Every time he wrapped up a case, he felt filthy, foul, in need of a shower or a couple of days away. As if he were the murderer. As if it were somehow his fault that those two idiots had killed Leone. It's just that you can't touch horror without becoming part of it. And he knew that. He necessarily had to plunge his hands into that viscous slime, into that disgusting swamp, if he wanted to catch crocodiles. And in order to do so, he was inevitably obliged to transform himself into a creature of those unclean places. He had to get dirty. Mud became his abode, the stench of decay his deodorant. But the marsh—with dragonflies skimming the water's surface, the venomous snakes, the gray sand that so resembled an elephant's diarrhea—Rocco just couldn't find any way of bringing himself to like it. It was the ugliest, darkest part of his life, and going back there was painful and exhausting. And all this—the investigations, the murders and the murderers, the falsehoods—it all forced him to reexamine his reckonings. He, who was struggling to leave behind the ugliest things he'd lived through. Who was trying to forget the evil committed and the evil received. The blood, the screams, the dead—who presented themselves behind his eyelids every time he shut his eyes. Every time he had someone like Luisa Pec or Luigi Bionaz in front of him. Sons of bitches, filthy individuals, the fauna to be found in those swamps. Who dragged him down with them, down into the quicksand of life, forcing him back into the swamps. And it was worse than a nightmare. Because there's one good thing about nightmares: they usually vanish in the first light of dawn. But the swamp was always there. Real, tangible, alive, and pernicious. Awaiting him. In the swamp, Rocco Schiavone was no different from all the others. No better and no worse. In the swamp, the boundary between good and evil, between right and wrong, no longer exists. And there are no nuances in the swamp. Either you plunge in headfirst or you stay out. There is no middle ground.

The house in Provence was as distant as Halley's Comet. Who could even say if it would ever return.

"Shitty line of work," he snarled a second time. Then he left his office and headed over to the press conference.

There was no need for a question from any of the professional journalists, either print or television, on the issue of Rocco Schiavone and the findings of his investigation. It was none other than Chief of Police Corsi, finally present in flesh and blood and no longer just a voice on the telephone, who beat everyone else to the punch. "Dottor Schiavone will now tell you how he managed to work his way to the point of requesting arrest warrants for Luisa Pec and Luigi Bionaz."

Usually the press conferences run by Chief of Police Corsi were simply monologues. He'd give the reporters a chance to ask one or, at the most, two questions, and then he was gone. He was the star of the show, and anyone who tried to steal the scene from this prima donna found that out at their own expense. So it was a gesture of great generosity—as Rocco immediately understood—to give him the spotlight. A generosity that was every bit as pointless as the press conference itself, because there was nothing that meant less to Rocco Schiavone than the spotlight, and the attention of public opinion in general. Corsi had stood to one side, next to Schiavone, arms folded across his chest. He was highlighting the point that this was his deputy, a member of his team, an extension of his own identity. The chief's face was beaming, his suit was impeccable, his hair was neatly gelled, his titanium-frame glasses were gleaming, and, above all, he was exuding joy from every pore.

Rocco cleared his throat. "*Buona sera*. Considering how late it is, I'll try to keep this brief ..."

Everyone was concentrating on him. Notebooks in hand, TV cameras running. There was just one pitfall he needed to avoid: the thighs of the cute blonde in the front row. With her tip-tilted eyes, like those of an Asian kitten, she seemed to be there to make Rocco's job just as challenging as possible.

Why is she in the front row? Couldn't she have found a seat a little farther back? thought Rocco as he prepared to address the room.

"I'll start from the beginning, if you have no objections. Thursday. It's about five in the evening. Leone is heading down the mountain to town. A pack of cigarettes, a conversation: in short, he heads out. Three-fourths of the way down the main piste, in the middle of a clearing, right where the shortcut runs through, there's someone waiting for him. That person calls his name. Leone leaves the run and heads over to talk to the person. It's a friend, there's no doubt about it. So he heads over. The friend offers him a cigarette. Leone takes it. He takes off his gloves—he takes them both off," and here Rocco paused and looked around at the press. "He starts talking to this man. Then the conversation turns into an argument, and the mysterious individual hits Leone Miccichè. But he doesn't kill him. Leone is just knocked unconscious. So the man shoves a handkerchief into Leone's mouth to keep him from shouting and leaves him there, covering him with snow to make sure no one can see him."

"Why would he do such a thing? Does he want to let him freeze to death?" asked a bespectacled reporter with a prominent nose, prompting a sneer of contempt from Police Chief Corsi.

"No. The mysterious man has a very specific plan. He leaves him there, unconscious, under a foot and a half of snow with a handkerchief in his mouth. But that's not his handkerchief. The mysterious man stole it. To be exact, he stole it from Omar Borghetti. Omar Borghetti is the head ski instructor up at Champoluc. Everyone knows him."

"Sure, but why would he steal it?" asked the cute blonde with the thighs.

"The son of a bitch—forgive me, the murderer," he said, correcting his gaffe, to the ill-concealed embarrassment of the police chief, "wanted to make sure it was found on the scene of the crime, no? Leone dead, with Omar's handkerchief stuffed in his mouth. Omar Borghetti. The longtime boyfriend of Leone's wife, Luisa Pec. In other words, the murderer did it to frame that unlucky wretch."

"A crime of passion?" asked the blonde with the thighs.

"Sure. A crime of passion. A crime of jealousy, anger, frustration, and so on. That's why I said that the killer committed what was clearly premeditated murder. That handkerchief speaks loud and clear. What do we know about him? First of all, that he's no fool."

"Right," broke in Police Chief Corsi, who'd held back until then. "He must have read a few detective novels or seen a few TV shows."

The reporters all nodded in unison but turned their eyes back to Rocco. Who felt it his duty to proceed with his explanation. "My superior officer just stated a great truth. This guy must know something about DNA. Which is why he takes great care to get rid of his and Leone's cigarette butts."

"Okay, that's all clear up to this point," said the reporter with the big nose. "Then what?"

"If you'd just give us a chance to explain, Dottor Angrisano!" The police chief scolded him, with the cold indignation of a headmaster visiting the worst class in the school.

Rocco resumed his explanation to keep the atmosphere from deteriorating further. "All right. But at this point I asked myself a question: What did they argue about? Debts? I don't see that. This is no ordinary argument. The killer was there for the specific purpose of taking Leone's life. So I came to this conclusion: there never was an argument. You don't need an excuse to commit premeditated murder. If you've decided to kill a person, you just go straight for the target. Our mysterious man strikes Leone and knocks him unconscious because his victim has discovered something."

The roomful of journalists waited in silence. Pens poised over their notebooks. The smartphones blinked as they recorded.

"That's right. He'd suspected something that he then confirmed with further analysis. His wife, Luisa, was pregnant. But Leone Miccichè was sterile."

"Oh, Jesus …" someone blurted.

"Who got her pregnant, then?"

"If you ask me, the murderer," volunteered the blonde in the front row.

"If you all don't mind," put in the police chief, "why don't we let Dottor Schiavone finish."

"No, no, you're perfectly right, ma'am. Now we only need to figure out who he is."

"Well, all you'd really need is a DNA sample from the fetus, no?" ventured the reporter with the big nose.

"True. But there's another way of finding out, without even falling back on forensic science. The crucial point has to do with the cigarettes. I really racked my brains over that one, you know? The whole question of the gloves just didn't add up. The victim took off both gloves. But you only need to take off one glove to smoke a cigarette, no?"

The reporters all nodded their heads.

"But Leone took off both gloves. Why?"

"To light the cigarette?" theorized one reporter, bald as a cue ball.

"No. You only really need one hand for that," Rocco replied. "Then I understood. It was so simple. A person has to take off both gloves to *roll* a cigarette. Right? That's why," he said, and he mimicked the act of rolling a cigarette.

"So the murderer who gave him the cigarette smoked loose tobacco?"

"Bravo!" Rocco replied to the schnozzola. "We even know the brand: Samson. The same brand that Luigi Bionaz smokes."

Cue Ball nodded. So did the blonde with the thighs. But the schnozzola bit his lip. "Wait—wait just a minute. Fine, so he smokes that brand of tobacco. But that alone isn't grounds for murder charges, is it?"

"Listen here, you and your questions!" broke in Police Chief Corsi. "This isn't the first time you've made a special effort to trip up the findings of my office."

"But all I—"

"And that's *not* all. Just pipe down. Let us hear what the deputy police chief has to say. Maybe then we'd finally have a chance to read something sensible in your newspaper, too."

"That's sheer insanity," blurted the reporter. The other members of the press snickered. There was no mistaking the fact that the big-nosed reporter and the chief of police had grudges that went back even further than any of the others.

"Pardon me," Rocco Schiavone broke in, "could I ask what paper you work for?"

"La Stampa."

Now Rocco smiled too. It was all as plain as day. It wasn't the reporter who got on Corsi's nerves; it was the paper. *La Stampa.* The same paper where the man who had stolen the police chief's wife so many years ago had worked.

"Let's get back to Luigi Bionaz." Rocco resumed the thread of his story. Then, to make sure he wasn't annoying his boss, he asked, "If I may, Dottore?"

Corsi nodded seriously.

"There's another reason we have Luigi Bionaz dead to rights. He's the head snowcat operator. He decides who goes out and where. Which pistes need grooming, what shortcuts to take. Most important of all, he buries Leone Miccichè, still alive, right in the middle of one of those mountain lanes that those treaded monsters use to head back to town. And in fact, at his earliest opportunity, he sends poor Amedeo Gunelli up there. And Amedeo, unsuspecting, runs his snowcat right over Leone's living body, lying under a foot and a half of snow, and shreds him into a thousand pieces."

"Maybe he was already dead," ventured the schnozzola from *La Stampa*.

"No. Leone was still alive. Our medical examiner, Fumagalli, is positive."

"In that case, it's a murder without a murder weapon!" concluded the bald-headed reporter.

"Exactly. But the real murder weapon is the knowledge that Luigi Bionaz had of the schedules and routes of the snowcats. He was the one who directed all that traffic. And that night, he insisted that Amedeo leave the work he was in the middle of doing and head back down to town. So Leone was buried and half-frozen, but he still could have dug his way out of his hiding place. That could have become dangerous for Luigi, no? Think it over. If a monster of that size runs you over, what are the odds of tracking down the weapon, the object that clubbed Leone over the head when he was still alive, knocking him out? Well, I can tell you. The odds are zero! That was Luigi Bionaz's stroke of genius."

"How did he steal Omar Borghetti's handkerchief?"

"That's a whole different matter. Luigi has access to Luisa's chalet when and however he wants. Omar Borghetti, as Pec's ex and longtime friend, would go to see Luisa almost every night after work. Among the things that bound them together, aside from their friendship, was a matter of money. Luisa owes a large sum of money to the head of the ski instructors. Stealing Omar's house keys was child's play for Luigi."

"But what proof do you have?" asked the blonde with the thighs. Her fellow journalists nodded collectively. Police Chief Corsi felt called upon to intervene. "The proof is the tobacco, Luigi Bionaz's absolute lack of an alibi for five o'clock, when the killer knocked Miccichè out, and eventually the child that will be born. And DNA evidence is stronger than fingerprints."

"What do Luisa Pec and Luigi Bionaz have to say for themselves?" asked the bald reporter as he jotted down notes on his pad.

"Luisa Pec has already offered a spontaneous confession. Luigi Bionaz, on the other hand, insists he's innocent."

Only then did Rocco notice that standing behind the journalists was Magistrate Baldi. He was smiling. Rocco returned his silent greeting.

"*Bravo*, Dottor Schiavone. Excellent work. Fast and precise," said Baldi, giving him a slap on the back as the journalists filed out of the conference room.

"*Grazie*, Dottore."

Baldi looked at him seriously. He nodded. "I asked and you provided."

"Provided what?"

"The murderer. Better yet, the murderers. You kept your promise."

"Very true, Dottor Baldi. Now how about you? Are you going to keep your promise, too?"

The judge smiled. He looked over at the chief of police, who had stopped to talk to a woman. "Sure. I'll keep my promise. I'm a man of my word, you know? But can I just ask you one thing?"

"Go ahead."

"Where were they from?"

Rocco nodded. "Sri Lanka. There were eighty-seven of them. And they had an appointment with someone who had jobs for them. I couldn't bring myself to round them up as if they were weapons themselves."

"Sri Lankans," murmured Maurizio Baldi. "Excellent work, Schiavone. But don't forget: you owe me a favor."

Rocco nodded.

"Maybe in the end, you and I really will find a way of becoming friends," said the judge, flashing him a radiant smile. "Tomorrow morning, come by and see me in my office. I want to hear your opinion. I told you about it, no? I've got a nice big pile of tax evaders on my desk. I'd really like to know what you think."

Rocco heaved a sigh. "Certainly, Dottore. I'll be there tomorrow morning. But could I give you a piece of advice?

The less you're seen with me, the better it will be for you. I'm just saying—for your career and for your future."

"Future? What future, Schiavone? We're in Italy, hadn't you noticed?" And he left the deputy police chief standing there. Rocco put a hand in his pocket and pulled out his pack of Camels. It was empty. He cursed through clenched teeth and glared at the cameramen, who were stowing their video cameras in their canvas cases and aluminum suitcases. He looked around for the blonde with the thighs and the eyes of an Asian cat. But she was gone, without a trace.

When the car driven by Italo reached Brissogne, it was past nine. The exterior lights of the prison were all on. The other windows seemed like dead, menacing eyes. An icy wind was blowing, whipping whirlwinds of snow off the asphalt in the glow of the headlights.

"Is this going to take long, Rocco?"

"No more than a few minutes."

There Luisa sat, her arms resting on the table, a water bottle beside her. Rocco walked into the room and looked the woman in the eyes. Her eyes were weary and bloodshot, clearly hoping for nothing better than sleep, and an end to that shitty day. Luisa's head slumped onto her chest as if she'd suddenly fallen asleep.

Rocco placed his forefinger under her chin and lifted her face. "Why?" he asked.

Luisa dropped her gaze. "For a while now, things between me and Luigi … had been a little out of control. Leone was jealous. Life with him was just hellish."

"But you kept telling yourself, *We have debts; this guy owns property down in Sicily* … No?"

"I didn't want it to end like this. Luigi had promised that he'd just talk to him."

"Luigi had already made up his mind to kill him. He had a very specific plan. Didn't you know that?"

"He was only supposed to talk to him, to see if he could settle things peacefully. That was the understanding. Luigi took the initiative."

"That's a technique as ancient as Rome, you know that? The idea of dribbling the ball back and forth between the two of you."

"You don't believe me?"

"No. I say that the two of you planned it out together. You may now be sorry that you did it, but Luisa, you did it. Listen to me. You're nailed on this one. And you know perfectly well what it is that nails you: the evidence that you're carrying in your belly. Right?"

Luisa touched her midriff.

"Get it off your chest now, and then we won't have to talk about it again. At least try to get out of this situation with a shred of dignity—that is, if you ever had any to start with."

Luisa Pec was crying now. "If I tell you one important thing that pins this on Luigi, then will you give me a hand?"

"What kind of a hand?"

"I mean, will you talk to the judge?"

"We'll see. What are we talking about?"

"Thursday evening, at five fifteen, Luigi called me on his cell phone. He was freaked out. He told me to go up to the Crest shortcut. He said that something disastrous had happened."

Rocco remained silent.

"I was there, too, that night. I got there afterward. Luigi had already buried Leone." Her tears started pouring out, as if someone had left the faucet open. "And he told me that it was too late, there was nothing he could do now. That he was dead. And that the only thing left to do was to try to protect each other as best we could."

"Leone was still alive, under the snow—do you know that?"

Luisa looked the deputy police chief in the eyes. "Leone …?"

"That's right. He died two hours later. Run over by Amedeo Gunelli, in a snowcat that ripped him up into eighteen thousand pieces."

Luisa hid her face in her hands, and her chest heaved in an explosive series of sobs. Rocco waited for the woman to calm down. Then he pulled her hands away from her face. "Who was there, besides you and Luigi?"

"No one else. Just the two of us. And … Leone."

"Where was Omar Borghetti?"

"I don't know. He'd come to see me half an hour earlier. I owe him money."

"Yes. I know about that. But what is this supposed crushing proof you have against Luigi?"

"Get my cell phone—the prison guards have it."

"What would I find on it?"

"Search through the pictures. There's one that leaves no doubt."

"What's in this photograph?"

"It's Luigi, standing in front of the pile of snow where Leone was buried. He has a shovel in his hand and he's looking down at the ground."

"Did you take the picture?"

Luisa nodded her head.

"That meant you had him by the balls, didn't it?"

"I don't know. It was an awful thing, just terrible. I didn't know what to do. I hadn't wanted to kill him, and it just seemed that if something went wrong, that photo might help me out, no?"

Rocco lost it. "Fuck you, Luisa Pec, you and your son-of-a-bitch eyes. I never want to speak to you again. I'll take a look at your cell phone, I'll enter it as an exhibit, but I'll do everything I can to make sure you do time behind bars."

"I didn't want to—"

"Again? There are at least two reasons that I'm pissed at you. First, you've made my life a sequence of pains in the ass over the past few days that I just can't believe. Second, you force me to shove my hands into this shit right up to my elbows, and believe me, that's something I'd gladly do without."

He took two more steps. Then he looked Luisa straight in the eyes. "You know something a great English poet once wrote? 'I know that a woman is a dish for the gods, if the devil dress her not.'"

"Why, what are you, a saint, Dottor Schiavone?"

"No, I'm the worst son of a bitch there is, Luisa. But let me tell you, I face that reckoning with myself every blessed day. When I look at myself in the mirror, or a body of water, or when I drive, when I eat, when I go to the bathroom. Even when I look up at this fucking gray sky you have around here. Always. And sooner or later, I'll have to settle my account. But there are no innocent corpses on my conscience. And if you don't think that's enough, let me promise, I couldn't give a flying fuck about it." He started to leave, but stopped when he reached the door. "All the same, there is a compliment you deserve. You look like two great actresses, did you know that? And the performance you put on that first day at police head-quarters, when you found out that the body was your husband's, well, I fell for it. You just picked the wrong profession. You should have tried out at Cinecittà."

And he stormed out, slamming the interview-room door behind him.

"Should I take you home, Rocco?" asked Italo.

Rocco nodded. He didn't feel like seeing Nora, he didn't feel like going out to eat … He didn't feel like feeling like anything. All he wanted was a shower, a fried egg, some hypnotic channel surfing, and then falling asleep on the sofa, in hopes of a long, dreamless sleep.

"Why did they kill him?"

"For the money. Because they were lovers. Because they were expecting a child and Leone had found out it wasn't his. Because they're cowards. Because they're a pair of shitheads."

Italo touched his lip, where a scab had formed. "Listen, Rocco. That thing we did with Sebastiano."

"Right."

"Do you think we'll do it again?"

"Are you sorry you did it?"

"No. I just want to know."

"If a good opportunity rolls around, sure. We can try. Why? Did you have something in mind?"

Italo heaved a deep sigh. "Yeah, I have something in mind. But we'd have to talk it over."

"Not tonight."

"No, we've done enough for tonight."

"Perhaps you don't understand what I'm trying to tell you ... If the Confindustria axiom holds true, then ..."

"Cut the potatoes into thin strips, along with the red and yellow peppers."

"Still, even playing with a 4-4-2 formation can be risky against a team as powerful as ..."

"All the major stock market indexes have dropped, pointing to a ..."

"Is Robin Hood, prince of thieves, capable of love?"

I wonder if it's possible to change channels so fast that you still get some complete sense out of what you hear. Or at least something no worse than what they're actually broadcasting. It's started snowing again. Hard. Look at how the flakes are hitting the window. They say that no snowflake is identical to any other. But who did they have check them? That is, did someone sit down and sort through twelve million snowflakes before they could melt? Or maybe not. Maybe snowflakes aren't like fingerprints. Everyone has a fingerprint. Every snowflake is different. My eyelids are starting to droop. I need some sleep. Here on the couch? In front of the television set like an old drunk? But what if I close my eyes and I see the pictures?

The pictures?

And then they turn into a movie.

Piazza Santa Maria in Trastevere. Marina is sitting by the fountain and talking to some boys from Oslo. I still remember. It was a July night. The first time I ever saw her. I decided straightaway: I'm going to marry her. Right then and there, I made up my mind, to the sound of the splashing water of the fountain and the gutter punks' dogs that were howling at the moon. This couch is so comfy. And I can't, I shouldn't ... Should I let myself go? Sure, it's soft, and warm, too. Outside, I think it's still snowing. But I don't want to have to open my eyes. I'll just let myself slip away, little by little. I wonder if this is what dying is like. I've heard that when you freeze to death, you just fall asleep, gently, and never even realize it. That's better than having a tank run over you and crush your head, I'd have to say. Definitely much better.

"I heard the whole thing. You caught them," Marina tells me.

"Yes."

"Did some idiot suggest you go out and celebrate tonight?"

"No. Luckily, no one did."

"There's nothing to celebrate."

"I'd have to say you're right."

She sits there, beside me. Outside, it's stopped snowing.

"Are you all right, Rocco?"

"Yes."

Marina laughs. "You're good at catching lies, but you don't have the slightest idea how to tell one."

"You feel like going somewhere, Marì?"

"Why? Where do you want to go?"

"To go take a look at Provence. It's not even an hour's drive from here."

"And we could indulge in a few fantasies?"

"Right. We could imagine some things."

"Like we are right now?"

"Like we are right now."

"Rocco, you do this far too often, do you know that?"

"Yes, I know."

"It's not good for you."

"Yes, but without it I can't live."

"You should try, Rocco. You have to live."

The rocket that Sylvester Stallone fired into the Vietcong encampment woke him up. Rocco opened his eyes. It was snowing outside. He was stretched out on the sofa, and Rambo was slaughtering a fucking Charlie army.

He switched off the television set. He got up. It had to be two in the morning. Or three. He went over to the window. The snow was still falling, but the flakes were smaller now. The road was white, except for the tracks of a car's tires that had punctuated the blanket of white snow with black patches of asphalt. The streetlamps were dotted with frozen drizzle, and the green sign outside a pharmacy blinked. One frozen hand gripped his heart. The other seized his throat. He leaned his head against the glass. He shut his eyes.

He hadn't taken flowers to Marina in four months now. He decided that next weekend he'd go to Rome. But only for her. For Marina.

"I'm going to take a shower. Marina, would you make me an espresso?"

"Are you leaving so soon?"

"Before the swamp can swallow me up again, my love."

ACKNOWLEDGMENTS

A few necessary thank-yous. To Patrizia, who believed in it before anyone else. To Luisa, for her patience, and with thanks for all the things that she explained to me, helping to keep me from putting my foot in my mouth. To Patricia, who gave me the push that started it all. To Toni, who in the meantime has become my wife and who makes my life fulfilling. To my father and his paintings, pictures that have stayed with me since I was a little boy, and to my mother, for her mathematical mind. To Marco and Jacopo, who, with my sister, took me up to an elevation of five thousand feet. To Nic and Lollo, whom I can never thank enough, and who stubbornly continue to believe in the things that I do. To Mattia, for the energy and pure talent that helped me to make the book so much better. Last, but not least, Nanà Smilla Rebecca and Jack Sparrow, who illuminate my home with love.

And then a special thank-you to the village of Champoluc and especially to Luigi, Carlo, and the Livres et Musique bookstore, to the Vieux Crest hut, where I started writing this book, and to Le Charmant Petit Hotel, where I finished it.

ABOUT THE AUTHOR

Born in 1964 in Rome, Antonio Manzini is an actor, screenwriter, director, and author. He studied under Andrea Camilleri at the National Academy of Dramatic Art and made his debut in fiction with a short story he co-wrote with Niccolò Ammaniti. He is the author of two murder mysteries that feature Deputy Police Chief Rocco Schiavone, a cop who thinks outside the box and disrespects both his superiors and police department regulations. *Black Run* is the first of these novels to be translated into English.